come
what
maybe

Entangled Publishing, LLC
644 Shrewsbury Commons Ave., STE 181
Shrewsbury, PA 17361
Visit our website at www.entangledpublishing.com.

Amara is an imprint of Entangled Publishing, LLC.

Edited by Liz Pelletier and Lydia Sharp
Cover design by Elizabeth Turner Stokes
Stock art by Jee1999/Shutterstock
Interior design by Toni Kerr

Print ISBN 978-1-64937-141-6
ebook ISBN 978-1-64937-160-7

Manufactured in the United States of America

First Edition February 2023

AMARA

come
what
maybe

KERRI
CARPENTER

ALSO BY KERRI CARPENTER

SOMETHING TRUE

The Dating Arrangement
The Wedding Truce

OTHER ROMANTIC COMEDIES FROM KERRI CARPENTER

Her Super Secret Rebound Boyfriend
Flirting with the Competition

For John, my very own happily ever after!

CHAPTER ONE

*"You do not really understand something unless
you can explain it to your grandmother."*
-Albert Einstein

Lauren pulled into the driveway, put her car in park, and picked up the white throw pillow she'd bought, with the navy-blue hand-stitching, and re-read the quote. Yep, that Albert Einstein sure was smart, because his words pretty much summed up her relationship with her grandmother. The grandmother whose house she'd just arrived at. The grandmother she was staying with for the next couple months. The grandmother with the eagle eye, who not only had a real talent for finding faults but also pointing them out.

Repeatedly.

As Lauren did with all areas of her life, she'd been documenting this road trip from her home in Arlington, Virginia, on social media. She turned off the car now and opened Instagram. She'd posted a story of the pillow she'd bought for Grams at a quaint general store she'd stopped at earlier. Lauren smiled, seeing her recent story was already getting quite a few views. One direct message asked *the* question.

Why are you in Maine?

She answered this particular follower with the truth. Or, at least, the most general, simplistic version of the truth.

I'm from Maine. Visiting family.

True enough, she thought. She'd been born in a very small beach town on the Maine coast called Seaside Cove, not far from Kennebunkport.

Seaside Cove, population twenty.

Okay, maybe it wasn't that tiny, but she'd definitely felt that way growing up. Everyone knew everyone else. If she got her hair cut after school, the employees at the grocery store would know all about it by dinnertime.

Yeah, it was *that* kind of town.

Growing up in Seaside Cove wasn't all bad, though. It was beautiful, actually. The fall foliage was to die for. Summers were full of long days and beach parties. Lauren was convinced you couldn't find better seafood anywhere. The houses that were lucky enough to line the coast had an absolutely magnificent view of the ocean that extended out for an eternity.

Her grandmother's house was one of those. Lauren stretched and twisted as she got out of the car. Then she simply stared at the gorgeous house in front of her as she took in the familiar and comforting sounds and smells. The birds, the waves crashing on the beach, the salty sea air mixing with the sweet scent of Grams's countless hydrangea bushes.

"You gonna stand there all day gawking or come in?" a rough, scratchy voice called from the front door.

Lauren rolled her eyes even as she grinned. She grabbed her purse, her phone, and the present for

Grams, and made her way to the house. She'd get the rest of her stuff later.

Halfway to the porch, she stopped, a perfect picture presenting itself. She crouched as she aimed her phone and snapped a beautiful shot of a row of white daisies fluttering in the breeze as the ocean glistened in the distance.

"What the hell are you doing?" Grams asked from the porch, hands firmly placed on her hips.

"Taking a pic for social," Lauren replied simply.

"Don't put me online," Grams yelled. "I don't want some hacker to get my address off that picture. I know about cybersecurity."

Sure, she did. Lauren shoved her phone into the back pocket of her jeans and continued toward the house, bounding up the three steps onto the wraparound porch. She was met by Grams's assessing stare that always lasted three seconds too long, or just long enough to make you feel awkward.

Even though they hadn't seen each other in person in over two years, Lauren knew there would be no hugs. That wasn't their relationship.

Grams huffed and walked into the house. Lauren followed, her gaze darting into every room, down every hallway, soaking in the familiar and noting any new touches. The same Tiffany lamps on the piano in the front parlor. A new runner in the hallway. The china cabinet displaying the dishes that had belonged to Grams's mother in the dining room.

Grams was standing at the kitchen sink, a dish towel slung over her shoulder and a discerning look on her face. Rose Catherine Josephs wasn't the lovey-dovey-hugging type of grandma who kissed boo-boos and crocheted afghans. Neither did she offer words of affection or wise anecdotes. Although she did offer plenty of words, which she probably thought were wise. But to Lauren, they were usually direct, no-nonsense, and occasionally biting.

Grams looked at her watch. "Surprised you're here already."

"Why?" Lauren put her purse on the table. "I texted you from the last rest stop with my ETA."

"Figured you would stop at the local bar on Main Street before you came here."

Here we go. One freaking time in college, she'd stopped to have lunch with a girlfriend before coming home, and Grams never forgot it.

She could reply with something like, *Oh Grams, you know I wanted to see you first.* But what fun would that be? Instead, she said, "I was afraid the bar would be closed on a Sunday."

Grams's eyes narrowed. "Your hair's too short."

"Nice to see you, too," she replied drily.

"Why'd you cut it? If I had pretty, long hair like you, I would have never chopped it."

Lauren ran a hand through her dark brown hair. It wasn't like she'd given herself a buzz cut. She was sporting a trendy bob, her natural curls cut into layers, so they fell in perfect waves just above her shoulders. "Because I like to experiment."

"I liked the long hair." Grams turned to the sink, ran the towel around the edge, and then neatly hung it back up.

"So you said." Taking a long, fortifying breath, Lauren presented the bag she'd picked up at the gift shop. "For you, Grams. Happy Mother's Day!"

She waited while Grams removed the pillow from the bag and undid the tissue paper Lauren had asked the clerk to wrap it in.

"What the hell am I supposed to do with this?"

Completely unoffended, Lauren jumped to sit up on the counter. Grams snapped her fingers, and Lauren immediately got down. Not even two minutes in her presence and she already felt like a scolded child.

Leaning back against the granite counter, she said, "Oh, I don't know, Grams, maybe you could put it on the couch or in your bedroom. Maybe you could just say, 'Thank you, Lauren, favorite granddaughter, for thinking of me on Mother's Day.'"

"I'm not your mother," she said, turning her back and walking toward the living room.

"You're as good as," Lauren said under her breath, secretly hoping Grams heard it.

She followed her grandmother into the living room, then went to the window and looked out at the garden.

"And you're not my favorite granddaughter, either."

Lauren snorted. "Keep telling yourself that. You know you love me the most. Hydrangea look amazing this year."

"Yes, they do."

Turning from the window, Lauren faced Grams and studied her. "If I'm not your fav, who is? Brooke is too self-absorbed, and Gabby is too flighty."

"And you're too presuming," she said with finality. Then, "How is she?"

Lauren didn't have to ask who *she* was. They were all concerned about Gabby. Her youngest sister was the reason for Lauren putting her own life on hold and staying in Maine for a couple months.

"You should know," Lauren said. "I know you talk to Gabby all the time."

Grams leveled a look at her. "I'm her grandmother. You're her sister. She tells you things that she keeps from me."

Gabby was an amazing actress. She'd put in her time at local playhouses, theater in the park, basically anywhere that had a stage and a script. When she'd moved to New York City, she'd auditioned her way to roles in the chorus, understudies, bit parts, and secondary characters. She danced, she sang, she acted her little heart out.

Finally, after all those years, Gabby did it. She won a coveted starring role in a new musical that everyone was talking about. But then a worldwide pandemic swept in, and Gabby lost her job. Her dream.

Adding insult to injury, one of her roommates had been caught trying to sell antibacterial wipes on eBay for exorbitant prices and had to pay a huge fine. Not to worry, he'd been able to pay the fine…by stealing from Gabby and their other roommates.

Now, her sister was out of work, out of money, and out of an apartment after the landlord evicted her.

Even though Lauren worried about her sister, she wasn't completely on board with her decision to leave everything she'd built in New York and return to Maine. Lauren was a firm believer in rising to the challenge. She was sure that if Gabby just took some time and came up with a plan she would be able to fix anything that had happened to her in Manhattan.

Lauren shrugged. "I still think she should stay in New York. Figure a way out of her mess."

Grams eyed her. "And I think you're wrong. Gabby needs her family right now."

Lauren rolled her eyes. "She's going to be fine."

"Gabby is resilient. Still, everyone needs help from time to time."

As the youngest, Gabby had often been spoiled by all of them. Lauren was afraid Grams was following in that tradition now, allowing Gabby to move back home. Or, maybe Grams needed someone, too.

Lauren worried her lip. Another reason she came back to Seaside Cove. Two birds, one stone, she would make sure both Grams and Gabby were okay.

Grams was stubborn, outspoken, strong-willed, and completely capable of taking care of herself. She'd been running a business that she'd started way back in the day, Rose's Café, a small café and coffeehouse. Naturally, it had closed during the worst waves of the pandemic. Grams claimed she was great, health-wise and financially. But Lauren still wanted to see with her own eyes that everything was okay.

"She'll be just fine after a little rest," Grams said with authority.

Lauren thought so, too. But she couldn't just *agree* with Grams. If she did, her grandmother would assume Lauren was up to something and make her life hell trying to figure out what it was.

"You're babying her," Lauren said. "Again." Grams was also inserting her nose into a situation that didn't concern her. Not the first time.

Grams quirked an eyebrow. "She's broke. That stupid roommate of hers really screwed her over."

"If only she'd listened to me and asked for multiple references," Lauren said. "That's what responsible people do when they're searching for roommates. Not to mention giving that shady roommate access to the rent, utilities, and cable money. Who does that! Now, she's in debt."

Lauren had already created a very detailed plan to help Gabby get her finances under control. She couldn't wait to show it to her.

"A lot of the country is in debt. We'll pull through it. And you should have picked her up on your way up here."

Lauren deflated. "I tried, Grams. You know I tried." She'd practically begged and pleaded with Gabby. But her sister definitely had this whole independent streak that was as big as...well, as Lauren's own independent streak.

She fell into the cushions of one of the soft, comfy couches. "So, what's for dinner?"

"I don't know. What are you making?" Grams replied, sitting in her usual spot, a gray wingback chair. "It's Mother's Day. I'm not cooking."

"Seriously? There's nothing to eat? I've been driving for hours." Uncomfortable, she shifted, then remembered her phone. She stood and removed it from her back pocket before sitting again.

"Those jeans tight enough?" Grams asked wryly.

"Well, Grams, you know what they say. The tighter the jeans, the closer to God."

Grams's rebuttal came in the form of a word that would have seen Lauren with a bar of soap in her mouth.

To the casual observer, it might seem like Grams was the typical grumpy older member of society. And those observers would be right. But she was also more than that. Grams had raised Lauren and her two sisters after their mother died.

Every year, Grams discounted Mother's Day. She made it seem like it wasn't that big of a deal. Only, it was to Lauren. It was a day to thank the person who had stepped into the mother role for her. The person who had kept her fed and clothed. The person who liked to bitch about how tight her jeans were.

"These jeans are not that fitted." They were a dark-wash skinny jean. They were snug but nothing extreme.

"Are you wearing underwear?"

"Grams!" She grimaced. "Yes, I'm wearing underwear."

"Don't know how in those pants. They're so tight you would think I'd see your panty line." Grams peered at her. "Unless you're wearing a thong. Are you wearing a thong?"

Lauren felt her face heating up and knew her ears were turning red. "We are not discussing my underwear."

"You know what I've always told you about thongs." Grams pointed at her. "What have I always told you?"

She covered her face with her hands. "I can't."

"Lauren Rose." Grams's voice had that stern, don't-mess-with-me tone to it.

Lauren looked up. "Wearing a thong gives you a UTI," she dutifully recited. "Which, by the way, isn't even true."

"How would you know? Did you become a doctor lately?" Grams crossed her arms.

"You're not a doctor, either." She didn't know what she felt more uncomfortable about. The fact that her grandmother was talking to her about thongs or that for years she'd always wondered if the whole thong-UTI thing was true.

"I mean, if you want to basically wear dental floss up the crack of your butt—"

"How about we talk about something else?" Lauren racked her brain. Coronavirus, a root canal—literally anything would be better than talking thongs with Grams. "Gabby said she's going to work in the café with you."

Grams nodded. "What about you? You have a job yet?"

Lauren ground her teeth. "I've never *not* had a job." In fact, she'd been working since she was a little girl.

She used to work in Grams's café. After school, weekends. Grams had said it was her job and she had to learn responsibility. It wasn't until Lauren was older that she realized Grams was watching her while her mom was sick.

"Oh, I forgot. You go on Myspace."

Sure, if they were living in 2006. "Grams, I've explained this a million times. I'm a social media strategist. It is an actual job." She crossed her arms over her chest. "And guess what? I get paid to do it. I also do online coaching, classes, and talk at conferences."

She did so much more than that, really. But it was useless to try and explain her job to Grams. She'd been trying for years, and it always ended up with Grams throwing out insults and Lauren getting defensive.

Grams waved a hand in the air. "What the hell does that even mean?"

"I teach people how to optimize social media for their businesses."

Grams raised one eyebrow. "You go to college, get your degree, and then what? You could have become a teacher."

"I kinda did."

Leaning forward, she said, "You speak at conferences, you say?"

"All the time. Well, more so before COVID. But yes, I've spoken to crowds of thousands of people." Right before the pandemic hit, she'd been tapped as the keynote speaker at a prominent marketing conference in San Diego. It had been a highlight of her career for sure. She received the full VIP treatment, hotel suite, limo from the airport, autograph session after her speech. She only wished her grandmother and sisters had seen it. Maybe then they would understand how hard she worked.

Grams sat back in the chair again and shrugged.

"Those people probably liked your long, curly hair."

That's it. She couldn't take it anymore.

Lauren glanced at her phone. Wow, twenty minutes. That might be a new record for them.

She stood. "I need to go out."

"You just got here," Grams said in a flat voice.

"I'm hungry. I'm going to go get some food. And a very large drink," she added under her breath.

Of course, Grams had the hearing of an elephant.

"You shouldn't drink on a Sunday. It's God's day."

Lauren knew without a doubt that if God were in this room, He would have already opened the wine.

She snatched up her phone, grabbed her purse from the kitchen, and headed toward the front door. "I'll be back in a bit."

Hopefully Gabby would be there by the time she returned. Lauren and Grams always did better when they had a buffer.

"Don't go to that bar on Main Street. No good happens there," Grams called after her.

And with that, Lauren knew exactly where she was heading.

CHAPTER TWO

"You're in a good mood."

Ethan McAllister stopped whistling and looked up from his beer, into the eyes of one of his closest friends and the current bartender at The Thirsty Lobster. "Hm?"

"I don't know," Joe said. "You've gone from tapping your fingers on the bar to humming and now to whistling." He replaced Ethan's old beer with a fresh, cool mug. "Not to mention the grin. There is something…" Joe leaned forward and lowered his voice. "You got laid."

Ethan rolled his eyes. But he didn't correct his friend. Let Joe think what he wanted to think.

The truth was, he *should* be happy. Memorial Day weekend was right around the corner, and that would kick off tourist season, which would hopefully translate into copious drinks bought and lots of revenue for the businesses of Seaside Cove.

Total happiness. Except…

Today would have been his anniversary. His ten-year wedding anniversary. Ethan wasn't sure how to feel about that. Getting divorced had been the right move; he had no doubt. But he wasn't proud that he had a failed marriage under his belt. He also didn't like thinking back on that relationship. So, he'd woken up with a clear goal of being positive today instead of moping around and questioning his life. Even if he didn't fully feel that way.

"Who was the lucky lady?"

Ethan turned toward Stu, another friend and Thirsty Lobster regular, who was sitting at the bar, watching the baseball game and eating a hot dog. Stu apparently had no problem hearing over the noise of the bar, the TV, or anything else.

"There was no lady," Ethan said.

"Sorry," Stu said, holding his hands up in front of him. "Who was the lucky guy?"

"No guy, either."

"I'm not judging. Man, woman—you do you, bro. We just want you to be happy."

Ethan shook his head. "I appreciate that. Actually, today would have been my anniversary with Veronica," he explained to Joe and Stu, and also Peggy and her sister, Wendy, the two older women sitting on the other side of him.

Peggy and Wendy owned the beauty salon across the street, and when they weren't getting their gossip fix among the hair dryers and nail stations, they came over to the bar for even more. They were twins who had just turned sixty, and Ethan suspected they'd been gathering the gossip in Seaside Cove for most of those six decades. But, despite their rumormongering ways, he loved them. They never ceased to make him laugh.

Wendy waved a hand nonchalantly at Ethan. "That's nothing to get worked up over. Today would have been my anniversary with my second husband, too."

Peggy snorted. "No, it isn't. You got married in April, not May." She rolled her eyes. "You don't even know your own anniversary date."

"It's hard when you have so many." Wendy had been married three, or maybe four, times. Ethan wasn't really sure. He just knew she liked to refer to herself as the modern-day Elizabeth Taylor, and he'd had to look that name up on Google to understand what she meant.

"I could always acquire a new anniversary date. Young men like you are in." Wendy winked at Ethan.

He chuckled and winked back. "I don't think I could keep up with you, Wendy."

He wouldn't mind getting married again someday. He would just be a hell of a lot pickier about the bride the second time around. He'd make sure he chose someone who actually wanted to get married, who actually loved him. Someone who wasn't using him to get what they wanted.

"I'm not worked up about the date," he explained to everyone. "Actually, I'm doing okay. I'm looking at the positive."

"Good for you. Glass is half full. Speaking of..." Peggy said, waving her half-filled glass at Joe, who moved to top her off.

"I love an optimistic man," Wendy said, practically licking her lips.

"Marrying my sister isn't going to help anything. Trust me."

"Rather than going straight to the altar with Wendy, why don't you try dating again?" Joe suggested. "You know, dinner and a movie. Hanging out. You haven't dated anyone in a while."

"Hey. I date." Ethan pulled the bowl of pretzels toward him.

"No, you don't," Joe said and refilled Stu's beer. "I'm not talking about hooking up or casually seeing women. I mean actually forming a relationship. You haven't dated anyone seriously since your divorce."

Wendy grinned. "All you need is a good roll in the hay." She pointed at Stu. "Like this one. I heard you've been sniffing around that Carson girl. The one who moved in with her cousin last year."

Stu's mouth dropped open. "What? How did you—"

"They always know," Ethan supplied.

"You need to be careful with that Carson girl," Wendy said. "She seems like the type who's always going to want more. Pick someone else to get wet dreams over. You too," she said directly to Ethan.

He didn't know about wet dreams, but it might be nice to go out to dinner and have some good conversation with a woman. The problem was that Seaside Cove wasn't exactly swimming in young, single ladies. Fishermen? Yes. People his parents' age? Absolutely.

Ethan rose and jumped up on the step that led to the door so he could face them all at once. "I know everyone in town. Where am I supposed to meet someone new?"

Peggy tapped a manicured finger against her lips. "I don't know, Ethan. I just have this feeling that you're about to meet the woman of your dreams."

The door to the bar suddenly flew open as someone rushed in like their life depended on getting inside. In their effort, they slammed into

Ethan, who almost fell off the step. He righted himself and turned to face the person. Everyone in the bar looked in that direction.

A gorgeous woman stood there. With the door open behind her, she was framed by orange and pink light from the setting sun. The colors did amazing things to highlight her hourglass figure and dark hair.

Ethan did a double take. It was an hourglass figure and dark hair that he knew very well. Or, at least, he used to.

"Holy shit," he blurted. "Lauren Wallace. Wow, I haven't seen you in years."

"Ethan freaking McAllister." Her hands went to her hips. "Funny running into *you* of all people."

He took a step back. "'Running into' *literally*. First time opening a door, Lauren?"

She placed a hand over her heart and batted her long eyelashes. "What can I say? I'm just used to men opening them for me."

His mouth quirked. Same old Lauren. He hadn't seen her in ten, maybe fifteen years, and she immediately defaulted to her usual banter. *Their* usual banter.

Despite having basically gone to school together since kindergarten, the real connecting factor between Ethan and Lauren had been his best friend, Robbie. Also known as Lauren's serious, steady boyfriend.

The three of them had spent most of high school together. Football games, movies, hanging out at Lauren's grandmother's coffee shop. From all outward appearances, it would seem like Ethan and

Lauren were best friends. In reality, they'd spent more time bickering and antagonizing each other than anything else.

Looking at Lauren standing in front of him in his bar caused several new feelings to crop up. On the one hand, it was his default to be overcome with a certain annoyance. On principle.

Yet, the way his body was responding…well, that was something he didn't want to think too much on.

Ethan gestured toward the bar. "Why don't you come in and have a drink with a 'real man?'"

She made a big show of looking all around the bar. "Good idea. I'll go find one." With a laugh and a pat to his arm, Lauren jumped down the steps and waved to their audience at the bar. "Hi, everyone," she said sweetly.

"Huh, look at that," Stu said in Ethan's ear. "Peggy called it."

"Called what?" Ethan whispered back as he watched Lauren.

"The woman of your dreams. That didn't take long at all."

Ethan snorted. Lauren Wallace as the woman of his dreams? "Not likely," he said.

Stu stared at him. "Are you sure? Look at her." He whistled long and low. "If you're not going to go for it, maybe I will."

Ethan slapped a hand on Stu's chest as he took a step toward Lauren. "I don't think so."

Stu grinned. "That's what I thought."

Before Ethan could comment on that, his attention was diverted to the bar, where everyone was focused on Lauren.

"Well, well, it's Lauren Wallace," Peggy said, being completely obvious as she assessed Lauren from head to toe.

Not that he could blame her. Lauren had definitely been one of the prettiest girls in their school. But now, she was drop-dead gorgeous. Especially wearing those fitted jeans.

"When did you get back in town?" Peggy asked.

"About an hour ago."

There was a long pause, during which no one seemed to know what to do. Then, the silence broke, and a million questions were flung at her in a matter of seconds.

Lauren turned her head quickly in the direction of each new question, looking from person to person like she was watching a tennis match.

Ethan held up a hand, even though he was just as curious about the answers to those questions as everyone else. "One at a time, guys. Let's give her a minute."

"Thanks," she said with an ornery smile leveled at him. "But I do have the ability to multitask. And speak for myself."

Point taken. He clamped his mouth shut.

"How's Rose?" Wendy asked. "She hasn't been in to get her hair done in a while. We should call her this week," she said to her sister. Peggy agreed.

"Grams is good." Lauren paused, cocked her head as if considering. "Well, she's the same, anyway."

Everyone nodded. The whole town knew Rose Josephs's disposition. She would yell at you at the drop of a hat and never shied away from offering her opinion to pretty much anyone, in any position, at any time, but she was also a valued member of the Seaside Cove community. Everyone respected her. And feared her. A powerful combo.

"What about Brooke?" Stu asked. "Is she married?"

Lauren smiled and rolled her eyes at the same time. "I see you haven't changed, Stu. Still lusting after my sister?"

He grinned and saluted her with his beer mug. "Hell yeah."

"Sorry to tell you that Brooke is engaged."

Stu dramatically clutched at his heart and collapsed onto the bar, making Lauren laugh. A sound that made Ethan suck in a breath, just like it had back in high school.

Peggy circled her. "I don't see a ring on *your* finger."

"I'm not married," Lauren said, attempting to back away from Peggy. "Or engaged."

"Got a boyfriend?"

Lauren narrowed her eyes. Just slightly, but Ethan noticed. "Occasionally."

"Do you have one right now?" Wendy asked from the bar.

"Nope, not at the moment."

Peggy slapped Ethan on the back. "Great news. Because we want you to get Ethan out of his dating slump."

Ethan choked as everyone at the bar nodded and voiced their agreement. These people were supposed to be his friends.

"Oh really," Lauren replied with a twinkle in her eyes. "Having trouble finding a woman? Hm, I'm not surprised."

Ethan gave her a hard look. "What's that supposed to mean?"

"I seem to remember that you never could hold down a serious girlfriend in high school."

"That's because I was too busy playing the field."

"That was one lonely field," she quipped. "Who was your prom date again? Oh right, you didn't have one. Julie Winster dumped you the night before."

Ethan growled under his breath. That was one of his least pleasant memories from high school. "Julie Winster missed out."

"But Robbie and I didn't, since you had to tag along with us to prom."

"You can't deny you were impressed by my dance moves."

Lauren's lips twitched. Everyone in town knew Ethan loved to dance even though he was absolutely horrible at it. He was a local legend.

"You don't have to marry him or anything," Wendy said to Lauren. "You could just, you know…" She shimmied her shoulders and winked.

"Wow," Lauren said, patting his arm again. "That's so sweet that you have the good people of Seaside Cove pimping you out."

"Ethan's a catch," Peggy said.

Ethan had had enough. He cleared his throat. "Okay, that's fine. You've all had your fun. But let's table any further discussion of my dating life. I'm sure Lauren would rather sit down and enjoy a nice, *quiet* drink."

Before any of the troublemakers could protest, he put a hand to Lauren's back and lightly led her to the end of the bar, leaving a couple empty seats between them and the nearest customer. "Let's get you away from the heathens that like to frequent this place."

"Love you, too!" Peggy yelled.

Lauren was laughing at the whole situation. He wanted to be irritated by it, except she looked even more beautiful when she laughed. She always had.

He held out a stool for her. Lauren took her time sitting down, placing her tiny purse on the bar.

"What can I get you?" He gestured to the bar, unable to keep his smile under wraps.

"Alcohol."

"Fine choice. There's a variety."

Joe appeared at that moment with a fresh beer for Ethan.

"Can I please have a gin and tonic? And if you wanted to go light on the tonic, I really wouldn't mind," Lauren said.

Ethan raised his eyebrows in a silent question even as he sat back comfortably.

"Grams," Lauren answered.

"Some things never change." He said it casually, but he put his hand on top of hers and squeezed as he did.

Back in high school, the two of them had thrived on ribbing each other. Verbally sparring with Lauren was one of his favorite hobbies, much like watching baseball games, fishing, and dreaming of traveling.

But you couldn't razz someone the way he did Lauren without getting to know them. How else would you know what to tease them about?

He was aware that she'd had an antagonistic relationship with her grandmother. He didn't know why the two of them were at odds. For the most part, he sensed Lauren enjoyed it. But sometimes it seemed deeper, almost hurtful. Like now.

Lauren sat next to him, stiff as a board. Her posture was rigid, and she was staring straight ahead.

"Want to talk about it?" he asked.

She shrugged. "Oh, you know. Same old. Were you aware that Grams wouldn't have cut her hair if it looked like mine?"

"I wasn't, but I feel like it was the piece of information missing in my life."

The side of her mouth twitched. "Or that my jeans are way too tight?"

Ethan glanced down. "They look just the right amount of tight to me." He winked, and she batted a hand at his chest.

"Shut up." She chewed on a fingernail for a moment before continuing. "Grams also said I should have picked up my sister on the way home. But Gabby didn't want me to pick her up. I tried, dammit." She slapped a hand on the bar and then fidgeted in her chair. "I mean...ugh. Gabby shouldn't even be coming back here, in my opinion."

He wasn't sure what to say to that. Or what was even going on.

Joe set a glass with clear liquid and two lime wedges in front of her. He also grabbed a fresh bowl of pretzels and a bowl of nuts and placed them next to her. "I'm Joe. I grew up in Chesterfield."

"Nice to meet you," she said. "I'm Lauren. I went to high school with this loser." She chucked a thumb in Ethan's direction.

"Nice," he said drily.

Joe grinned. "We were just kidding about *you* dating Ethan. Although, Ethan does need a woman, if you know someone."

She faced him, her eyebrows going straight up. "Oh, really?"

Ethan rolled his eyes. "Don't listen to him. Joe is recently married, and he only wants everyone to be as happy as he is."

"Is that such a bad thing?" Joe asked.

Lauren smiled big at Joe, and Ethan almost fell off his barstool. That smile of hers lit up her entire face. It made her blue eyes sparkle. And she had these two tiny dimples that winked. It used to undo him as a teenager. Now, high school came rushing back in bold, vivid colors.

Lauren had been that rare teenage girl who was popular because she had friends of all shapes, sizes, personality types, interests, groups, you name it. She'd always made the extra effort to talk to people, say hi to the new person, include the loner. And everyone loved her for it.

Then there was Ethan.

It wasn't that the two of them had a contentious relationship. It was more of a yo-yo situation. What they now called frenemies.

They'd lost contact over the years, though. Ethan sat back in his chair and racked his brain. He tried to stay in touch with friends from high school the same way the rest of the planet did…through social media. But he couldn't remember the last time he'd seen anything about Lauren in his feeds.

While Joe showed her some of the wedding photos on his phone, Ethan pulled his own phone out of his pocket and opened an app. He scrolled through his friend list and didn't see Lauren there. That was odd. Maybe she'd left social media.

"What are you doing for a living?" Joe asked.

"I'm a social media strategist."

Well, there went that theory.

"Basically, I help people strategize how to market their businesses while utilizing social media," she said in answer to Joe's blank stare.

"Do you work with large companies?" Ethan asked.

"I have a couple of big ones on my roster. But to be honest, I work more with mom-and-pop places and solopreneurs."

Lauren leaned toward Joe, and those dimples shone again. "You wouldn't happen to have any french fries, would you?"

"We sure do. You want to see a full menu?"

"No, thanks," she said. "Fries will do it for me."

"I'll put that order in right away," Joe said, then left them alone. Finally.

Ethan took a pull of his beer. "How long are you in town?"

She lifted her drink to her lips. Perfect

heart-shaped lips painted a light pink. Those perfect lips pressed together in a narrow line. "I'm not sure. I have some family stuff to deal with." She glanced around the bar slowly with a faraway look on her face.

Ethan followed her gaze. The people, the pool table and dartboards in the back corner. He was proud of this place. He'd rescued it from Old Man Henry Monroe, who'd owned The Thirsty Lobster for decades.

Once Ethan took over, he'd tried to preserve the dive-like quality that the locals loved, while also updating it with touches he knew young people and families would appreciate. He'd found a pinball machine and placed it in a special spot in the corner. He'd spent a little too much buying TVs, but they looked good mounted around the walls. Plus, he was able to play a variety of sports and other shows, so everyone was happy.

The old wooden bar had been about to collapse, so Ethan had saved as many pieces of it as he could. Then he mixed those pieces with reclaimed wood from an old fishing boat. He expanded it into a large U shape, offering much more seating.

Lauren was now examining all of the dining tables on the other side of the room, half of which were full of people who didn't want to cook on a Sunday. That was something else he'd been working on—updating the menu. He wasn't going to remove any of the fun bar foods, but he did want to offer some family-friendly food and healthy options.

Joe reappeared. "You two ever date back in high school?"

"Each other?" Lauren asked incredulously as Ethan choked on his beer.

"No way," Ethan insisted.

"Did you hate each other or something?" Joe wasn't able to wait for the answer because he got called to refill a drink order.

Ethan turned to Lauren. "Hate is kind of a strong word. And not exactly the best way to describe our relationship."

Tilting her head, Lauren appeared thoughtful. "You're right."

"It was more of a dislike."

Lauren shook her head. "Nope, that's not it."

"Okay, if you're so smart, what was it, then?"

"Well…" She bit her lip. "Back in high school…"

"Yes?" he prodded.

She leveled an intense stare at him. "I kind of had a thing for you."

CHAPTER THREE

Ethan blinked. Other than that slight eye twitch, he didn't move a muscle as he took a moment to let Lauren's words sink in.

I kind of had a thing for you.

He sat back and took her in. Lauren appeared completely unaffected. She sipped her gin and tonic and played with a strand of her hair.

Lauren Wallace had a thing for him in high school? Un-freaking-believable. Sure, they'd hung out almost every single day, thanks to their mutual relationships with Robbie. But they'd also fought every single day. They'd annoyed each other every single day. They'd provoked, irritated, riled up, and aggravated each other *every single day*.

To hear this now was shocking.

Almost as shocking as the fact that he'd had a thing for her, too.

"You..." Ethan straightened. "You were into me?"

She snorted. "Don't let it go to your head."

He grinned as he leaned toward her. "What level of lust are we talking about here? Were you scribbling my name in your notebook, or were you having naughty dreams about me?"

She closed the gap between them, so they were practically nose to nose. "First of all, I just had a harmless little crush on you at some point. No big deal. Secondly..." She broke off and took her time giving him a long, sexy once-over.

"Secondly?" he prompted, his pulse picking up in anticipation of what she might say next.

"You didn't have *that* body in high school." She bit her lip as she finished ogling him. "You look good, McAllister."

He swallowed. Hard. "Thanks, Wallace. You look okay, too."

She tilted her head, and a piece of her hair fell over her eye, making her look even more sexy. "Just okay?" she asked primly.

Way more than okay. She was smokin' hot. But beyond that luscious dark hair and those penetrating blue eyes, the bangin' body and the gorgeous face, Lauren was funny and witty, and he liked being around her.

Joe showed up with the fries she'd ordered, and Ethan was saved from having to voice any of those incriminating thoughts.

"Think you two can sit any closer?" Joe asked as he placed the plate of hot fries in front of Lauren.

"Huh?" Ethan asked before realizing that Lauren was practically in his lap. When had that happened?

They scooted apart, and Lauren's face broke out into a light red blush.

"We haven't seen each other since graduation," he said.

"We're just catching up," Lauren added.

Joe gave them a look that clearly said he didn't buy any of that. "Is that what we're calling it now? Well, don't forget that we're in Seaside Cove, Land of the Gossips." He gestured to the other side of the bar, where all eyes were trained on the two of them.

"You're going to be the hot topic of conversation tomorrow," Joe said.

Ethan shrugged. "Looks like we already are."

Lauren popped out of her seat and leaned over him to grab a bottle of ketchup. As she did, he couldn't ignore her breast brushing against his arm, no matter how gentlemanly he reacted to her on the outside. The rest of his body noticed, too, a rush of awakening washing over him.

"Excuse me," she said in a breathy voice before returning to her fries.

Ethan's mind went blank, and his throat went dry, unable to speak. All he could do was stare at her. God, she was really stunning. He remembered that she'd been pretty in high school. Maybe the prettiest girl in their class. She'd had long dark hair that fell in loose curls down her back. Her hair was a lot shorter now, but the way the layers fell over her eyes was damn sexy. And those eyes... They were the lightest shade of blue that popped against all that dark hair and long lashes.

"What are you doing?" Lauren asked, pulling Ethan out of his own head. She jabbed a fry in his general direction. "You're staring at me, weirdo."

He rubbed a hand over his face. "I'm not a weirdo. I am a business-owning, law-abiding, responsible—"

"Responsible?" She interrupted with a noise that was a mix between a huff and a laugh. "How can you say anything about responsibility, when you used to run around doing whatever you pleased, whenever you wanted? You didn't take anything seriously. What did you know about responsibility? What do you know about it now?"

She wasn't wrong. Ethan had been irresponsible, careless, unreliable, unpredictable—you name the appropriate synonym. That innate recklessness had taken him around the world. He'd met Veronica, another American, in Budapest and found out the real consequences of flying by the seat of his pants.

"It so happens that I have become a very dependable citizen of Seaside Cove."

"Doubtful."

He defensively gestured around the room. "I own this bar."

"I know." She popped a fry in her mouth.

Once again, she caught him off guard. "How?"

She ate a few more fries, taking her time about it, then said, "Grams sends me newspaper clippings about anyone I've ever met. Marriage announcements, obituaries, any mention of a classmate. She's made it impossible for me to forget my past. Sometimes I think she's secretly trying to get me to move back here."

"You wouldn't want to live in Seaside Cove again?" he asked.

She shrugged. "I wouldn't mind Seaside Cove. But it would make Grams too happy."

"We can't have that." Ethan held his chuckle in.

"Besides, I would probably just become her personal torture object."

"Oh." Honestly, Ethan didn't quite know what to think about Rose Josephs. The older woman looked at him as if she knew every single one of his secrets, and that was unsettling as hell.

"Sometimes I get the feeling your grandmother is spitting in my latte," he said.

"I wouldn't put it past her," Lauren replied casually.

Fantastic.

She downed the rest of her drink, then held it up to Joe to signal a refill.

"You might want to go a little easy. How about you switch to water now. Or maybe coffee," he suggested.

"Thanks, Mom."

"As the owner of this establishment, I have a responsibility—"

"There's that word again. Does it feel weird coming out of your mouth? Unfamiliar? Alien?"

He shook his head. "You're really on a roll tonight. Anyway, you're messing up the whole equilibrium of our relationship. You're supposed to be the responsible one. I'm the carefree goofball. When did *I* ever have to warn *you* about drinking too much? *Never*."

"Maybe I need a night off from obligations. Let my hair down a little." She met his eyes, bit her lip. There was a long pause between the two of them. Long and significant. "A night to be bad," she finished.

Ethan swallowed hard. He was glad they hadn't stopped drinking, because his throat became massively dry again. *Lauren Wallace wants to be bad?*

She may not be acting like her old self right now, but he was still the same person, only with more experience. And he wouldn't be Ethan McAllister if he didn't *just go with it*.

• • •

Lauren had a nice warmth running through her body, thanks to the multiple gin and tonics.

It had been a long couple of days driving up to New England, with stops to visit various friends along the way. She should be exhausted, yet sitting here, going back and forth with Ethan, was actually giving her a second wind.

She was both thrilled and shocked that Ethan had taken over The Thirsty Lobster. It couldn't be denied that he'd done wonders to the place. But she couldn't get her mind around the fact that Ethan was a business owner.

He'd always been laidback, which had mostly annoyed her, since it was completely opposite of how she viewed things. At the same time, she'd also coveted that casualness and been attracted to him.

Actually, it had been more than a harmless crush. She'd had some major feelings for him. But Ethan had ended that.

Lauren had been hanging out with both Ethan and Robbie a lot. They were both cute guys, and she'd enjoyed spending time with them. And, okay, she'd enjoyed flirting with the two of them as well. But she'd been leaning toward Ethan, which made zero sense. Robbie had been the smart, safe bet. Robbie had a plan.

Ethan, on the other hand, had no plan, no ideas of what he wanted to do with his life. He didn't even know if he was going to go to college. He was a "fly by the seat of your pants" kind of guy, which was against everything Lauren believed in.

Then came the Sadie Hawkins dance in the tenth grade. She remembered approaching him to feel out his interest. But he'd been aloof. He'd suggested she ask Robbie instead. Lauren had been really embarrassed.

After that, she'd had to pretend that she'd never asked him to the dance, never wanted to go with him, never been interested at all. Maybe that was when the antagonistic side of their relationship started. Her pride had taken a pretty big hit.

She watched his throat bob as he swallowed hard. Lauren knew she was flirting with him tonight, and she was enjoying his reaction. There was no harm in a little innocent flirting with an old friend. Especially one who'd turned her down all those years ago, she thought with a silent laugh.

Of course, her thoughts weren't exactly innocent, and Ethan was more of a frenemy.

"You want to be bad tonight?" he asked, gulping.

She smiled slowly. "Maybe."

"You want to knock off a liquor store or something?"

She laughed. "That might be a little *too* bad."

"You could always go skinny dipping in the harbor," he suggested.

"You want me to jump into that water? Naked?" Was she yelling? Her teeth were becoming a little numb. But quite a few heads turned in her direction when she said "naked."

Lauren cleared her throat. "I should probably keep it down."

Ethan glanced over his shoulder and sighed. "I knew I should have kept this place closed on Sundays." He took a big swallow from his beer. "No bar, no gossips."

"No bar, no reconnecting with me," she said.

His smiled faded. "That would have been awful."

"Yeah?"

His face softened. "It's been really good to see you, Lauren."

It was a simple statement but a powerful one. Lauren felt warm again, and this time it had nothing to do with the alcohol.

"I see a lot of people from high school around here," Ethan continued. "It's nice. But you and I hung out almost every day. Even though you were a total pain in the ass—"

"Thanks," she interrupted with a wink.

"With all of your rules and your lists."

She glanced at her phone, knowing he would make fun of the amount of organization and lists she kept in there. "Better than you with that whole 'it'll work itself out' attitude you had."

He let out a half laugh, half snort. "God, you're so structured. I bet you still follow every single rule. I bet you make lists about the rules you have to follow, and rules about how to make your lists."

Once again, she snuck a glance at her phone, pushed it farther away on the bar top. "And I bet you still breeze through life, paying your bills late and living without a five-year plan."

He laughed. "You're such a Goody Two-Shoes." He leaned toward her, daring her to contradict him.

She met him halfway, moving closer so she could really see into his light brown eyes. Eyes that she was pretty sure she'd labeled as "dreamy" when she was a teenager.

"You think you're insulting me? I take pride in my Goody Two-Shoes–ness, which is a hell of a lot better than being a flaky slacker with no plan."

He placed a hand on her thigh, and every nerve ending in her body woke up. "Now you're playing dirty, Wallace."

She slapped a hand on his chest, pausing to feel the muscles underneath. Damn, Ethan was built. "You always were a little instigator."

He leaned in even closer. "And you…"

"Yeah?" she asked with an edge to her voice.

"You were always my favorite person to fight with."

Maybe it was the alcohol. Maybe it was the pure exhaustion. Lauren had no idea. But she was suddenly feeling very sentimental…if not other things toward Ethan.

Somewhere, in the far recesses of her mind, she was aware that they were in a public place. A good portion of the town was sitting on the other end of the bar, surely watching their every move.

She knew all of this.

Yet, she didn't seem to care.

Lauren closed the gap between them by pressing her lips to Ethan's. If he was surprised, he didn't show it. Instead, his hand came up to the back of her head, holding her close to him as he took over the kiss. And all Lauren could focus on were Ethan's lips on hers.

His hands moved from framing her face into her hair, where they held her head in place so he could do wonderful and magical things to her mouth.

Damn, the guy could *kiss*.

She could taste the beer on his mouth. As she pressed herself even closer to him, she picked up his scent. He smelled of soap, like he'd just come from the shower. And there was a hint of some kind of aftershave. Very subtle, yet very potent.

He slid his tongue into her mouth, deepening the kiss, and she actually moaned. Or maybe that was him. She had no idea.

The way his lips felt against hers was mind-blowing. But then she heard some whistling catcalls in the background. *Uh-oh*. She pulled back a little. "Please tell me they're watching some sporting event and something extraordinary just happened," she said, keeping her eyes trained on Ethan.

His gaze flicked over her head to take in the customers at the bar. Then he met her eyes again.

"We probably shouldn't have done that *here*." He ran a hand over his jawline.

She hadn't meant to flirt with him. She hadn't meant to kiss him. And she certainly hadn't meant to do it in public, in front of enough townies that by tomorrow morning her name would be on all of Seaside Cove's residents' tongues.

Hell, that was going to happen anyway, just by her showing up here. But there was a difference between "you'll never guess who I saw at the bar last night" and "you'll never guess who I saw kissing at the bar last night."

She definitely didn't mean to suggest they get

outta there. But she *had* suggested it. Even more unbelievable, he agreed. He threw some bills onto the bar top, waved goodbye to Joe, and took her hand in his. Pulling her toward the door, he ignored all the questions and comments thrown at him.

Lauren tried to block out what people were saying, but she heard someone mention Grams. She paused for a moment, hesitant. Grams was going to hear about this.

"You okay?" Ethan asked.

She faced him. Damn, he was handsome. Tall, with broad shoulders and tanned skin. He had light brown hair that was slightly in need of a trim, and his brown eyes were big and sexy and focused directly on her.

The truth was she knew exactly what she was doing, and Grams didn't have a say in it. When it came to her life, her career, Lauren ran a tight ship. She'd been planning for weeks just to come up to Maine and help her sister. So, maybe for just one night, she could do whatever the hell she wanted — and right now, she *really* wanted this. For once in her life, she could take a risk. Couldn't she?

"Yep," she answered.

With a grin, Ethan pulled her out the door. As soon as it closed behind them, he grabbed her face and kissed her long and hard. Good thing he was holding her so tight, because her knees went weak.

"I live nearby," he said as their kiss ended. His voice was gruff, and those brown eyes were emanating lust.

She nodded and allowed him to lead the way.

Ethan lived in a small Cape Cod house only a

block away from the bar. Once they crossed that threshold, clothes started flying off. Their hands became increasingly more frenzied.

There were no words exchanged between them. Only contented sighs and satisfied moans.

For someone who prided herself on being a planner, Lauren wasn't doing a great job sticking to the plan. She'd come to town to take care of her sister and check on her grandmother. Instead, she ended up in bed with her frenemy from high school.

What was that expression about best-laid plans? She'd have to figure that out later, because right now she was too busy enjoying the thrill of this to care.

CHAPTER FOUR

There were only two reasons why someone would be up this early in Seaside Cove. Either they were a fisherman, or they were doing a walk of shame.

Lauren groaned loudly. Not like there was anyone around to hear it. When was the last time she'd started the day wearing the same clothes she'd had on the night before?

Well, at least she got to see the sunrise. How often could she claim that? And it was a phenomenal sunrise that morning. The sky looked like it was on fire, all reds and yellows and oranges.

Lauren chewed on her lip as she continued her walk back to Grams's house. She couldn't believe she'd actually slept with Ethan McAllister. What in the hell had she been thinking? She sighed. What's done was done, and she'd had a good time. Even better than good. Ethan had been…quite amazing, really. And she had no regrets about enjoying that.

The only thing was that now she had to face the music.

Or, more precisely, her grandmother.

Her stomach turned. While she'd like to think it was from one too many cocktails, she knew the real source of worry lay at the end of the driveway in the gorgeous Victorian house.

She'd texted Grams the night before and said she was hanging with a friend. Grams was way too smart to believe that. Lauren might as well enjoy these last few moments of peace.

There was another thing to think about, too. She hadn't exactly been discreet last night. Half the town had watched her suck face with Ethan and then leave the bar together, their intentions as clear as the alcohol in all those gin and tonics she'd been downing.

It was only a matter of time before the gossip train dropped off the news of her hookup.

What Lauren expected to see as she made her way up the driveway to Grams's house were some fishing boats out on the water and a dark house still fast asleep. She did not anticipate running smack dab into her sister, who was sprawled across the porch on a yoga mat. Lauren wobbled, tried to right herself, but went down hard on the porch with a big *thud*.

"Owww," she moaned, rubbing her wrist. "What the hell, Gabby?"

"Namaste." A big grin spread across Gabby's face.

Lauren would be annoyed, but her youngest sister was so damn hard to get mad at. Gabby was a petite dynamo with pretty auburn curls that trailed past her shoulders, big blue eyes, and the most endearing smile known to man.

Currently, she was wearing black yoga pants and a pink fitted top. Her feet were bare, and her hair was piled on top of her head. A few curls had snuck out to frame her face. She looked like she could be posing on the cover of a fitness catalog.

Gabby had always been into yoga, Pilates, and dance of all forms, and she'd had a body to reflect those interests. But Lauren couldn't help but notice her sister was looking a little thin.

That made reality race back and slap her in the face.

"You okay?" Lauren asked, after she untangled herself from Gabby and helped her stand up.

"I think I'm the one who should be asking *you* that question."

"Me?"

"She who stays out all night long and does the walk of shame home in the morning." Gabby's grin grew even wider.

Lauren leaned back against the railing of the porch and crossed her arms over her chest. "I didn't say anything about a walk of shame." Nothing shameful about what happened between her and Ethan last night. "That's your opinion."

"Whatever you say." Gabby grinned. "By the way, Brooke arrived late last night."

Lauren tried to remember her sister's flight details. She couldn't, but she was positive Brooke wasn't supposed to get here for another week or so. "Seriously?"

Gabby shrugged. "She might as well still be in Chicago, though. She's been on the phone with her fiancé since she arrived." Gabby tilted her head, a mischievous look on her face. "One sister is all about her fiancé, and the other sister spent the night with a mystery man."

"What if I slept in my car?"

"Oh please. Your car was parked here all night. Besides, Grams said you were hanging with 'a friend.'" Gabby used air quotes to emphasize her point. "Neither of us bought that."

Great, just great. Lauren grew serious. "I'm sorry I wasn't here when you arrived."

She took a closer inspection of her sister. Gabby put on a good front, but Lauren couldn't miss the pallor of her skin, the dark circles under her eyes, and worst of all, the sadness in those eyes.

"That's okay," Gabby said, not quite making eye contact. "Really. I got in late. Grams and I made some ice cream sundaes, then I went to bed."

"Ice cream at night? Damn, she must be softening. She would have never let me eat ice cream for dinner. She always went easier on you."

"Maybe she just likes me better."

"I wouldn't doubt it." Lauren grinned. She reached over and lightly tugged on one of Gabby's loose curls. "I see you're back to your normal hair color."

Gabby shrugged. "I was doing purple for a while, which I really liked, even though Grams told me I looked like Barney the dinosaur when I FaceTimed her. But I was kinda missing being myself."

"Speaking of being you…" Lauren began.

Gabby narrowed her eyes. "Were we?"

With her sweetest smile, Lauren continued. "Yes. Now, I've come up with a plan for you." When Gabby simply raised her eyebrows, Lauren went on. "I have a few simple items to help you get your life back on track."

Gabby snorted. "A life plan, huh? Does it have bullet points?"

Lauren ignored the sarcasm. "Of course it has

bullet points. And sub-lists and color coordination."

Gabby stretched her arms over her head. "If it's not in an Excel spreadsheet, I'm not doing it."

"Make fun all you want," Lauren said. "But I'm not just in Seaside Cove for vacation. Neither is Brooke," she said through gritted teeth.

Lauren's feelings about Brooke had never been simple. While she knew that Brooke coming to Maine was going to add a lot of frustration to her life, she also knew that Gabby needed both of her sisters.

"We're here to help you, Gabs. There's no better way to do that than by getting organized."

As she began to readjust her yoga mat, Gabby frowned, a gesture she rarely did. Before she could talk herself out of it, Lauren decided to drop the "Gabby life plan" and give her sister something to make her smile again.

"Is it technically a one-night stand if you've known the person for a really long time?"

"I think my yoga practice is done for the day." Gabby dropped her mat. "You had a one-night stand? With who?" She was practically jumping up and down. "Tell me. Tell me!"

Gabby's phone started playing "Here Comes the Sun." She picked it up, and her smile faded quickly, then she hit a button and the Beatles' song abruptly ended.

"Everything okay?" she asked, trying to be as nonchalant as she could. But her sister's entire demeanor had changed in a second.

Gabby didn't say anything.

After another few moments, Lauren tried again.

"Gabs?"

"What? Oh, it's nothing." She pasted a smile on her face, but it didn't reach her eyes. "Back to you and your little sexcapade."

Lauren had a million questions. She studied her sister. Again, Lauren decided to stay quiet and give Gabby something else to focus on. Even if it was at her own expense.

She wiggled her eyebrows. "I don't know if I should kiss and tell."

"Oh, please. You're dying to tell, and I'm dying to hear. Spill!"

Lauren took a seat on one of the wicker chairs, and Gabby joined her on the adjacent one. Almost in sync, they both pulled their legs up so they were sitting cross-legged. And Lauren told her sister all about last night.

When she was done, Gabby tapped a finger to her lips. "Didn't you used to fight with him all the time? Am I making that up?"

"No, you're right." That was the complicated part. Lauren rose and walked to the porch railing, watching a bird fly gracefully overhead until it made a swift dive into the ocean to retrieve its next meal. Mother Nature held no answers for her, though.

She turned back around to face her sister. "We hung out all the time because I was dating Robbie, and Ethan was Robbie's best friend. But we kind of had this whole frenemy thing going on. Right up until we kissed."

"So, how did you go from hate to lust?" Gabby asked, then shook her head. "No, that doesn't matter. Here's the real question. Are you going to see him again? And by 'see' I mean get down and dirty with him naked?"

Lauren shook her head as she laughed. "You need to get your libido in check. And I don't know about Ethan. I mean, I don't live here, and it was kind of just this spontaneous thing that happened. Totally not in my plans. In fact, he already wreaked havoc on my plans by keeping me away from here when you arrived."

"Who kept you away?" Grams, who had just appeared right behind Lauren out of freaking nowhere, asked.

Lauren jumped a mile. "Holy grandma ninja! Aren't you supposed to be at work?" Grams usually started her day hella early to get into the café and start baking.

"Kelsey is doing the morning shift today." Grams pinned her with a stare, and it took all of one second for Lauren to start squirming. "Six o'clock in the morning," Grams said.

Lauren looked to her sister, but Gabby stayed planted firmly in her seat.

"I realize it's early," Lauren said.

"Or, one could say it's late. As in, you stayed out all night, Lauren Rose Wallace."

This was ridiculous. Lauren was thirty-three years old. She shouldn't have to explain to her grandmother, or anyone else, where she was and what she was doing.

"I sent you a text so you would know that I was with a friend. And I was fine." Better than fine. Especially with Ethan's muscular arms wrapped around her.

"A text message? That's what your eighty-year-old grandmother deserves? Someone could have stolen your phone and sent that while they were harvesting your organs."

"When did you get so dramatic?"

"When did you start lying?"

Her head snapped up at that question. Her heart started beating rapidly, too. Oh shit. *She knew.* She had to know. Grams was pinning her with one of *those* stares. Those "I know exactly what you were up to, and I've been standing here letting you lie to my face" stares.

"But speaking of text messages, I've received quite a few this morning." Grams waved her phone in the air.

Shiiiiiit.

"How do you think it feels to find out my eldest granddaughter is out there offering her body up to Ethan McAllister?"

"Ohmigod, Grams!"

"Everyone in Seaside Cove knows that you shoved your tongue down his throat in the middle of a crowded bar."

"Well, um, it was kind of an accident," Lauren said. As far as excuses went, this was one of her worst.

Grams crossed her arms over her chest. "Was leaving the bar with Ethan also an accident? Because it doesn't sound like it was."

"Um, well…"

"I'm assuming you ended up at his house. Or did the two of you get a room at a pay-by-the-hour, seedy motel off the highway?"

And Grams wondered where Gabby got her dramatic chops from.

"We went to his house. It's not a big deal," Lauren said.

"Not a big deal? It's becoming a big deal as the entire population of Seaside Cove is waking up to your escapades on the front page of the newspaper."

Grams was exaggerating about the newspaper, but just barely. Lauren knew it, yet she was still annoyed. "All I did was hang out with an old friend."

"'Hang out?' Is that what we're calling sex these days?"

"Are you judging me, Grams?"

"No." She pointed to Lauren and then to Gabby. "I have never judged one of you. Not ever."

Lauren exchanged a look with Gabby, who had one eyebrow raised.

"I didn't judge you when you decided to double major in theater and philosophy," Grams said to Gabby.

With a minor in Latin, Lauren silently added.

Gabby took a drink from her water bottle. "You told me I didn't have a lick of sense and that I'd never find a job."

"And I didn't judge this one," Grams continued, hooking a thumb toward Lauren, "when you quit your well-paying job with benefits and a 401(k) to go off and start your own business dabbling in Instagram."

"I don't dabble," Lauren said, hearing the defensiveness in her voice. "I am a social media strategist." She didn't mention that she'd pulled in a six-figure salary last year and had to hire two people, with more staff coming in the future. "You called me a damn fool."

Ignoring both of them, Grams went on. "Have I said anything judgy about your sister's long string of jackass boyfriends?"

"You called her fiancé a 'cheese dick' last night," Gabby said, using air quotes to make her point.

Grams shook her head. "Speaking the truth is not judgmental. It's just the truth. Brooke's fiancé *is* a cheese dick."

Lauren opened her mouth to say otherwise but quickly shut it. "Yeah," she agreed. Gabby nodded. None of them were fans of Brooke's fiancé, Lucas.

"Now, if we're done here, I'm going to go make a pot of coffee."

"And some blueberry scones?" Gabby asked hopefully.

Grams narrowed her eyes. Gabby dazzled her with her biggest, brightest smile. As usual, Grams caved. "And blueberry scones."

Gabby pumped her fist in the air.

But Grams wasn't quite done. "I'll also be playing your PR assistant as I continue to receive calls about your…untoward behavior."

Lauren groaned.

Grams pointed at her. "Make sure you take a shower. God knows what you got on you sitting at that bar for hours last night."

"Hey, I heard you go into that bar all the time," Lauren said.

"And I take a shower afterward." Grams started

to walk back into the house, but she paused in front of Lauren, placed a hand on her shoulder, and lowered her voice. "You okay?"

She wanted to say something sarcastic or snarky, but she knew this was Grams's way. "I'm fine. Don't worry about me."

Grams's eyes softened as she looked her up and down. She gave a definitive nod. "Good." Then her scowl returned, and she continued on into the house.

"As much as I'd love to stay here and keep talking about your 'untoward behavior,'" Gabby said with a wry grin, "I gotta go meditate. I need to find my center."

Gabby wasn't the only one who needed to find her center after last night. At least she was done with the "telling Grams" portion of this nightmare. Now, she just needed to decide what to do about the man she'd never in a million years imagined she'd be having a morning-after conversation with.

• • •

Ethan had woken up with a big ole smile on his face. That grin got even bigger as he'd taken in the messy blankets, the twisted sheets, his boxer shorts hanging over a lamp in his bedroom…

Then he'd realized he was alone.

Had Lauren Wallace used him and then snuck out?

He snagged his phone and saw that she'd sent him a text message. Thank goodness he'd remembered to exchange numbers with her.

Had to run. Didn't want to wake you. Great to "catch" up. ;-)

A text message wasn't the most ideal end to such a great evening, but it was better than nothing. Although, he couldn't shake an uneasy feeling as he showered and cleaned up his bedroom. Since he didn't have to be at the bar for a couple hours, he decided to take a walk.

But as he made his way around town, he couldn't stop feeling disappointed. He didn't want last night to be a one-time thing. He'd love to see more of her.

Sure, he knew Lauren lived out of town now. Not to mention, she probably had some list about why getting involved was a bad idea. But what if… He couldn't help but ponder.

Ethan circled around to the docks. He'd always liked walking around this area, checking out the boats, taking in the activity of the local fishermen. The sound of birds chattering as they tried to feast on the findings of the fishermen. It was comforting to hear the boats banging against their docks as the water lapped against the shore.

After taking a good long time to brood, he finally pushed away and turned. That's when he spotted Lauren walking out of The Fish Hut. Tourists always stopped in The School to pick up their fish when visiting. It was a nice, clean seafood restaurant on the water that also sold raw fish for cooking. But the residents of Seaside Cove favored The Fish Hut, the local fish market, where the prices weren't jacked up and the fish were always freshly caught. That's where Lauren was exiting, a bag in her hand.

He knew he should let it go. No reason to go over to her. Yet, his brain wasn't relaying that information to his feet, and he found himself picking up the pace to meet her.

"Lauren," he called when he was close enough.

She stopped in her tracks, slowly turning to face him. She'd obviously showered and changed. Ethan thought she looked fresh and beautiful in a long flowery dress and sandals. She had a scarf tied in her dark hair, and her face was clean and free of make-up, which, in his opinion, she didn't need anyway.

"Ethan, hi," she said, shuffling her feet and biting her lip.

"Good morning," he replied easily. "What are you doing down here?"

She held up the plastic bag. "Grams sent me to pick up some fish for tonight. She's making a big dinner for me and my sisters—they both got in last night. Although she claims it's only for her."

He studied her, surprised at her behavior. For someone he'd seen at their most intimate last night, it was a bit odd that she wasn't meeting his eyes. Might as well get straight to the point, then. "I never would have taken you for the love 'em and leave 'em type."

She blushed. "I'm not. Not usually, anyway."

He took a step closer. "Should I be honored or offended by that?"

She made a choked sound. "Excuse me?"

"One little text message." He shoved his hands in his pockets. "That's all I get after everything we did together last night?"

"*Shhh*," she hissed with wide eyes. "I've already gotten an earful from Grams, who claims that everyone in town knows what happened." She glanced toward the water for a long moment. "Anyway, I'm sorry I didn't wake you this morning. It was kind of shitty of me."

"Apology accepted," he said easily. "But next time, I expect a handwritten note."

She arched a brow. "Next time?"

"Yes." He knew she wasn't going to go for it, but he would try anyway. "I'm not sure how long you're planning on staying in town, but rumor has it I'm going to ask you out."

"Oh really? I haven't heard that rumor yet."

Ethan rocked back on his heels. He tried to decipher her body language. His gut was telling him she was interested, but he also suspected this wouldn't be an easy sell.

He took another step closer. "What do you think?"

"You and I are very different."

"Hm, seems to me we were on the same page last night."

She twined her fingers together. "Look, last night was…"

"Hot? Erotic? Fun? Sexy? All of the above?"

"Unexpected," she said.

"Sometimes the best things can be found in the unexpected."

"Thank you, walking fortune cookie." Her sarcastic smile faded as she took a moment to chew on a fingernail. "Listen, Ethan, last night was…a one-time thing. Okay?"

"Unless we do it again," he said, "and then it can be a two-time thing."

She rolled her eyes dramatically.

"Did you have fun?"

She offered a small smile and kept her voice low when she answered. "You know I did."

"Then what's the issue?"

"This"—she gestured between them—"was not in my plans when I decided to come home to Seaside Cove."

"Do you always stick to the plan?"

"Ah, yeah," she said as if this was the most obvious thing in the world. "Why would you make a plan if you didn't intend to stick to it?"

"Maybe a better opportunity comes along."

She narrowed her eyes. A cute little wrinkle formed on her forehead. "Hmm. I guess I didn't really take the time to ask you many questions last night."

He offered his most charming grin. "You know what's a good place to get to know me? A romantic candlelit dinner with wine and snotty waiters."

She sighed. "Ethan McAllister."

"So that's a hard no for dinner with me on Wednesday?"

"The fact that I didn't wake you up and did the whole sneaky-sneaky, get-out-of-Dodge-the-morning-after act should have really clued you in to my future intentions."

"Lunch instead of dinner, then?"

Finally, she broke. She laughed, forcing her dimples to make an appearance, and Ethan got the feeling he was getting through to her.

Just then, a loud whistle from halfway down the

street broke through the intimate bubble around them. One of the guys Ethan recognized from the bar last night was giving them a thumbs-up.

"Right there," Lauren said. "That's another reason we can't go out again."

"We didn't really go out," he said. "Technically. We went outside but then walked straight to my house. Not a date. Not an outing."

The corners of her mouth twitched. "You're ridiculous." She shook her head, and her face grew serious. "I really don't want to be the center of the gossip gazette. And I'm only here temporarily."

He took in her words. "I wasn't in your plan, and you never change plans."

She blushed. "Exactly, yeah."

"You seriously don't want anything else to happen with us because of your plan?"

A long silence stretched between them. Ethan had the feeling they were both willing the other to give in.

"Friends?" she finally asked.

"We've always been friends," he replied, trying hard not to let his disappointment show.

And he must have succeeded, because she smiled and blew out a breath, like she was relieved. "Great," she said, nodding, then stepped back and started to turn away. "Great. See you around."

He waved her off with a smile, but after last night, there was no way Ethan could go back to being friends-only. Or frenemies-only. Or whatever they'd *only* been that they definitely weren't anymore. But until Lauren figured that out, he would let it go and respect her decision. Because that's what friends did, even if it hurt them to do it.

CHAPTER FIVE

Lauren had slept late. Again.

The last few weeks had passed by in a blur. A very busy, somewhat chaotic, slightly emotional whirlwind.

As a favor to a friend, Lauren agreed to be a workshop presenter at a virtual social media conference. That meant she'd had to drop everything else and put together a couple workshops, including making slides and promoting the conference to her followers.

She'd been so swamped that she hadn't been able to give Gabby her full attention. They'd only had time to talk about her finances a little, even though Lauren had outlined a full-fledged financial plan to help her sister get out of debt and start saving money.

Of course, Brooke took every opportunity to chastise her. "I thought you wanted us here to help Gabby, and now you're doing your own work."

Lauren was frustrated. Not to mention tired and just...depleted. Maybe she was getting a cold or allergies or something, because her energy had been decimated.

She'd been waking up late, and even once she was awake, she had a hard time getting out of bed. That's why she'd decided to finally take it easy today.

Way later than she typically woke up, she made

her way down to the kitchen for coffee. Still bleary-eyed and tired.

"Look who finally decided to grace us with her presence." Brooke smirked. She was wearing a tailored pantsuit, her makeup flawless, and tasteful pearl studs at her ears. She had on a headset and was carrying her iPad.

Lauren couldn't deny that Brooke was the most gorgeous woman on the planet. She had long, thick hair a shade lighter than Lauren's. She could definitely be in a shampoo commercial. Plus, she had the same blue eyes that Lauren and Gabby had inherited. But where Gabby was adorable, Brooke was…graceful. Sophisticated, classy.

Even from the doorway, she could smell Brooke's expensive perfume. While Brooke was Chanel, Lauren would choose something new and trendy, and Gabby would make her own organic scent.

Yet, the three of them were sisters.

Lauren yawned. "Sorry. I am so wiped out."

"You've been tired a lot lately." Gabby was stirring some eggs at the stove. "Want some scrambled eggs?"

"A little late to be making breakfast," Lauren said, slumping into a chair.

"I've already been at work at the café," Gabby said. "Brooke started early this morning too and forgot to eat," she said, waving a spatula at her sister.

"I didn't forget. I rarely eat breakfast," Brooke said. "Eggs are good, though. High protein. I'm doing a low-carb diet right now. Lucas thinks it's a good idea."

Lauren loved scrambled eggs, but for some reason her stomach turned at the idea of eating them. She shook her head. "None for me. Maybe just some toast."

"You have mono or something?" Grams asked, coming into the kitchen. Her terse question was followed up by the obligatory hand-to-the-forehead move. Grams stared down at her for a long time. "No fever. But you have been sleeping a lot the last couple of days. Your eyes look clear. But there is...something."

"What?"

Grams shook her head. "I'm not sure," she said slowly.

Something about the way Grams was eyeing her was unnerving. She rose. "I'm gonna grab some coffee and then a nice, long shower before I hop online for work."

After her shower, Lauren felt even more tired, as if she'd just run a marathon. She sat down on the edge of the bed and toweled her damp hair. She wasn't feeling too great all around.

She picked up her coffee but paused with the mug in midair. Suddenly, her taste for it dissipated. She felt kinda queasy.

This better not be a stomach bug. Those were the worst.

Brooke stuck her head in the door. "Hey, do you have any tampons?"

Lauren put the untouched coffee on her dresser and scrounged around in her purse and then in her makeup bag. *That's weird...* She must have forgotten to pack them. "No, sorry. Try the linen closet in the bathroom."

"We've been here for over three weeks now. Guess we'll have to do a big tampon run for both of us. I'll see if Gabby has any." Brooke dashed out of the room.

"Right." Lauren sat back on the bed. Her coffee was growing cold, yet she still didn't want any. Strange, since she considered herself a coffee addict.

She dressed quickly and ran a comb through her hair, deciding to let it air dry today. As she considered putting on some light makeup, she couldn't get something out of her mind.

What was it? What was bothering her?

Grabbing her laptop from the desk, she flopped onto her bed and decided to work from there for a couple hours. She set up her pillows and made herself comfortable. But something was still stuck in her brain.

"Hey, Brooke," she called. Maybe she'd missed something her sister said.

Brooke reappeared in the doorway. "What's up?"

Brooke was correct. She had been in Maine for over three weeks.

Her sister was waiting in the doorway, holding a tampon. "Gabby had one," she said.

Lauren rubbed the back of her neck. When was her last period?

Oh my god! Lauren's hand flew to her mouth, and her eyes widened.

"Lauren?" Brooke asked. "Are you okay?

What's wrong?"

"No, no, no," she said, shaking her head back and forth.

Gabby came running into the room. "What's wrong?"

Lauren had thrown her laptop to the side and was kneeling on the bed. Her hand was still over her mouth.

"I don't know," Brooke said, rushing forward and taking Lauren's other hand. "She called me in here and then started freaking out. L, you're so pale."

"Are you gonna be sick?" Gabby asked.

"Oh yeah," Lauren said but made no move toward the bathroom. She couldn't move as a certain possibility ran through her mind.

She'd been here for three weeks. Her last period had been five weeks ago. At least five weeks. Maybe six. She was crazy tired, and she'd been feeling queasy.

How soon did pregnancy symptoms start?

"Oh my god," she said again, her eyes welling up.

Brooke and Gabby were on either side of her, their arms coming around her.

"Grams just left to meet her friend Ruth. Do you want me to run after her?" Gabby asked.

"No!" she squealed. "I can't tell Grams."

Brooke leaned back and peered at her. "Can't tell Grams what?" she asked with narrowed eyes.

Damn, Brooke had always been perceptive. Lauren shook her head again and took a few deep breaths. She would not cry. This wasn't a situation to cry over. Besides, crying didn't solve anything. Look at her mother, who had spent more time in tears than not and still had a million problems.

"If you're sick…" Gabby began.

Brooke cut her off. "She's not sick."

"Well, something's obviously wrong."

Brooke eased Lauren back down to a sitting position. "Yeah, something's definitely wrong."

"How do you always figure stuff out so fast?" Lauren asked her sister.

"Context clues." Brooke twirled the tampon still in her hand.

"Can someone please fill me in on the context clues of this situation?" Gabby complained.

"I think I might be pregnant," Lauren spit out, then watched as her sister's face mirrored the shock she felt.

• • •

At the advice of Brooke, they all piled into Lauren's car and headed to a pharmacy thirty minutes from Seaside Cove. If anyone saw them buying a pregnancy test in or near town, the gossip train would go into warp speed.

The three of them stood in the family planning aisle, staring at the vast array of options.

"Which one do we pick?" Gabby asked.

Lauren didn't know how to verbalize her gratitude over the use of the word *we*. She may disagree with her sisters—or even wonder what planet they were born on, in the case of Brooke—but it meant so much to her that they'd come on this nerve-racking quest with her.

Lauren grabbed one of the store-brand boxes. "How about this one? I think it's on sale."

Brooke sighed loudly. "This is not the time to go cheapies. Here." She took a box done up in pink and white and handed it to Lauren. "Let's buy two, so you have extras on hand."

"Why does she need extras?" Gabby asked as they made their way to the front counter.

"In case there are any errors, or she wants to take multiple tests."

"Have you done this before?" Lauren asked. She'd been joking with the question, but the dark shadow that passed over Brooke's face was not funny. "B?" she asked.

Brooke shook her head and yanked the two boxes out of Lauren's hand. "Here, I'm going to buy them. Consider it an early birthday present."

Lauren was about to object when her phone went off. Ethan's name came up on the screen. He'd been texting her every so often to see if she wanted to go out somewhere with him—as friends. She'd said no every time, because she really had been too busy since they last saw each other, and thankfully, he didn't get pushy or clingy. But now...*oh god*.

She groaned. What in the hell was she going to tell Ethan? He was the only person she'd slept with in the last six months. If she truly was pregnant, Ethan was definitely the father.

Ethan, who was still spontaneous and carefree. Mr. Go With the Flow. He who must not plan. Sure, he owned a business now, but that business was a bar. A bar with odd hours and seedy characters.

Seedy characters like…her. Going into The Thirsty Lobster and hooking up with Ethan, which resulted in a trip to a pharmacy for a pregnancy test.

Gabby stepped up next to her and put an arm around her shoulders. "It's going to be fine, L. We don't even know if you're actually pregnant yet."

"Shh," she hissed. She glanced around the store. Even though she didn't recognize any of the shoppers and they were about thirty miles from Seaside Cove, she still felt completely paranoid. She even shoved her cell phone into her back pocket, just in case Ethan could somehow hear them through the messaging app.

Brooke shook a bag in front of them. "I got the goods. Let's go home and pee on some sticks, shall we?"

The drive home went by way too fast, in Lauren's opinion. She walked through the foyer and up the stairs in a complete daze. She knew her sisters were following her, yet she still felt completely and utterly alone.

When they reached her bedroom, Brooke removed one of the boxes from the bag. "Do you know how to use this?"

"You pee on it?" Lauren asked.

"Hold it under your urine stream for at least five seconds. Then put the cap on and lay it flat on the counter. It should tell you on the box how long it will take. Some tests are two minutes, some are three."

Gabby narrowed her eyes. "You get a job in a doctor's office recently?"

"It's all in the directions," Brooke said. She

pushed the box at Lauren.

Lauren went into the bathroom and read the instructions. *Here goes nothing...only the biggest moment of my life.*

When she was done, she brought the test into the bedroom, where Brooke and Gabby waited on her bed. She laid it on the dresser.

"So," she said.

"So," Brooke echoed.

"We just have to wait," Gabby offered.

A long silence filled the room. Lauren had so many emotions rushing through her she didn't even know which one to focus on.

"Aren't you on birth control?" Brooke asked, breaking the quiet.

Lauren flinched at the judgment in her sister's voice. She wanted to believe Brooke wasn't trying to hurt her feelings, but the question still stung.

"I was taking it. For a long time. Then there was this whole mix-up with my insurance. After that, I decided to take a break, since I've been on the pill for years."

Gabby stepped closer. "Didn't you use condoms? You're the one who talked to me about condoms in high school."

"Of course we did." Lauren thought back. She remembered Ethan grabbing a condom from his nightstand. She recalled that distinctive crinkle sound of the foil and the heady anticipation within her as he rolled it on.

Well, at least she remembered all of that the first time they'd had sex. She felt her cheeks heating.

"Why are you blushing?" Brooke asked, tilting her head.

"Um, it's just that Ethan and I sorta had sex a bunch of times that night."

"Woo-hoo!" Gabby exclaimed.

"Shut up, Gabs," Brooke reprimanded. She focused on Lauren again. "Did you use a condom each time?"

"I can't quite remember. I know we did the first time," she quickly added. "But after that, it was kind of a blur." She started chewing on a nail.

Gabby put an arm around her shoulders. "It's going to be okay, L. No matter what that test says, we're here for you."

She offered a half smile. "Thanks."

Brooke rose and walked to the window. She stared out for a moment before turning back to them. "If it's positive, what do you think you'll do?"

"I'll keep it."

Lauren dropped the finger she was chewing on. She actually blinked at how fast she'd answered her sister's question. Or maybe it was the fact that she hadn't even needed to think about it.

She would keep the baby.

Lauren hadn't really thought too much about having kids. Sure, the idea of being a mother would pop into her head when she was at a baby shower or with one of her friends who had children. But when it wasn't right in front of her like that? It just didn't come to mind.

Glancing down at her phone, Lauren realized it was way past time for the test results. She tiptoed to the dresser and looked down at the test.

She froze in place, not even blinking. Her whole body went numb.

"Well?" Gabby pressed.

"It's…" Her tongue felt all wrong, too thick and dry. She tried again. "It's…positive."

Brooke's eyes widened as they locked onto Lauren's.

Gabby pumped a fist into the air. "I'm going to be an aunt. All right!" She jumped up and drew Lauren into a long, tight hug.

Lauren patted Gabby's back, even while she looked at Brooke over Gabby's shoulder. When Gabby finally released her, she sunk back down on the edge of her bed.

"I know this is totally unexpected," Gabby began. "But it's a baby. Babies are amazing. They're so little and cute."

"And expensive and life-altering," Brooke added. Then she faced Lauren and her features softened.

Brooke crouched in front of Lauren and squeezed her hand. The two of them had been sniping at each other their entire lives. Sometimes it just seemed easier to bicker than to even attempt to get along. After all, they were so different.

But there were times—times like this—when they had a moment. It usually didn't last long. There was a silent understanding between them. Something was changing or scary or anxiety-producing, but they were there for each other. Just like when their mother died. Or when Lauren was about to leave for college.

"Congratulations," Brooke whispered.

Lauren squeezed her sister's hand back. Just like that, the moment ended. Brooke stood again and went back to brooding, her hands placed firmly on her hips. Lauren wasn't surprised or hurt. She'd expected it.

"How do you feel?" Gabby asked.

Lauren pondered that. "Tired. Shocked. Kind of like I'm going to puke."

"That's probably normal," Gabby said. "We need to get some books. And check out some blogs and articles."

Brooke blew out a breath. "We need to get her to a doctor's office so they can do a blood test and confirm that there is, in fact, a baby in there."

Gabby's eyebrows drew together. "She just took a test."

"More than likely that test is probably accurate, but the next step is still to confirm the pregnancy with a doctor. Do you know the first day of your last period?"

"Uh…" Lauren had no idea off the top of her head.

"They'll use that date to figure out your due date."

Gabby was grinning from ear to ear. "And then we can go shopping for a crib, and a bassinet, and a stroller. Oh, and baby clothes. Little baby shoes are so adorable."

Brooke nailed Gabby with a no-nonsense stare. "Gabrielle, will you calm yourself? There are more important things to do first."

"What's more important than shopping? And setting up a registry." Gabby's eyes were sparkling.

If Lauren wasn't in such a daze, she would totally laugh at her sisters' different reactions.

"How about going to the doctor's office, getting Lauren on prenatal vitamins, making sure she rests and eats right, and…" Brooke averted her eyes and spoke slowly. "Telling the father."

"Oh right," Gabby added. "What about Ethan?"

"Ethan, yeah." Right, she wasn't completely alone in this. There was someone else involved. "I'll tell him. Of course I'll tell him," she said softly, more to herself.

"He might not have a good reaction," Brooke said slowly. "Are you prepared for that possibility?"

Gabby shoved Brooke's shoulder. "What the hell, Brooke? Of course she's not prepared for that. She just found out she was pregnant two seconds ago. How can she be prepared for anything?"

All of this was overwhelming. Lauren was a planner, and an unexpected pregnancy hadn't exactly been an item on her to-do list this year.

But she was also pragmatic, and it didn't matter if she'd intended to have a baby or not. A baby was coming in nine months. She would deal with this. She would make a new plan.

Lauren put a hand over her stomach. A baby. *Her* baby.

Financially, she was in good shape. She could support a child.

"I'm just saying," Brooke said defensively, still arguing with Gabby. "There's a lot to consider right now." She turned to Lauren. "Where are you going to live?"

Lauren opened and then closed her mouth.

"What do you mean? I already live in Virginia."

"By yourself. Maybe you should consider living up here, closer to family."

"In Maine?" she asked.

"No, in California," Brooke retorted. "Of course in Maine. Grams is here. And, ya know, the father of the baby is here, too."

"And Auntie Gabby is here. At least for now. For the foreseeable future. Probably forever." Gabby frowned.

Brooke tapped a finger against her lips. "You always say you can work from anywhere."

"True," Lauren agreed.

"When are you going to tell Grams?"

Lauren felt the color drain from her face. Grams! Her pulse skyrocketed. Grams was going to kill her. And then she would kill Ethan. This was so not good.

"L?" Gabby asked, eyeing her with worry.

She had to tell Grams that she was pregnant. An unplanned pregnancy. Grams was going to try and force them to get married, just like she had with Lauren's parents.

She couldn't marry Ethan. They weren't even dating—and they weren't even truly friends; they were frenemies. If they had to live together, they would kill each other. She couldn't subject a helpless infant to that kind of messed-up relationship.

This was a disaster.

"Maybe I don't *have* to tell—"

Brooke cut her off with a stern look. "Don't finish that sentence. Of course you have to tell Grams. And you have to tell her soon," Brooke added.

Yeah, okay, maybe she did. This wasn't something she could hide from her. Although she could attempt to if she didn't ever talk about her child and swore her sisters to secrecy. And she returned to Arlington before her pregnancy started showing and never visited Seaside Cove again. And removed herself from social media. Which might interfere with her job on social media, but—

She had a sinking feeling in her stomach. A sinking feeling that was actually rising up to her throat.

"Lauren?" Gabby said. "Are you okay?"

"I...um...uh..." Then she was up like a shot, running into the bathroom.

I'm having a baby, and I have to tell Grams.

She heaved into the toilet.

CHAPTER SIX

Ethan was in a groove. He was working behind the bar, there was one waitress serving the lunch crowd, and a cook was in the back. Business was light but steady. It gave him time to catch up on paperwork, clean up behind the bar, and, of course, think about Lauren Wallace.

Despite his many offers, she was still refusing to go out with him, even as friends. At first, he'd thought the whole busy-with-work thing was made up. But then he ran into Brooke the other day, who confirmed that Lauren truly was swamped with some conference.

All he wanted to do was hang out again. Okay, sure, he'd love to sleep with her again, too, but he would also like to grab dinner and drinks, catch up. Nothing fancy.

He got that she wasn't staying in Seaside Cove forever. But why not enjoy the time she was here? There was nothing standing in their way.

"You with us today?"

He snapped out of it at the sound of his waitress and let out a quick laugh. "Sorry, Dawn, I was lost in thought."

Dawn shook her head, causing her long, blond ponytail to swish back and forth. "From what I saw, seems like you were lost in a very good thought." She winked.

He ignored the innuendo. "What do you need?"

"Two Diet Cokes and an iced tea." She leaned against the bar while he filled the order. "Light day," she commented.

Ethan placed the drinks on her tray. "It is. Sorry about that. I know you're saving up for grad school." There were currently three tables with customers, a pair of fishermen at the end of the bar, and a few sandwich orders he was filling for guys down at the dock. That would hardly make a dent in Dawn's future tuition cost.

She shrugged. "It's okay."

Ethan made a snap decision. "If you want, you can stay on for the night shift and work with Sherry. There are a bunch of different games on tonight. Should bring in a crowd."

She grinned. "That would be great. Thanks, Ethan." She picked up the tray and headed back to her customers.

The door opened, and the streaming sunshine wasn't the only thing to brighten his day. Lauren waltzed inside, looking amazing in a bright red top and light blue capri pants. Her hair was loose around her face, which was practically glowing. Her lips were painted the same color red as her top, which made her blue eyes sparkle even more than usual. A computer bag was slung over one shoulder, and she was carrying a delicate-looking purse in the shape of bright red lips.

Maybe she was finally going to agree to go out with him.

"Hey, you," she said as she took a seat at the bar in front of him.

"Right back at ya." Out of habit, he immediately

filled a glass of ice water and placed it in front of her as she took her laptop out of the bag. "Did you come in for a late lunch? Or was it to ogle me and my biceps?" He flexed for her.

She let out a mirthless laugh. "Seeing your biceps was the first thing on my to-do list today."

"First thing?" He glanced at his watch. "Getting a late start?"

She cast her gaze down, seemingly enthralled with the bar. "It's been an...odd morning. Anyway, I thought I'd do some work here today. That okay?"

"Not that I mind, but don't you usually work at your grandmother's café?"

She opened the computer and tapped a couple keys. "How do you know that?"

He gestured around the room.

"Right," she said. "We're in Seaside Cove. Everyone knows everything I do." She sipped the water. "I needed a change of scenery today." She tapped a finger, also painted bright red, against her lips. "And... I wanted to see you. But not your biceps."

A warmth spread through him at her words. "Then I definitely don't mind. Want something to eat?"

She frowned. "I do, but..." Her hand flew to her stomach.

Ethan leaned forward. "Are you feeling okay?"

"My appetite has been all over the place lately."

He grabbed a menu. "Since it's not busy this afternoon, if there's something specific you want that's not on the menu, we can make it for you."

She perused the menu while he refilled one of

the fishermen's beers. When he returned, she'd closed the menu. "I'll just wait a little to order."

"You sure you're okay?" he asked.

Her lips parted, and she leaned forward slightly. Ethan waited. It definitely seemed like something was on her mind. Lauren's eyes darted around the room. Finally, she sat back in her chair.

"I'm fine. Um, exhausted from all the work last week."

He eyed her for another long moment. He was thrilled to see her at all, but she was definitely acting a little odd. He couldn't put his finger on it.

Lauren bit her lip. Again, her eyes roamed the bar, landing everywhere but on his face. "I have a lot on my mind. You wouldn't happen to have some saltines?"

He grabbed a few packets from behind the bar and placed them in front of her. "You coming down with something?"

She tore a packet open. "I'm fine, really."

"What are you working on today?"

She glanced up, and her entire demeanor changed. At the question of work, she went right back into her usual confident, self-assured, very-Lauren-esque state.

"I'm going to be featured on a colleague's podcast next week. We're talking about the use of videos on different social media platforms. I'm trying to get some general thoughts together so I can make a presentation."

"A presentation for a podcast?"

"Well, I figured I could repurpose the info and use it to teach my followers. I've been wanting to do a master class on video for a while. This will be a good segue."

He nodded. "Maybe you'll be able to convert some of the podcast listeners."

She perked up, and her dimples appeared. "Exactly."

He filled another drink order for Dawn. Then he returned to Lauren.

Leaning on the bar, he asked, "So, what is there to say about video on social media these days?"

She narrowed her eyes. "Don't tease me."

Interesting comment. A tad bit defensive, too. "I'm not."

Her brows drew together, her face tightened. But Ethan didn't waver. He waited her out.

Finally, she relented. "Sorry. I'm used to my sisters and Grams not understanding anything I do. They tend to either blow off my work or make fun of it."

"That sucks. I don't really understand everything about your job, but I think it sounds interesting."

Her eyes brightened. "It is. Social media marketing changes every five seconds. Or so it seems. It's kind of like the Wild West right now. But it can be so powerful in helping people's businesses. I mean, I've seen people rake in six-figure sales purely by following my lead. And then there's…" She stopped, offering a small smile. "Sorry, I could seriously go on for hours."

He liked seeing her passionate about something. "Don't apologize," he said. "It's amazing that you feel that way about what you do. You're lucky. Most people aren't satisfied with their jobs."

She tilted her head. "Are you?"

That was a loaded question.

Like so many things in his life, Ethan had bought The Thirsty Lobster on a whim. Against the advice of his parents, his friends, and his lawyer, he'd jumped on the opportunity without any real business plan.

If he said that to Lauren, he was pretty sure she would explode. Even as they talked, she was making a list.

He did enjoy working at the bar. Way more than he'd ever thought he would. And he wanted it to succeed, both for himself and for the town. This light afternoon aside, it was well on its way to be firmly in the black. That was important to him.

But after it was in a good place, he didn't really know what was going to happen.

"Uh-oh, we're losing him," Lauren said, amusement in her voice.

He slung a rag over his shoulder. "Sorry. I've been doing that all day."

She steepled her hands and set her chin on top of them. "I never would have guessed you would open a bar. Yet, it suits you."

He wouldn't have imagined it, either. But certain things in his life brought him to this point. Certain people. Certain ex-wives.

"I bought this bar after I returned to Seaside Cove last year."

Not a total lie. Not the complete truth, either. After he returned home, which was after his time traveling the globe after meeting his ex and his divorce. Following that event, Ethan had taken time to travel again and get his head together. Until the pandemic put an end to that. He'd returned to his hometown.

"Returned from where?" she asked, taking another sip of water.

"All over the place. I traveled a ton in my twenties. When I came back to the States, I lived in Florida for a while."

After Veronica had bled his bank account dry and then divorced him.

"What did you do before? For work, I mean."

Noticing she'd gone through all of the crackers, he set a few more packets in front of her. "A little of this. A little of that."

She waited, obviously wanting more of an explanation.

"I went to community college. Then I worked on the fishing boats." He pointed toward the window that faced the docks. "I waited tables, bussed tables, filled in as a sous chef. I've had jobs in hotels; I've driven cabs. I did a couple stints in offices. When I was in Europe—"

"Where in Europe?"

"A couple different countries, but I spent the most time in Hungary, right outside of Budapest. For almost two years. I did tons of jobs. I taught English. I worked in the tourism industry." *I met my ex-wife.* He frowned.

She pointed a finger at him and swirled it around in the air. "There's a story there."

With a nonchalant shrug, he played it off. "There are many, many stories there. Essentially, when I inventoried all of these random jobs I did over the years, the ones that made me the happiest were those in the food industry."

"Ah."

He waved at a group of women who were leaving after their lunch. "Thanks for coming."

He turned his attention back to Lauren. "I came back here right at the onslaught of the pandemic. Seaside Cove was a mess."

She nodded. "Grams told me. The local businesses really took a hit."

He glanced out the windows. There were still many storefronts that were boarded up, unable to survive. Some new businesses had moved in, but the community was still rebuilding.

"I came into this bar in the very early days, before we all realized what was happening. Henry, the man who used to own it, was so great with everyone. You could tell his employees respected him. And he had this way with the customers. People were scared about the pandemic, but he was doing his best to ease their fears."

The bar had been in somewhat of a disorderly state, though. It had needed a little TLC. Badly. But the drinks had flowed, and people were enjoying themselves. Ethan remembered that specifically. The vibe was so inclusive and calming.

"That was the last night this bar was open. It closed the next day for quarantine, and it never rebounded. I heard that Henry retired. When I saw the *For Sale* sign, I made a few inquiries and ended up with a bar."

"Just like that?" She shook her head in disbelief.

"Pretty much."

"You said you had a lot of jobs working in restaurants and bars, but did you ever run one?"

"I had helped out plenty."

"But—"

"No." He cut her off, not wanting to talk about his lack of planning. "I did not have any direct experience owning an establishment."

She sat back in her seat, studying him. "That's an incredibly ballsy move. Opening any kind of food establishment is always risky. Weren't you scared? Especially given the timing of the pandemic."

When he allowed himself to think about it, he'd been terrified. But his usual MO was to chug along, concentrating on the day-to-day and not think too far ahead.

"I didn't buy this place until almost a year after everything started. The economy was starting to rebound at that point. People were getting vaccinated."

"Still..." She let her words fade off. A line formed on her forehead, and he could tell she was thinking hard about all of this. "Did you talk to anyone? Do you have a mentor or a strategist?"

His palms were dampening at her questions. Time to change the subject, and he knew just the tack to take.

"Actually, I could use a mentor. Someone to help me with marketing and advertising. I've done a little, but it's not my area of expertise." He tapped the top of her laptop. "Maybe you could give me some tips. Some marketing tips," he clarified.

She smiled. "I would be happy to do that."

"I can pay you, of course. Not much, but I do have some money set aside for publicity."

She tilted her head and nailed him with a stare. "Ethan, are you serious? I think you and I are past that point. I mean, you've seen me naked."

"And yet, we still haven't been on a proper date," he added.

"You know why."

"I know why," he said wryly.

Still, it was great to see her again. He couldn't even count how many times he thought about her throughout the day. Especially knowing that she was nearby.

It wasn't the best thing to do, but he couldn't stop himself. He leaned over and kissed her. Shockingly, she didn't pull back.

"What was that for?" she asked.

"You're sexy."

"Obviously," she deadpanned.

He laughed, which faded at her next statement.

"We're still not going out on a date."

"Fine. If all you want is a purely sexual relationship, I guess I can do that."

She threw a packet of crackers at him. "Ethan," she began, leaning forward.

He waited as she opened her mouth, closed it. She clutched at the silver necklace she was wearing. "Yeah?" he prompted.

"There's something I need—"

A group of high school girls burst through the door, accompanied by the sound of giggles and slang words that Ethan couldn't figure out. He watched as Dawn intercepted them and showed them to a table.

"Sorry. You were saying?" he said to Lauren.

She bit her lip. "I, um…so, you traveled all over the place."

He got the feeling that's not what she was going to say.

"You ended up in Budapest," she continued. "Then you said you were in Florida after that. What made you return to Seaside Cove?"

He didn't want to say it. He really wanted to keep it to himself, although pretty much everyone in town knew his story. Or thought they did.

Before he could stop it, the words tumbled out of his mouth. "I got divorced."

"Ah," she said.

They'd already established that she knew he'd been married and divorced. Her gaze flicked down to take in his empty ring finger.

"That's pretty much all there is to say on the subject."

Her brows drew together as she peered at him. "I don't think so."

He ran the rag over a clean spot on the bar. "I was married, then divorced. After that, I moved back home. The end."

"I'm sorry. That must have been hard. But I doubt the story is that cut-and-dried."

That usual lump rose in his throat. It always did when he was reminded of that time with his ex. A time when he'd ignored all the warning signs.

She didn't push, but again he found that the words fell out of his mouth anyway. Maybe it was because she didn't ask for the full story.

"There were a couple years when I was a serious poker player. Texas Hold'em," he clarified. "I met Veronica at a poker club outside of Budapest."

She had been vivacious and passionate and so full of life when they'd first met. She'd made him laugh and kept him on his toes with midnight picnics, spontaneous day trips, wine tastings, and dance lessons. Ethan had been fascinated by her love of both classic literature and pop culture. She could just as easily quote Chaucer as she could a Kardashian.

"The night we met, I had just won a big tournament." A big tournament worth a lot of money. Warning sign number one, he thought bitterly.

"Veronica was from the States, too—some posh beach town in California. She was 'backpacking' through Europe with a friend."

Lauren cocked her head. "Why did you just use air quotes for the word backpacking?"

Ethan let out a small laugh. "Because Veronica's version of backpacking involved staying in hotels, flying first class, and dining at the best restaurants. She may have had a backpack…tucked somewhere in one of her Louis Vuitton suitcases."

Lauren closed the lid of her laptop, all attention focused solely on him.

"Despite her disdain for traveling light, we fell for each other." Or, at least, he'd fallen for Veronica. Her feelings hadn't been quite the same as his. "We got together really fast. Everything was intense and exciting. No time to breathe, young love, and all of that. We just kept leaping without looking." He glanced at Lauren, saw her eyebrows draw together. He laughed.

"I realize our lack of planning is probably giving you a heart attack."

She scrunched her nose. "Just small heart palpitations. What happened next?"

"I got wind of a new poker tournament with big stakes. The buy-in was more than I'd ever spent, but the payoff was huge. Veronica and I ended up leaving Budapest for South America."

Lauren's eyes widened. "I like the way you talk about hopping from one exotic location to another. It's the same nonchalant way I talk about running an errand at Target."

He grinned, but it didn't last. "Before the plane even left the runway, I'd proposed," he said. Ethan still didn't know how that had happened. He blamed the champagne and Veronica's big green eyes. "As soon as we landed in Ecuador, we married."

Lauren leaned her chin on her hand, a dreamy look in her eyes. "An international relationship between two Americans in Europe and South America with an amazing poker player and a young woman on vacation." She sighed. "Sounds like a romance novel."

It may have started as a romance novel, but it devolved into a horror story.

"I believe romance novels end with the couple living happily ever after. In my case, the romance ended after the poker tournament."

Lauren scrunched up her nose. "Another man?"

He shook his head. "Lack of funds. I lost money

in one of the tournaments. A lot of money. All of my money," he explained.

"Ah." Lauren ran a hand through her hair. "I take it that didn't go over well with the missus."

"Not so much." He shrugged. "I wasn't that worried. I was content working odd jobs. That's what I'd been doing before I started playing cards in Europe. I liked that kind of life. I found a great job in a hotel bar. Fun people, good tips, and all the alcohol I wanted."

"I'm guessing Ms.-I-don't-own-a-backpack had a different kind of life planned?"

He pointed at her. "Bingo." To say Veronica had her own agenda was an understatement. "When the money ran out, so did she."

"She left you?"

"She left the nonexistent money she'd assumed I had."

Lauren reached out and intertwined her fingers with his. She squeezed, and he squeezed back. He needed the support. "I'm so sorry, Ethan. That's horrible."

It was also humiliating. He'd been so embarrassed that he hadn't seen it. Of course, they'd had a whirlwind romance. When in that very short time would he have noticed that her intentions weren't the same as his?

"I don't want to feel like that again," he said. "That trapped feeling because someone is using me for something."

Lauren deflated. She pulled her hand away from his and shrunk down in her seat. He wondered if she'd been through a rough breakup, too.

"Well, this bar needs you. You must be planning on staying in Seaside Cove," she said.

He shrugged. It was a tough question to answer, because on the one hand he had the bar, his friends, and a life that he was currently enjoying. But he'd always had a side of him that craved the ability to pick up and go. To travel with no specific destination in mind. To meet new people and have unique experiences.

"You own a business now," Lauren said, peering closely at him. "You can't just leave it."

"I would never do anything to jeopardize my employees or this place." Or his hometown. Seaside Cove had been through enough with the pandemic. "But once we really get going and the books are looking good, there is a possibility of hiring a responsible manager."

She glanced down. "And you would be free to travel or do whatever you wanted. No commitments. No obligations."

No one able to rip his heart out. He nodded.

She blew out a long breath. He studied her, and it seemed like there was something really bothering her.

"You know, ever since you came in today, I've felt like you've been trying to say something."

She tilted her head and placed a hand to her stomach. "I, uh…"

"What is it?" he asked, concern growing.

"Ethan, I'm—"

A loud crash sounded near one of the tables. He saw a tray of toppled food and a sheepish-looking toddler. Then he heard the scolding tone of said toddler's mom.

"Hold that thought," he said to Lauren. "I need to—"

"Go," she finished for him.

Her lips were downturned, and there was a certain sadness in her eyes.

"Lauren?" he asked.

"It's nothing." She turned her attention back to her laptop and began typing furiously. "I need to do some work."

With that, he grabbed a fresh rag and the broom, heading toward the spilt food. The uneasiness he'd felt in Lauren was now firmly transferred to him. Yet, he had no idea why.

He glanced over his shoulder at her. Why did it feel like something in his life had just changed?

CHAPTER SEVEN

A wave of disappointment washed over Lauren as she drove back to Grams's house.

She'd been right on that precipice of changing someone's life forever. That was a lot of power to have. "Hey, Ethan, you're going to be a father. Your life will never be the same again." That's all she had to say.

But she'd chickened out. Something had stopped her. Not just a little "something." Kind of a big something.

Ethan didn't want to be tied down by a woman. After hearing about his experience with his ex-wife, Lauren couldn't really blame him. She didn't want him to be the reason he felt—what had he said? *Trapped.*

She pulled into the driveway, put her car in park, and then just sat in the front seat, staring out at the gardens.

This house had been her most favorite thing growing up. She had a lot of memories of running around the yard with her sisters. They would play hide and seek throughout the three stories for hours. Or they would walk along the beach below the property.

She remembered dancing with sparklers on the Fourth of July with her sisters; making out with her high school boyfriend, Robbie, on the porch; her mother's bell-like laugh as Lauren rode her bike up and down the driveway.

Of course, with the good memories always came the bad. Fighting with her sisters, Robbie breaking up with her right after graduation, losing her mother.

Through it all, the three-story house stood tall and proud and unwavering. It lasted through snow and hurricanes and nor'easters. It had been there for holidays and sicknesses and everything in between.

The home had been built in the 1880s and stayed in her family ever since. The long driveway curved slightly as it ascended a small hill. Lined in colonnade fashion with her grandmother's famed hydrangea, it made for an impressive start. But honestly, that was nothing.

When you made it to the end of the driveway, the view was absolutely breathtaking. The Victorian house sat on the rocks overlooking Seaside Cove Beach. With stunning ocean views in every direction, Lauren's fingers itched to grab her phone and start shooting.

Then there was the house itself. Muted grayish-blue cedar shingles covered the outside, which was accented by white gingerbread trim. Her favorite part of the house was the wraparound porch that Grams kept decorated with a multitude of flower boxes and wicker furniture.

Waves crashed on the shore below. There was a small lighthouse just visible to the north. Lauren remembered its guiding light that shone brightly every night.

She needed that guiding light now. She'd meant

to come home a million times over the last couple years. But she'd been so busy starting her new business it had been near to impossible to find any time to visit Seaside Cove.

Now that she was here, everything felt like it had been turned upside down. She'd never dreamed she'd be pregnant. Not in this way.

But she was having a baby. And she'd decided she was definitely keeping it and raising it. If Ethan wanted to be part of the baby's life, that was great. But if he didn't, she was still moving forward with her plans.

Although, the idea of being a single parent definitely made her feel queasy. The memories of her mother raising her, Brooke, and Gabby were hard to ignore. Her mom's crying spells, her depression and anxiety, the frustration, the unease.

Not that she couldn't handle it. She totally could. Her mother was a completely different person than Lauren. Their personalities were almost completely opposite.

It was hard, though, not to think of her own upbringing. For almost seven years, she'd had a mom and a dad. Then her dad, claiming he was fed up with her mother, took off. Lauren always wondered if he'd been fed up with her, too. Brooke and Gabby had been too young to have done anything to irritate him, but Lauren was the oldest—and her existence was what had forced her parents to marry. She couldn't help but feel that maybe her father had resented her a little for that.

After he left, she'd been with an emotionally fragile single mother. Of course, Grams had stepped in and done her best. Just as her mom started to get back to her usual sweet and kind self, they found the cancer.

Lauren went from a life with a mom and a dad to a life without either.

Her mom hadn't had a choice in the matter. The cancer had the final say. But her dad stepping out of her life? Well, that had been his decision, and Ellie Wallace had paid for that choice.

There was the distinct possibility that Ethan wouldn't want to be part of their child's life. Or, as she'd learned today, he may just pick up and go at any moment.

Like her dad.

Could she expose her child to that kind of upheaval and heartbreak?

Of course, she'd already come up with several lists. There was going to be a lot to prepare in the next nine months. All of the Ethan stuff aside, if she stayed organized, she would be fine. Just fine.

She didn't need a partner to raise a child. She could do this on her own. Anyway, what did it matter? She lived in a different state. Even if Ethan wanted to be part of the baby's life, he wouldn't be seeing it that much.

"Ugh," she said, her shoulders drooping with what felt like the weight of the world on them.

Maybe she needed a new list for possibly staying in Maine. She quickly grabbed her phone and typed in the notes section. After a few items, she decided to finish that list later.

Finally getting out of the car, she walked toward the porch. Grams was sitting on one of the rockers.

There was a book in her lap, but her head was tilted back, her eyes closed. She looked really peaceful.

Grams's eyes flew open and her loud, gravelly voice cut through the silence of the air. "About time!"

Lauren jumped a mile as she placed a hand over her heart.

"You forget how to get out of a car or something?" Grams asked with an arched eyebrow.

Lauren sighed. "No, Grams. I was just…" What had she been doing?

While she tried to figure it out, Grams placed her book on the table next to the rocking chair. She clasped her fingers together and looked directly at Lauren. "Something's going on."

Lauren took a step backward, running into one of the porch railings, hard. What? How? How did she know?

Lauren peered at the house. Even though they didn't always get along, she knew neither Brooke nor Gabby would have revealed this news. It was too big.

Grams arched an eyebrow. "Well?"

"Well, what?" Lauren said, her throat suddenly very dry.

"You're not ignorant, so don't act like it. I know something is up with you."

Lauren rolled her eyes in an attempt to throw Grams off. "Nothing is—"

Grams waved a hand in the air. "Don't even finish that sentence. I know you like the back of my own hand. And I know when you're acting differently. I'm not ignorant, either." Grams gave a definitive nod.

She hadn't lived with Grams since she was eighteen years old, so how was it that her grandmother could still stare her down and evoke that feeling of fear? Lauren averted her eyes as her brain went into overdrive, desperately trying to think of something to say. Instead, all she could do was stutter. "But…but…"

"But, but," Grams echoed back. "A mother knows."

"You're not my mother," she whispered, not meeting Grams's eyes.

"I'm as good as. Besides, I was your mother's mother. You can bet your tight little jeans that I knew when something was up with her, too. You've been acting weird the last week or so. Your appetite is different. You're exhausted all the time."

Lauren fell into the chair next to Grams. She was going to have to try a different tactic, because denial seemed to have no effect. "I have been really tired," Lauren admitted.

Grams sat back in her chair, rocking, waiting.

"That conference really wiped me out. I know you have no idea what I do, but trust me when I tell you that I was up late every night, working."

As Grams opened her mouth, Lauren quickly jumped in. "And I think I may be warding off a cold or something. Maybe a little bug."

"Perhaps you got something from that Ethan boy. Your little escapade with him has consequences."

Lauren almost choked. Grams had no idea.

"You need to take care of yourself, Lauren

Rose." Grams's voice was still stern, but she placed a hand over Lauren's.

Sometimes Grams really surprised her. Maybe she should just tell her the news. Maybe she would be happy or supportive.

On the one hand, she was a thirty-three-year-old woman who was handling a delicate situation. But this was still her grandmother. She didn't want to disappoint her. Lauren had always been the perfect grandchild. She got straight A's and excelled at extra-curricular activities. She continued her success at college and had always worked hard. Not that Grams outwardly praised her or anything, but she knew Grams appreciated her work ethic.

She'd been exemplary in Grams's eyes—until she'd started her business. The irony was that while she worked hard for every employer, warranted praise and bonuses and glowing referrals, the true success happened when she went out on her own. She was raking in the cash.

"That bar is dirty. You could have picked up any number of diseases," Grams said, apparently still hung up on that.

"Grams, Ethan's bar is not dirty. It's perfectly clean and well-run."

"I didn't say anything about how it's run. All I know is that you have gone there how many times now? You could be bringing some Corona-type virus back to me."

Lauren was pretty sure that even Coronavirus would avoid Grams.

"Weren't you just at The Thirsty Lobster?"

Lauren rolled her eyes for real this time. "How

did you know that?"

She picked up her cell phone from the table between them and waved it in the air. "Several people informed me that you were once again seen there with that Ethan boy."

Suddenly exhausted, Lauren rested her head against the porch column. "First of all, could you stop calling Ethan a boy? He's in his thirties." She rubbed at her temples. "And can you also please just *stop* in general? I was working at the bar today."

"Why don't you work from here? You have a perfectly peaceful house to get your work done." Grams used air quotes when she said "work." Lovely.

Lauren could work from the house, which was peaceful. Grams, however, was not. And she'd been off today. Not to mention, Her Highness Princess Brooke had commandeered several rooms while she planned out whatever wedding she was organizing.

"Don't you want to date Ethan? You did sleep with him."

"Thanks for the reminder. I like Ethan. I do. It's just that…"

"What?" Grams asked. "Not good in the sack?"

Lauren started coughing. "Jesus. No. I mean yes. I mean, no to your question. Er, yes, he's good in the sack. Ugh. I can't talk to you about this."

"Embarrassing you is so much fun."

"You are so incorrigible."

Grams guffawed. "Are you going to tell me why you aren't dating Ethan? Why my oldest granddaughter thinks it's appropriate to have sexual relations with someone but not call that person her boyfriend?"

"He doesn't have a plan," she said desperately.

Grams nodded slowly. "A lot of people live perfectly wonderful lives without planning every teeny tiny detail."

She knew it was a slight toward her. Lauren was too tired to care.

"Ethan is a business owner. Who starts a bar and restaurant without a plan? I would have consulted so many different people before I just opened a bar. I would have talked to people who have gone through it. I would have run risk analysis. I would have done research."

"Not everyone acts the way you do," Grams countered.

How true that was. If Lauren ran the world, it would be more organized and efficient. She had no doubt.

"He has a business with employees and bills, yet he would consider leaving to travel the world or whatever. Just leave." *Leave me. Leave our baby.* "He told me that. Today."

"Maybe he doesn't have a reason to stay put." Grams leaned forward, reached over, and pushed a hair off Lauren's face. "I'm going to make you tea."

"I don't want tea."

"You need some tea. You're getting over a cold, and you need tea and soup and a good night's rest."

Fighting was futile. She would drink the damn tea. "Fine."

Grams stood. Before she left, she said, "Do I

need to make you a doctor's appointment?"

Lauren's hand flew to her stomach before she remembered that Grams wasn't talking about her pregnancy. She thought she had a cold.

"No, I'm fine. Or, er, I'll be fine in a couple of days." She would be really fine once she told Ethan, her carefree and completely spontaneous hookup who didn't make plans or think about the future, that he was going to be a baby daddy.

She wanted to puke. And it had nothing to do with morning sickness.

Grams pointed at her. "Get some rest."

Lauren scrunched up her nose. "You're being so bossy."

"Where do you think you get it from?" With a wry smile, Grams walked into the house, leaving Lauren alone to fret.

• • •

Ethan loved nights like this. The bar was slammed, the restaurant was packed, laughter was loud, drinks were flowing, and the money was rolling in.

After making a handful of mixed drinks, he tuned one of the TVs on the wall to the Yankees game, eliciting a loud round of boos.

"Customer request," he called out.

"Screw the Yankees," someone yelled.

He chuckled, not surprised. This was Red Sox country. He immediately moved to fill a drink order for one of his waitresses.

Samantha, his chef, stuck her head out of the kitchen door. "We're running low on the special."

"Seriously?"

She nodded. Her apron was covered with various food items, and there was a light sheen of sweat on her face. Everyone was working hard tonight.

"I'll let the other waitresses know."

Another hour went by, and the bar continued to keep Ethan on his toes. He helped out everywhere he could.

When the door opened again, he didn't even have time to look up to see who came in. He was too swamped, running a couple of the checks with multiple credit cards. Then he heard Joe call out a big hello and ask how Rose was doing.

Lauren.

He continued taking care of the credit cards in the register but gave a quick glance to his left. Lauren stood there, talking with Peggy and her sister. But she kept sneaking glances at him. Two times in one day. He wondered if she was changing her mind about seeing him.

A few minutes later, he had all the checks worked out and distributed back to the proper waitresses. Lauren appeared in front of the bar near the end. He sauntered down, wiping the bar as he did.

"Twice in one day. I'm honored."

She smiled, but he noticed that it didn't reach her eyes. Her dimples stayed dormant, too. He frowned. Now that he was noticing, she seemed worried. She was wringing her hands together.

"You okay?"

"Um." That was all she said before she began gnawing on her lower lip.

"What's wrong?" he asked.

"Hey, Ethan, we need more clean glasses," Joe said.

He held up a hand for Joe to hang on. "Lauren?" he asked.

"I can see it's busy, but I do need to talk to you."

At least, he thought that's what she said. Hard to tell with the music pumping out of the speakers and his customers reacting to a home run by someone in the Red Sox game.

"What?" he yelled.

"Ethan, we also need more forks," Joe called.

Lauren leaned over the bar. "Can we talk later?"

Close up, he saw the worry written all over her face. Her features were pinched, and there were bags under her eyes. He hadn't noticed that when she was in the bar earlier today. "What's wrong, Lauren?"

She glanced around the bar. "You're so busy. I'll come back." She turned to leave but just as quickly faced him again. "I'm sorry. It's important. We need to talk tonight."

The hair on the back of his neck stood on red alert. He couldn't imagine what could have happened since he saw her earlier in the afternoon. But something was really wrong.

"Is your family okay?" he asked.

She nodded.

He scratched the back of his neck. "Want something to drink? A gin and tonic?"

"What?" she asked as the crowd responded to another play in the baseball game.

"Do you want a gin and tonic?"

"Yes." Her eyes went wide, and she shook her

head vigorously. "I can't. I mean, um, no thank you."

"Ethan, Ryan Kilpatrick has had way too much to drink, and he's trying to drive home," Dawn told him as she whizzed by, tray in hand.

Ethan grumbled under his breath. "Second time this week. Jeez, what is with him? Just give me one minute and call his brother." He faced Lauren again. "Tell me what's going on."

She glanced around the bustling bar. "No, really, this isn't the time or place. But promise me we can talk later?"

"I'm worried now." What in the world was going on?

Joe showed up right behind him. "Clean glasses, forks, very much needed," he said before hopping down the bar to fill orders.

They could have added two more bartenders and they still would have been slammed.

He noticed that Lauren began to back away. He couldn't let her leave like this. Not when she clearly needed him for something that was upsetting her.

Quickly, he came out from behind the bar, skirted a couple customers, and stopped in front of her.

"I'll come back." She began inching away.

He latched on to her arm. "Stay. Tell me. The longer it takes you, the longer I'm away from the bar, and the more stuff that will pile up. You don't want to be responsible for the fine people of Seaside Cove going hungry and thirsty, do you?"

She offered a half smile. "It's about us. About us being together." She shook her head.

"What?" he called. She was speaking so low, and

he was having a hell of a time hearing her over all the other noise.

"It's about that night we were together."

Something about them being together. He started to sweat as a bad feeling took over.

"Joe, can you turn the music down for a sec?" he yelled. Joe shook his head and put a hand to his ear. "Turn the music down," Ethan repeated.

He turned back to Lauren and gestured for her to continue. She placed a hand on his chest, then quickly removed it. She said something, but again he couldn't make it out.

"What?"

She tried again.

"Can you repeat that?" he asked.

Ethan always thought it was ridiculous when people said they stopped breathing. Or that their heart stopped beating. Or things happened in slow motion. Or that they were living something like a scene from a movie.

But when he finally heard what Lauren was try-ing to tell him, Ethan had to rethink his stance on all those ideas. Because all of a sudden, he not only stopped breathing as his heart paused, but both of those things happened in super-slow motion like a scene from an award-winning, blockbuster movie.

Ethan froze, and so did the rest of the bar when the music stopped at the exact moment that Lauren finally spit out what she'd been trying to tell him. Her words came out fast and loud, but then lin-gered in the air as the bar went silent and Ethan experienced all those clichés.

"I'm pregnant!"

CHAPTER EIGHT

If Lauren didn't move, maybe this wouldn't be real. Like how little kids thought if they closed their eyes, no one could see them.

Unfortunately, she wasn't a little kid, she had to move at some point, and this was all very, very real.

She shuddered. She knew her face was bright red because it felt like she'd stuck her head inside an oven. The entire bar was staring at her with open mouths and looks of shock. That spoke nothing of Ethan, whom she was avoiding at all costs. Her eyes darted around the room, landing everywhere but on his.

Had she really just told the entire bar, a good portion of Seaside Cove, that she was pregnant?

Shiiiiiitttttttt!

The bar remained quiet. There were hushed voices asking questions and the sound of the baseball commenters on in the background.

"You gonna hug her or what?" Peggy finally called out.

Lauren turned toward Peggy and Wendy, both watching her with matching expectant looks on their faces. She quickly took in Joe, who had frozen with a beer mug in midair. Diners at the tables were all focused on the two of them, and the people sitting at the bar had all swiveled on their stools to take in this new drama.

Lauren needed to do damage control. And fast.

She finally let out a breath and willed her body to function again. She pasted her best smile on her face, even emitted a little laugh.

"Oh my god. Don't worry, everyone. I was just messing with Ethan."

No one moved. This wasn't working.

"You're pregnant?" Wendy asked.

"Of course I'm not pregnant." Lauren waved her hand in the air. "Ethan, here, wasn't paying attention to me. I couldn't resist messing with him." She took a seat on the stool at the end of the bar. "How about a gin and tonic, Joe?"

People slowly started talking again. But she couldn't miss that some of the patrons were still watching her intently.

Joe placed a glass with clear liquid and a lime wedge in front of her. One sip. That's all she was going to take. One little sip wouldn't hurt the baby at this point. Right?

She rubbed her neck. But when she met Joe's eyes, he gave her a slight nod.

"Seriously, guys. I was only joking." She raised her glass in a toast. All eyes were on her.

People drank alcohol all the time before they knew they were pregnant. Hell, she'd been having wine. Still, her stomach clenched as she brought the gin and tonic to her lips, pretending to take a small sip, only letting it touch her lips. But she could still taste it.

And there was no gin in it.

Then she smiled and took a much bigger sip and dramatically swallowed so no one would miss it. Looking to Joe, she toasted him. "This is delicious."

Joe tapped a finger on the bar before returning to work.

"Did you see Ethan's face?" someone said.

"That was a good one, Lauren," Peggy called out.

Ethan. Right. The person she'd been avoiding. Despite the sips of tonic water, her throat was massively dry. At least everyone was returning to their former conversations.

She was staring down at her drink when she felt Ethan move to stand in front of her. "I will get you back for that," he said.

"Huh?"

"I can't believe you came in here to my turf and messed with me like that." Ethan was grinning from ear to ear. "I have to admit, though, you had me going for a second. I really thought you were pregnant."

What was worse? Having Ethan freak out about her being pregnant or having Ethan be ecstatic now that he thought she wasn't?

She was going to be sick.

"Lauren?" Ethan asked, his voice dropping. "You were kidding about being pregnant. Right?"

She flicked her eyes up to meet his. She'd learned her lesson and wasn't going to say those words again out loud. But she had to answer him…

So she shook her head. Ethan's eyes went wide, and all the color drained from his face.

He watched her for a long time. Finally, he leaned forward. Lauren wasn't sure if he was going to hug her or strangle her. In any case, he did neither. Instead, he took her drink and moved it away from her.

"It's just a tonic water," she said softly.

After what felt like an eternity, Ethan finally spoke. "You're..." was all he could eke out.

It didn't matter anyway because one of the waitresses came bustling over with a problem and Ethan was whisked away to deal with it. Good. She needed a moment before they had the real conversation she'd come in for.

"Lauren, come down here," Peggy called.

Reluctantly, Lauren joined the others at the end of the bar. She was met with high fives for fooling Ethan, who apparently was known for being the king of pranks around here.

Peggy pointed at her. "You're just like your Grams."

"I was thinking the same thing," Wendy agreed.

"What?" Lauren asked.

"Rose used to play jokes on us all the time back in the day." Wendy popped an olive from her martini into her mouth. "Remember the time," she began, looking to her sister.

Peggy laughed. "With the fish? Yes! That still makes me mad."

"But it was funny."

"Yes, it was."

Lauren wanted to hear more about Grams in her younger days, but Ethan returned. He stood next to her. Close, very close, as everyone at the bar continued to razz him.

"You turned a little green back there, Ethan."

"Imagine you becoming a daddy."

"Lauren's grandmother would kill you."

Peggy peered at Lauren. "She would kill you, too."

Didn't she know it. That's why telling Grams would be a very delicate situation. But first, time to talk to the daddy.

• • •

Joe cranked the music back up and ushered Ethan and Lauren outside, under the guise of getting something for him. Thank god for Joe. At least someone was thinking clearly, because Ethan could say without a doubt that he was far from being rational.

"Go talk," Joe said. "I have this covered."

Ethan knew he had been extremely busy right before Lauren entered the bar. For the life of him he couldn't seem to recall with what. Out of the special? Baseball games on the televisions, music blaring, tables packed.

"But—"

Joe didn't let him respond. He gave Ethan's arm a little shove instead. "Seriously, we have it covered in here." With that, he closed the door in Ethan's face.

Lauren crossed the street and collapsed on a bench facing the marina. She pulled her knees up, closed her eyes, and rested her head on them. Ethan followed, a hollow feeling in the pit of his stomach.

"I can't believe that just happened," she mumbled against her legs.

He didn't know what to do. His mind was

moving in a million directions at once while going a million miles an hour. Everything felt like it was happening simultaneously in warp speed and in slow motion. He placed an arm around Lauren's shoulders.

"I'm so embarrassed," she whispered. "The whole bar, everyone... They all heard... Everyone almost... Oh my god. What if they still think—"

He rubbed her shoulders for a moment, trying to calm her down. Finally, he managed to get her to shift so he could see her face.

"Don't worry about everyone else right now."

Lauren pointed back at the bar. "But..."

"You're pregnant?" he asked. "You weren't messing with me?"

Lauren nodded, a tentative expression on her face. "I was trying to tell you, but it was so loud. Finally, I screamed and everyone heard and I just had to save face." She shook her head back and forth. "This must be so confusing for you. I'm sorry." She inhaled deeply. "Yes, Ethan, I'm pregnant."

Okay, so he'd heard her correctly. Sadly, the entire town had heard her as well. Oh shit, that could have been so bad.

"It's, um, yours," she said, casting her eyes down.

He'd never had a doubt about that. "Of course it is."

Relief flooded her face. "I was hoping you wouldn't think... Well, some guys aren't... That is, they don't believe..."

Unfortunately, he followed where her thoughts were heading. "Some guys are dicks."

"I know we used protection, but maybe one of

the times we forgot." She bit her lip, that gesture he was coming to associate with her.

Ethan thought back. They'd been together several times that night. An amazing night. One of the best of his life. Maybe the condom had slipped their minds at some point. Or maybe one of the condoms had been defective. Hell if he could remember now. In any case, it didn't matter at this point.

She nudged him with her shoulder. "Say something."

He blew out a whistle between his teeth. "I'm at a loss."

"Are you mad?" she asked, looking down at the ground.

Mad? Oh shit. He was handling this whole thing wrong. Was there a right way to handle an unplanned pregnancy? His mind was spinning. First, she was pregnant, then she wasn't, now she definitely was. He was in such shock that he wasn't considering Lauren's feelings. The woman with the human being currently inside of her.

He faced her and gently took her hand. "No, I'm not mad. I'm surprised. But definitely not angry or anything like that."

Relief washed over her again, softening her features. He could tell, even in the dim lighting from the streetlights and storefronts behind them.

"I'm an impulsive, go-with-the-flow kind of guy, but I have to say, I'm literally stumped right now."

He'd created a life form. With Lauren Wallace. He had no idea how to handle this.

"Did you want kids?" she asked timidly.

"I, well…" He ran a hand through his hair. "I don't know. I feel like kids are such a grown-up thing to do."

"You're a grown-up," she pointed out.

"I don't feel like it at this particular moment."

"Yeah," she said. "I know the feeling."

To his astonishment, tears filled her eyes. *Dammit.*

"No, no, don't do that." He pulled Lauren against his side and squeezed her tightly. "Please don't cry."

"I'm not going to. Trust me, I'm good at holding tears in."

Hm, that didn't seem healthy.

They sat like that for a few moments, Ethan's arm around her, trying to offer comfort. The water was lapping gently against the docks. Occasionally, the bar door would open behind them and he'd hear people laughing, shouting, talking as they exited The Thirsty Lobster.

"I'm scared," she whispered softly against him.

Her words were so quiet, he almost wasn't sure that he'd heard them. But she pulled away from him.

"I'm scared," she repeated. "I've never been through anything like this before."

That's all it took for his protective nature to kick in. Immediately, feelings of incompetence washed over him as he racked his brain to think of ways he could help.

"What do you need? Do we need to take you somewhere? Get you something?"

"Something? Like what?"

"No idea. What do pregnant women need?"

"Besides a back massage and a milkshake?" She chuckled. "Brooke said the next step is to go to the doctor. I have to take a blood test to confirm the pregnancy."

He perked up. "You might not be pregnant?"

She rolled her eyes. "I haven't gotten my period in a long time. I'm nauseous and exhausted. Plus, I took four home pregnancy tests, all with positive results. I'm definitely pregnant, Ethan. It's just not in my medical record yet."

He felt like a jerk. "Sorry. I've never gone through this. Okay, so you need to go to the doctor."

"I'll have to find someone up here, since my normal doctor is in Virginia. I suppose I'll need to have all the records transferred back down to Virginia, too."

"Back to Virginia?" he asked.

"When I go back home in September," she said drily. "They'll need to know what's been happening."

A whole new issue just dawned on him. She didn't live in Maine. She lived in Virginia. But *he* was here, and *he* was this baby's father. "Don't you want to live here now?"

Her eyes widened to the size of beer mugs. "Live in Seaside Cove again?"

"Your family is here."

"My grandmother is here, too."

"I always thought grandmothers were included in 'family.' Huh." He took a deep breath. "And I'm here."

"Do you want to be involved? With the baby, I mean," she said.

"Of course." He couldn't keep the shock from coating his voice. Why in the hell wouldn't he be involved with his own child? "This is my baby," he said, trying but failing to keep the edge out of his tone.

Her eyes narrowed in on him. "We already went over this. Yes, it's your baby, Ethan," she said with a bite to her voice.

"If it's my child, then I want to be involved."

"How? Financially? Emotionally? Both?"

"In every way."

She pointed back at the bar. "You only recently opened a bar. How are you even doing financially?"

He straightened. "Don't worry about that. I'm just fine."

"I'm sorry, Ethan. I didn't mean to offend you. It's just that I make a good living, so I don't want you to ever worry about money in terms of the baby. I have it covered."

He could see that she was getting agitated. Hell, people in Canada could probably see it, too.

She took a deep breath. "I think that you need to take some time and process this information before we continue this conversation."

"I think you and I have an awful lot of big decisions to make," he countered.

"Listen, Ethan—"

He threw a hand up to stop her. "Don't cut me out of this part. This is my…kid, too. I want to be part of it."

His heart rate sped up. Suddenly, he was hit with

the very real idea that Lauren could take his child and live anywhere. An unfamiliar sensation filled every inch of his body: *panic*.

He hadn't been lying when he said that he'd never really considered having children. He supposed that by the time he did get around to starting a family, it would have been much later in his life — a decade or so.

"Ethan, you said it yourself earlier today. You don't like feeling trapped. You don't ever want to feel that way again."

He tasted a tinny, metallic flavor as his own words were thrown back at him. Yes, he had said that, and yes, he didn't like feeling stuck.

But the situations with his ex-wife and Lauren were completely different. He hadn't known Veronica very long before he'd proposed to her. It had been an impulsive decision.

With Lauren, he'd known her forever. Although, he hadn't seen her in over a decade. And he did kinda sleep with her the first night she was back in town.

Running a hand through his hair, Ethan silently cursed himself. He'd always liked to say that he was a spontaneous person. For the first time, though, he started to see that spontaneity as something else. He was borderline reckless, irresponsible, rash.

His lack of impulse control with Veronica had resulted in a divorce and countless dollars wasted in divorce lawyers. Now, his decision to sleep with Lauren—which he still counted as one of the best nights of his life—had created a baby.

His life would never be the same.

Lauren let out an annoyed huff, drawing him out of his thoughts. He glanced at her, and he could see the hard lines of irritation written on her beautiful face.

"You are suggesting that I drop my life in Arlington and move back to Seaside Cove so that I can raise our surprise baby with you. You, who told me hours earlier that you want the freedom to get up and go whenever the feeling grips you."

Frustration was starting to creep up his spine. "I know what I said. But I just opened this bar. I'm definitely going to be here for the next couple of years at least."

"Oh wow. A couple of years. Then what?"

"I…well…"

"Exactly. You don't know."

He rose from the bench, walked the few steps to the railing that separated the sidewalk from the water below, then turned back to face her.

"We could get married."

Her mouth dropped open. "Are you kidding me?"

Was he? Ethan hadn't had time to even consider the words that had flown out of his mouth. Good old impetuous Ethan. He'd just proven his own point.

He walked back to her and sat down again. "If marrying me makes you feel better, I say we can do it."

She emitted a noise that was somewhere between a gasp and an incoherent oath. "Oh, you say so, huh? You think marriage is the solution to all of this?"

"Wouldn't that prove that I'm in it for you and the baby?"

"It would only prove you're jumping into this without thinking. We've slept together a handful of times on one night. We don't even know each other."

He was about to counter when she barreled through. "And I don't want to hear that we knew each other in high school. That was fifteen years ago. I'm guessing you're not the same person as you were back then. Do you still think *Pirates of the Caribbean* is the best movie of all time? Are you still listening to 'SexyBack' by Justin Timberlake?"

"Hey. Keep it down." He made a show of looking around for anyone close by, which there wasn't, and pointed at her. "My love for JT was supposed to stay between me and you."

Her lips quirked for a split second before falling back into seriousness. "My point is that we're fifteen years older. We've both changed. We're only getting to know each other now. Marriage isn't the answer. Trust me, I know this firsthand."

He knew she was referring to her parents, but this was different. They weren't her parents, and Ethan was at such a loss at how to handle this situation. He wanted to assure Lauren somehow. He wanted some assurance himself. He wanted to be in his child's life.

"Well…it doesn't even have to be a real marriage."

She narrowed her eyes. "What the hell does that mean? You want to pretend to get married?"

"No, we can get married for real. But it doesn't

have to be anything more than a partnership to raise our child."

He was fairly positive that he was being nice. This was a tough situation, and he thought his solution was great. Lauren was clearly distressed, and he'd found a solution.

Only, she didn't seem happy or less stressed at the moment. In fact, if it were possible for fire to actually shoot out of someone's eyes, he would be burned to a crisp.

"Lauren?" he broached after a full minute of silence.

She put her hands on her hips. "It's clear you aren't taking any of this seriously."

"Yes, I am."

"Who just suggests a marriage of convenience as a solution to a problem in the twenty-first century? Is that what you did with your ex-wife?"

His ire went up. Now he stood so they were on an even playing field. He met her angry gaze with one of his own. "That's none of your business."

Lauren broke eye contact. "I'm sorry. You're right. Your past is none of my business."

"It's okay." He relaxed. Ethan wasn't one to hold on to anger. "My past may be my own business, but my future is all you. And the baby. That's why I really think you should consider my offer."

Her lips went into a pout. It would have been cute, but he had a feeling he wasn't going to like the next thing out of her mouth.

"Your offer? Your offer! You're unbelievable, Ethan McAllister. This is my baby, and I'll do what I think is right."

"Lauren—"

"I'm not going to wait around to see what whim you're having on that day of the week." She snatched her purse and turned. But something stopped her, and she looked over her shoulder. "Marriage? I can't believe...*ugh*."

With that, she stepped over to her car, which he noticed was parked quite close.

He watched her headlights turn on and then followed them as they drove down the street and made a left. He continued to stand there for what seemed like a long time.

"How'd that go?"

"What?" He turned to find Lauren's sister Gabby standing on the sidewalk next to him. "Where did you come from?"

"I came to check on my sis. I take it she told you the news."

Ethan nodded, swallowing a couple times. He was still speechless.

"Are you happy? Are you shocked? Do you need a drink?"

"Yes, to all of the above," he replied.

Gabby nodded. "I'm sure it's a lot to process." She glanced in the direction of Lauren's now-departed car. "Is she okay?"

"Define okay."

Gabby put her hands on her hips in a mirror image of Lauren. Ethan would have chuckled, but he felt too drained to laugh.

"What did you do?" Gabby asked.

"I don't think I said the right thing." Ethan ran through their conversation in his mind. "Yeah, I definitely said all the wrong things. I suggested we get married."

Gabby's eyes went wide. "Marriage?" She let out a low whistle. "You have met my sister, right? I mean, I'm assuming since the two of you have created a new life form that you've at least talked once or twice. Lauren is the most independent person on the planet. Not to mention she thinks through everything. To death! She makes a list when she wants to reorganize her closet. Why would you suggest marriage?"

Again, he ran a hand through his hair. If he kept that up, he was going to start going bald. "She said she's probably going back to Virginia. But I'm here. I thought…I just figured we could…you know?"

Gabby's face softened. She slung an arm around his shoulders. "Men are so incredibly ignorant, Ethan."

"Um, thanks?"

"You're welcome. But I appreciate your attempt with my sister. Even though it was utterly and completely wrong. You need to make up for it now."

She was right. But hell if Ethan knew what to do. "I don't know if I can say anything to make this better. Or if Lauren will even listen to me."

"Don't worry. I can help." Gabby gave him a squeeze. Her eyes were sparkling. "Here's what we're gonna do."

CHAPTER NINE

Get married. Get *married*?

Lauren huffed and sighed and cursed her way back to Grams's house. She'd been nervous to tell Ethan that she was pregnant. Not that she'd had any idea of what to expect, but she could firmly say that she hadn't expected some half-assed, completely random, unthought-out marriage proposal.

Marriage didn't solve anything. In her experience, it usually caused more problems. Wasn't that what her parents' marriage showed her?

Not to mention that her parents' marriage had been a forced arrangement because — *uh-oh* — her mom had gotten pregnant. And they had been miserable.

She got out of the car and slammed the door. Then she paused and covered her face with her hands.

The entire bar heard her say that she was pregnant. Even now she felt her stomach turning and the nausea rising. Wasn't it bad enough that the entire town knew she'd slept with Ethan?

She hoped that everyone bought her excuse of messing with him. She was fairly certain they had, but… Nibbling on a finger, she considered the situation. She'd know by tomorrow morning if she was in the clear. If she wasn't, everyone would be talking about how Lauren Wallace had gotten knocked up by Ethan McAllister.

Also, Grams would throw both of them off the cliff into the ocean.

Or a worse fate: Grams would join Ethan on the marriage bandwagon, just like she'd forced Lauren's parents to get married.

How could Grams be so progressive on some topics but a total old-fashioned crone on others? As soon as she found out about this baby, she was going to be on Lauren hard.

Already feeling protective, Lauren rubbed a hand over her stomach. Maybe this little dumpling wasn't planned, but she was going to give it the best life ever.

"And I don't need to be married to do that," she said defiantly into the darkness.

She stomped into the house and quickly found both Grams and Brooke in the living room. The TV was on low in the background. Grams was sitting in her favorite chair, flipping through a magazine, while Brooke had commandeered the entire couch and coffee table, surrounded by catalogs, magazines, fabric samples, and a color wheel. No doubt still planning the big Kennebunkport wedding she'd been working on since she got here.

They both paused in their activities and looked up expectantly as Lauren trudged into the room.

"How many times in one day do you need to see that Ethan boy?" Grams said before returning to her magazine.

"You don't even know where I went. I could have gone shopping. Or maybe I went for a drive."

"You went to see Ethan," Grams said without looking up. "I'm assuming you didn't enjoy it."

"I just went to The Thirsty Lobster for a drink," Lauren lied. "It wasn't a big deal."

"Then why do you seem irritated? Your face is so pinched you're beginning to look like a prune."

"Thanks, Grams," she said on a sigh.

"I'm just saying. You are at an age where you need to start paying attention to wrinkles. You might want to look into your skin care routine."

"Grams, I'm thirty-three, not one hundred and three. I don't have any wrinkles yet."

She waved a finger in the air. "It's right around the corner. I'm telling you."

Lauren shot Brooke a look. More of a plea, really. Luckily, and for once in her life, Brooke came through.

"Hey, Grams, didn't you say you were going to make tea?"

Grams perked up. "That's right. I have that new flavor to try." With that, she rose, gave Lauren one more long once-over, and walked out of the room.

Lauren collapsed onto the couch, next to Brooke.

"Watch the table linen samples," Brooke said, pulling something out from under Lauren.

"Sorry." Exhausted, she fell back into the cushion.

"How did it go?" Brooke asked. "I'm guessing not so great."

Lauren threw her hands up in the air. "Well, the entire town almost found out that I'm pregnant with Ethan's baby."

Brooke paused, magazine hovering in midair as she stared at her sister. "Excuse me?"

Lauren filled her in on the events of the night. "I think everyone believed me about joking, but who the hell knows."

There was a long silence that Brooke eventually broke. "What were you thinking, yelling out that you're pregnant?"

"I told you, B. It was so loud, and I was getting so frustrated." She ran a hand through her hair. "I just wanted to get it out. This is a lot to carry around."

Brooke sat up straight. "You shouldn't let people know you're pregnant this early."

"I wasn't trying to let people know anything. Are you even listening to me?" She was starting to feel as frustrated as she had in the loud bar.

"I'd wait until you're past the first three months. The risk of miscarriage is highest in the first trimester," Brooke added.

Gee, thanks, sister. "You think I don't know that? Of course I know that. I didn't mean for anyone but Ethan to hear me." Lauren crossed her arms over her chest.

Brooke put her color wheel to the side. "I'm sorry, L. On a different note, and more importantly, how did Ethan take the news?"

Lauren rolled her eyes as dramatically as she could muster, which was hard because her exhaustion increased by a hundred. "Ethan? I don't want to talk about Ethan McAllister." She drew on all her strength and sat up straight. "Let me tell you about Ethan McAllister and how he reacted."

She barely registered Brooke's chuckle at her quick turnabout.

"At first, he was great. Comforting and supportive. Of course, he was really surprised by the news."

"That's to be expected," Brooke said.

"Right." Lauren took a deep breath. "Then, the
jerk is all 'we should get married.' Married!" She
threw her hands into the air.

"It's always nice when two people who are going to raise a child together can actually be
together."

Lauren stifled the urge to throw something at
her sister—her very old-fashioned sister. Were she
and Ethan living in some other century?

"I don't even know where I'm going to be living," Lauren said.

Brooke pushed her shoulders back and tilted
her head. "You're not staying here in Seaside
Cove?" As if realizing she'd said something wrong,
she quickly shut her mouth and sat back.

Lauren narrowed her eyes. "I only found out I
was pregnant this morning. I have no idea what I'm
going to do or where I'm going to live. If I do go
back to Arlington, I'll need to get a bigger place. If
I stay here, I'll need to find my own space."

"You can always stay here. There's plenty of
room," Brooke said.

Yeah, Lauren could only imagine that scenario.
With the amount of criticizing Grams did with her
now, she couldn't fathom what adding a baby to the
mix would do. *You're putting that diaper on wrong.
Hold the baby this way.*

"My point is that I have a lot to think about at
the moment. But I know this. I'm not marrying
Ethan or anyone else." She chewed on her lip. "I

can't believe he suggested marriage," she grumbled under her breath.

"He was probably just trying to help," Brooke said kindly.

Lauren rolled her shoulders, irritation once again rising up from the pit of her stomach. Then she stood.

"Where are you going?" Brooke asked.

"I need some tea. Or chocolate. Or ice cream. Or cookies. Or all of the above."

She made her way to the kitchen, with Brooke following her. "I've been working for hours. I want some ice cream, too," Brooke said, opening the freezer and rummaging around. "I know I saw some mint chocolate chip in here."

"Hand me a spoon," Grams said from the kitchen table, "and I'll tell you where I hide the really good stuff."

While Grams got out the "good stuff," which was composed of various forms of ice cream and a huge jar of cookies, Lauren made a cup of tea. Her thoughts continued to bounce around from memories of seeing *pregnant* on the little stick upstairs to screaming her big news in front of half the town to telling Ethan to receiving the worst marriage proposal ever.

Wrapped up in her own thoughts and concerns, she didn't notice Grams watching her.

"Why are you drinking tea?" Grams asked.

"Because I wanted some," Lauren countered.

Grams pointed at her. "You drink coffee."

Shit. Why did she have the most observant grandmother on the planet? The woman couldn't let one thing go, either. "I drink tea, too, sometimes. I had some when you made it earlier."

"Not usually. Not unless I make it for you. You're a coffee person."

"I'm both." She wasn't.

"Since when?" Grams narrowed her eyes.

"Since…since…" *Don't say I'm pregnant. Don't say I'm pregnant.*

Brooke pushed the ice cream toward Lauren. "Since I told her about a study I read that detailed the value of drinking hot tea at night to help you lose weight."

Grams turned on Brooke. "Why are you so obsessed with weight? Doesn't that loser fiancé of yours tell you how beautiful you are?"

As Grams went on and on, and on some more, Lauren could only hold back a tear. Stupid hormones. Her sister really did her a solid. "Thank you," she mouthed to Brooke.

"Lauren! Lauren Wallace!" someone shouted from outside.

She dropped the spoon she'd been using to stir her tea. "What is that?"

"Lauren, this one's for you," came a man's voice.

All of a sudden, from somewhere in the front yard, someone began singing. Loudly. It only took Lauren a second to realize it was Ethan, and he was belting out "Unchained Melody" by The Righteous Brothers.

Why was Ethan here singing?

Well, "singing" was probably too kind of a word. Bellowing might be more appropriate. Or squawking maybe. Or…

What was it called when cats were in heat?

"Awww, he's serenading you," Brooke said, clasping her hands together with stars in her eyes.

Lauren pushed her tea away. "Ohmigod, I hate this song. I know every woman on the planet loves it, but it just grates on my nerves."

"Oops," Gabby said, rushing into the kitchen and making a contrite face. "I couldn't remember if it was you or Brooke who hated it. But I love it. It's so romantic."

"You told him to serenade her?" Brooke asked, amusement in her voice.

"I thought it would be sweet. Besides, you can't ignore someone standing outside your house, singing at the top of their lungs."

Grams snorted. "You say singing; I say shrieking."

Yes, shrieking. That's what Ethan was doing.

"The boy's not going to win *American Idol* any time soon."

"He wouldn't even make it past the first round." Brooke's eyes widened as Ethan hit a particularly bad, very loud note. "But the gesture is still sweet. It's the thought that counts, right?"

Lauren eyed her youngest sister. "How did you... *Why* did you?" She grumbled. "Why are you helping Ethan?"

Gabby offered a good-natured shrug. "Someone had to." She gave Lauren a little shove. "Go out there."

"No. You go out there." She pointed at her sister. "You're supposed to be on my side."

A big grin spread across Gabby's face. "I am.

That's why I helped." Gabby threw her arms around Lauren, just like she used to do when she was a little girl. She had to know that Lauren could never be mad at her when she did that, which just made her evil. "I walked down to the bar to check on you, and I saw you drive away all mad and stuff. You're my big sister, and I had to help."

"Lonely rivers flow," Ethan bellowed, er, sang. His voice was getting louder by the second. "To the sea, to the sea. To the open arms of the seaaaaa, yeahhhhhhhhh."

"For the love of god," Brooke said. "Wow. I thought you had a bad voice," she said to Lauren.

"Hey!"

"Sadly, it's true," Gabby added. She leaned in so Grams couldn't hear. "That baby has no chance of joining a chorus."

Ethan's voice cracked on the next note, but he kept going.

"Christ, Lauren, go talk to the boy," Grams said. "I didn't raise you to be rude."

"You didn't raise me to settle for less than I deserve, either," she countered.

Grams narrowed her eyes. "Are you psychic all of a sudden? You don't even know what that boy wants to say. Go hear him out. If he decides to be an ass, then let me know and I'll turn the hose on him."

"Also, it would be really great if he stopped singing," Brooke added. "He won't do that until you go out there."

"I thought you were all, 'It's so sweet and romantic and blah, blah, blah.'"

Brooke blushed. "It is. But my ears are starting to bleed. And anyway, I need to call Lucas."

Always about Brooke.

"Fine," she grumbled begrudgingly. "But give us a little privacy, please."

"No problem," Gabby said with a grin. "We'll just listen in discreetly from a distance. You won't even know we're eavesdropping."

It was near impossible to get mad at Gabby. Her intentions were always well-meaning. "That's all I ask."

When Lauren walked onto the porch, she found Ethan kneeling on the ground right below the railing. His arms were opened wide, a huge bouquet of red roses surrounded by lush greenery and perky white baby's breath in one hand. He continued singing the wretched song, but he smiled as he saw her emerge from the house.

Lauren crossed the porch quickly. She leaned against the banister. "Ethan, shhhh." They were so lucky they didn't have any neighbors who lived close.

Ethan finished the verse and gave a little bow. Then he stretched his arm out, offering the bouquet of flowers, which were gorgeous—not that Lauren would say that at the moment. She stayed put, not moving toward him or accepting his gift.

Ethan's arm dropped. "I can sense you're still mad."

"Ya think?"

"I'm very intuitive," Ethan said with a crooked grin.

"What are you doing here?" she hissed. Lauren couldn't help but glance over her shoulder.

"Grams is here."

"So? I'm here because you're here."

Her heart let out a little flutter. Damn heart.

Ethan took a tentative step closer. "Lauren, I know that I didn't react the right way when you told me about the baby. I'm sorry."

She snuck a quick gaze at the house before waving her hands. "Shh, keep it down. Grams doesn't know yet."

"Oh." He gave her a look but, to his credit, didn't question her. "I just want you to know that I'm excited," he said softly. He stepped onto the first step leading to the porch.

She shifted, suddenly intrigued. She met him halfway, moving toward the same spot.

"Don't get me wrong," he continued. "I was shocked to hear the news, but I'm happy. Really. The more I think about it, the more excited I get."

She paused as the wind coming off the ocean below blew her hair around her face, cooling off her suddenly warm cheeks. "You made me feel like you were trying to force me into something that neither of us wants."

He nodded slowly. "I understand. Proposing was an impulsive thing to do."

Her breath caught. Impulsive. That was the problem, wasn't it? Lauren kept too many lists and organized too many things. She didn't have room in her life for the spontaneous. She was running a very successful business singlehandedly. She hadn't gotten to this point by doing things on a whim. And Ethan was the opposite of all that. He was...well, he was just *impulsive*. In everything he did.

"We're not even dating," she said. "Hell, we're not even hooking up anymore."

"Not for my lack of trying." Ethan climbed the next step. "I never really thought about having a kid, but now that one's on the way, I know I want to be part of its life. I *want* to. I know that the same way I know I need air to breathe."

His words carried an honorable meaning. But more, she felt the emotion behind them.

"And you don't think we need to get married?"

"Not any time soon."

She had to ask the next question. "What if I do decide to go back to Virginia permanently?"

"We'll make it work."

He was saying all the right things, but still, her mind drifted back to her parents' many fights. More than the fighting, she recalled the aftermath. Her mother sitting in the kitchen—the same kitchen that was right behind her now. With tears in her eyes, her mom would talk to Grams after her father had stormed out.

"He never says the right things."

What if he had? What if her father hadn't been so rash? Would they have stayed together?

Ethan extended his arm, presenting the bouquet of flowers again. Lauren took her time about it. She had to make him sweat just a little bit more. Finally, she smiled and accepted the roses, dipping her head to take in the sweet, floral scent.

"These are beautiful. Thank you."

"I learned something tonight," Ethan said.

"What's that?"

"Always listen to Gabby. She suggested the

flowers and the singing."

Lauren let out a mirthless chuckle. "You might want to rethink that." At his raised brow, she scrunched up her nose and continued. "I kind of hate that song."

He frowned. "Well, damn."

She raised her hand, linking fingers with his. "But I did love the gesture. No one's ever sung to me before. And flowers are always a good move."

He relaxed. "You'll have to provide me with a list of your favorite romantic songs for future serenading purposes."

"I can do that. It will even be alphabetized and sorted by both song and artist."

He grinned. "I have no doubt." He squeezed her hand and then pulled her in for a sweet, soft kiss. "Lauren…we're having a baby."

A baby. *Wow*. Of course, she knew that, but hearing him say it was like hearing it for the first time. It felt more real now. She was going to be a mom, and Ethan was the dad. And none of this had been in her plans, but she couldn't just set it aside and deal with it later, when it fit better into her schedule.

She didn't like the uncertain feeling that swirled around her. All of a sudden, there were so many things in her life that she had no control over. That was not how she operated.

She put a hand on Ethan's chest. "We should come up with some rules."

"Here we go." He grinned again and leaned against the railing.

Lauren didn't care if Ethan or anyone else made

fun of her. Rules helped keep things running smoothly. They eliminated chaos and ambiguity. Maybe if her mom had set some rules, her early childhood would have been a little calmer. Maybe her dad would have said the right things, the things that her mom had needed to hear, and he would have stuck around a little longer.

"You know, just to make sure we're on the same page," she explained.

Ethan took a deep breath. "Okay. Hit me with some rules."

"Well, if we're having this baby together, I think we should agree that any discussion of marriage is off the table unless we're talking about true love."

"What you're saying is that marriage should not be offered as a quick fix to a problem."

"Exactly."

"What about the sex?"

Her insides did a little dance. In spite of everything going on at the moment, Lauren had to admit that she'd been thinking of Ethan every day. All she had to do was close her eyes and she could see his impressive body hovering over hers.

From his touches to his kisses, not to mention the way his skillful hands had moved over every inch of her body, she practically salivated every time she remembered their night together. She'd be crazy not to want a repeat.

She was somewhat surprised that he was being so blunt, but given the state of her condition, she supposed they were past subtleties.

"I was going to finally accept your offer for dinner. But, well, yeah, um, we could do *it* again."

He chuckled loudly. "I meant the sex of the baby. You know, finding out what it is before it's born."

Her cheeks heated up instantly. "Right. *That* sex. Well, I don't know. Do you want to find out early?"

"I can wait. It's not all that long. Kind of a fun surprise."

A surprise, right. Some people liked surprises, she reminded herself. Of course, she wasn't one of those people. After all, if they didn't find out the sex, she wouldn't be able to plan to the fullest extent.

"Do you care if we have a girl or boy?" she asked.

He shrugged. "Not really. As long as the little munchkin is healthy. But I hope the baby has your dimples." Lightly, he dragged a fingertip over the place where her dimples usually showed up. "And your striking blue eyes." He placed a soft kiss on one eyelid, then the other.

She sucked in a breath. He was charming her.

"What about you?" she asked, her voice coming out a bit breathlessly. "Which of your features do you think the baby will have?"

"I hope they have my height. We don't want another Smurf."

She slapped him in the chest, making him laugh. "Hey! I can't help that I am height-challenged."

Ethan grinned. "I like your lack of height. It makes you fit right where I want you."

With that, he grabbed her and tugged her toward him. His arms came around her, and she found herself being cocooned within Ethan's strong embrace. Her head fit perfectly under his chin.

Lauren took a moment to inhale his scent. It was a musky, manly aroma. She wasn't sure if it was his soap or shampoo, or maybe he was wearing some faint cologne. Whatever it was had begun mixing with the salty sea air from the ocean as the wind picked up, blowing her hair around her face. Ethan ran a hand over it, smoothing it down.

With a soft finger, he tilted her chin up and looked deeply into her eyes. "See, we fit together."

Then he kissed her. His mouth captured hers, and she wasted no time in kissing him back. If nothing else, Ethan was an outstanding kisser.

He pulled back only slightly. "We may not have planned any of this, but we do fit."

She opened her mouth to protest. She wasn't even sure why. Lauren just felt like she needed to disagree. Only, he didn't give her a chance to. He pressed his lips to hers again. Featherlight kisses, a whisper across her lips, eliciting the most delicious butterflies in her belly. She heard a sigh, then realized it had come from her. As she sank into the kiss, her arms came up and around his neck. She could smell the roses that she was still holding with one hand.

Ethan brought his arms around her waist, sliding his hands up her back as he deepened the kiss. Her mouth yielded to his, allowing his tongue to enter and meeting it beat for beat.

Dizzy when they pulled apart, she looked into his eyes. "Wow," she whispered.

"I don't want you to worry about anything," he whispered back. "We're going to figure everything out."

"That is oddly comforting," she said. Even though she couldn't imagine how they'd do it.

CHAPTER TEN

Lauren was in the middle of a surprisingly comforting dream where she and Ethan were pushing their baby in a swing in their backyard. They were all laughing as the sun shone down through the trees. Even unconscious, there was a feeling of serenity that permeated every inch of her.

Sadly, the sweet image dissipated as she was torn away from sleep. Someone walked by her room, talking way too loud for—she glanced at the clock on her nightstand—six in the morning.

What the hell? She knew Grams and Gabby would already be at the café, which left one person. Freaking Brooke.

Annoyed, she pushed the covers back and stalked into the hallway. She followed the sound of Brooke's voice downstairs to the kitchen.

"I know it's early," Brooke said. "You called me. Where else did you think I would be at this hour?" She paused, clearly listening to the person on the other end of the call. "Lucas, you were checking up on me, weren't you? Trying to catch me in some kind of trap. What the hell? I'm your fiancée, and you should trust me."

Lauren heard the scrape of a chair against the kitchen floor. "I'm sorry. Of course I'm sorry. I didn't mean… Yes, you're right. Fine, I'll check in again in a couple hours."

When Lauren was sure the phone call ended,

she entered the kitchen. Most of her earlier annoyance had dissolved after hearing her sister's end of that phone call. What the hell was up with Brooke's fiancé? If she was understanding the one side she'd overheard, Lucas was questioning Brooke's fidelity. Brooke wasn't the type to ever cheat or lie or steal. She was way too much of a goody-goody.

The two of them were so...different.

Lauren was driven and ambitious. She liked being independent and taking care of herself and her problems. Brooke, on the other hand, had been waiting for her Prince Charming to climb up to her window and save her from all the world's evils since she was a child. In her quest to find her happily ever after, she'd made herself a priority, oftentimes discounting her family's feelings in her search for her own happiness.

Some might say Brooke was a tiny bit selfish. Lauren would say that she was a whole lotta selfish with a dash of egocentric thrown in for good measure.

Still, Brooke was her sister, and the idea that some dickhead like Lucas wasn't treating her right made Lauren's blood boil.

"Morning," she called brightly as she sauntered into the kitchen.

Brooke practically jumped out of the chair, hand to her heart. "Morning," she mumbled. Then she took in Lauren. "Why are you up so early?"

Lauren was going to point out that she was often up at this time and enjoyed getting her day started early, recent pregnancy exhaustion aside. However, she was not in a good mood when someone's screaming with their possessive fiancé woke her up. But since Brooke already looked miserable, she decided to keep her thoughts to herself.

She crossed to the coffeemaker and started a fresh pot. "Well, you are always up at this hour, and you are typically in a great mood because you're an early bird. Yet, you're not looking so happy today." She pointed her finger in Brooke's general direction and twisted it in a circle. "What gives?"

Brooke raised a hand to her mouth and chewed on a nail. Then she quickly dropped her hand. *Good thing*, Lauren thought. *Don't want to mess up that pretty French manicure.*

"Nothing," Brooke said, pushing her cell phone around in a little circle. "I was working, and Lucas called. That's all." She picked up the phone, then quickly put it back down. "He likes to check on me in the morning."

Sounded more like he likes to check *up* on her. Had that jerk seriously been accusing Brooke of cheating on him? Lauren's fingers curled into fists.

Brooke rose, grabbed two mugs, and put them next to Lauren on the counter. She eyed the coffee still brewing, grabbed the sugar, then fixed her gaze on Lauren. "Things okay with you and your frenemy now?"

Lauren nodded, relieved that she could.

Brooke gave her a genuine smile. It was moments like this when Lauren was reminded that her sister did, in fact, love her. It was almost enough to make her forget about the other 99 percent of the time when Brooke got under her skin.

Brooke flitted back to the table. "At least one good thing happened from us all returning here. Because I'll tell you that me being here has really disrupted my life."

There was that other side of the sister she knew and loved. All. About. Brooke.

"What exactly has been so unsettling about coming to Maine for a little while? You're still getting to plan weddings. In fact, you're planning that big society wedding that you really wanted to do. What's the problem?"

Brooke tapped her phone, then pushed it around in a circle again. "You really have no idea about my life. About all the stress I endure."

Lauren poured two cups of coffee, fixed Brooke's the way she liked, and brought them to the table. "Oh, please inform me about all the stresses you have running around getting manis and pedis and socializing with your superficial friends and attending brunches and going to the theater with your posh husband-to-be."

A slight red blush filled Brooke's face, and a line formed on her forehead. Lauren knew what that meant. Her sister was working up a big old tantrum.

"Do you really think that's all my life is? Manicures and brunches?"

And dating her shallow fiancé. But Lauren decided to try and defuse the situation instead. "Listen, B, I know you work hard. I do."

"I love my job," Brooke said quietly. Then she looked up, and her eyes were filled with fire. "You have no idea what I deal with on a daily basis."

Lauren hated when she tried to be nice, but Brooke didn't give in. "Either tell me what these supposed stresses are or go out there and figure out how to deal with them."

Brooke crossed her arms over her chest. "You are so freaking bossy."

"Hey. You're here, aren't you? Our baby sister needed us."

Brooke rolled her eyes. "She's hardly a baby anymore."

"Gabby will always be the youngest."

"You're so annoying," Brooke retorted.

"Guys, stop."

Both of their heads snapped up to take in Gabby, who had just entered the kitchen.

"Gabs, why aren't you at the café?" Lauren asked.

"I'm filling in for Kelsey later, so Grams told me to go home and take a break for a couple hours. And don't change the subject. I hate when the two of you fight about me."

"We weren't fighting," Lauren said at the same time Brooke proclaimed, "She started it."

Gabby sighed. She went to the coffee pot and poured herself a cup, then sat down across from the two of them. "Not that I don't appreciate it, because I totally do. But I didn't ask for either of you to come back here and help me with anything. Just for the record."

Lauren reached over and squeezed Gabby's hand. "You had a really rough couple of years, Gabs. I was happy to come here. Plus, I wanted to see Grams, too." An idea began to form. "We should actually utilize this time to go over different job options for you," she said to Gabby. "Where are you on the vision board project I gave you a couple weeks ago?"

Gabby groaned. "Ground zero. I hate the vision board."

"That's okay. We can work on it together. I found a really good career aptitude test the other day. See," she said to Brooke. "I'm here to help our baby sister."

Brooke started shaking her head. "There you go again. Making yourself out to be the martyr."

Calling on all of her reserves of patience, Lauren faced her sister. "I'm not trying to be a saint here. It's been a sucky time, and I wanted to see my family and make sure everyone is doing okay. What's wrong with that?"

Brooke's response was a huff.

"*You* didn't have to come to Seaside Cove," she said to Brooke.

Mouth falling open, Brooke threw daggers in her direction. "You wanted me to return."

"Yes, I did. But that doesn't mean you *had* to do it," Lauren said rationally.

"The only reason Lucas let me come here was because his longtime family friends are having a wedding nearby and I'm helping them plan it."

Brooke's comment had Lauren sitting up straight while alarm bells went off inside. "*Let* you? What do you mean *let* you?"

"Oh boy." Gabby sat back, crossing her arms over her chest in a mirror image of Brooke.

Brooke blushed, but she kept going, jutting her chin out and pushing her shoulders back. "When you are in a committed relationship—something that neither of you know anything about—you don't just do things all willy-nilly. You consult the other person. You give them that courtesy."

"I've been in committed relationships," Gabby said as her lips puckered up into a pout.

Lauren ignored the relationship slight. "I agree with you, Brooke. You do need to give when you're with someone."

"You do?" Gabby asked with surprise.

"Yes. But there is a big difference between consideration and permission." Brooke narrowed her eyes, but Lauren kept going. "When you decided you wanted to come here, did you tell Lucas? Did you discuss it with him and have a mutual conversation? Or did you ask for his permission?"

Lauren already knew the answer, and it broke her heart. Her sister was a pain in the ass of the highest degree, but she deserved someone so much better than Lucas.

The red on Brooke's cheeks deepened to scarlet. "You don't know anything about my relationship, Lauren. You don't, either," she said to Gabby.

Gabby uncrossed her arms, her face softening. "We know what you just said, B. You said that Lucas 'let you' come here. That's not okay."

"Maybe I misspoke," Brooke stuttered.

Only, she hadn't, and they all knew it. Lauren felt like she should offer some big-sisterly advice. Something wise that would help Brooke see that she wasn't tied to Lucas.

"What is it you like about Lucas?" Lauren finally asked.

Brooke snorted. "Like you really care."

"I'm being serious. What attracted you to him?"

"I don't know. He's very handsome. I'm not going to deny that's what I noticed first."

Gabby wiggled her eyebrows. "Nothing wrong with that."

Brooke offered a little smile. "He was so cute and really smart. He's traveled quite a bit and has all of these interesting stories about other areas of the world. And he's romantic. He gets me lots of sweet things."

"Such as?" Lauren prodded.

"Flowers, candles, champagne."

Lauren huffed out a laugh. "Cliché, cliché, cliché."

"Sorry if my idea of romance isn't as passionate as getting knocked up by a one-night stand with the local boy you don't even like."

Well, Brooke always did know how to shut her up. Gabby's mouth dropped open. But Lauren knew she deserved it. Every mean, if not false, word.

She did like Ethan. Would she have sought him out if she hadn't come back to Seaside Cove? Probably not. Would she even be doing anything with him now if she hadn't gotten pregnant? Clearly no, since she'd been all but avoiding him until she saw that positive test.

Lauren and Ethan had always had that kind of push-pull relationship where they were fighting one second and agreeing the next. And that had nothing to do with Brooke's situation, anyway. No matter what Lauren did or didn't do, or how she was feeling in that particular second about Ethan, Brooke was still her sister and Lucas was still an asshole.

"For the record," she said, "I do like Ethan. I've never *not* liked him. We've always been some form of friends. You know this isn't about me and Ethan, though. I'm worried about your relationship with Lucas." When Brooke shifted, Lauren held up a hand. "I may not have anywhere near the same amount of long-term dating experience that you have. And you and I have always been very different people. But even I can tell you're not happy."

Not exactly what she'd been thinking of for wise, sisterly advice, but it was the only thing she could think to say. Brooke huffed, causing Lauren to roll her eyes.

Clearly, Ethan wasn't her only frenemy.

• • •

Not for the first time in her life—and sadly, it wouldn't be the last, either—Lauren felt unsettled after her little tiff with Brooke. No one knew how to get under your skin quite like a sibling. And a sister, well, she had a map that led straight to all of your trigger points.

Lauren took a quick shower and threw on some clean clothes. She used her favorite red headband to push her hair off her face. For good measure, she added bright red lipstick. The pops of red complemented the denim jumpsuit she'd picked out.

Wanting a break from Brooke, she did her best to sneak out of the house quietly. She got in her car and started driving to the café so she could vent to Grams about Brooke. Even as she parked the car across the street from the café, she knew Grams would just roll her eyes and tell her to get over it.

"You're sisters, and you will always be sisters. Work it out."

She'd only been saying that to them for thirty years.

She dashed into the café, and she was instantly assaulted by the aromas that reminded her of her childhood: coffee and warm baked goods. The scents were more comforting than she could ever say.

She glanced around and was happy to see that Rose's Café was pretty full. Most of the tables spread throughout the space were taken. People were also strewn about the oversize chairs and the two couches.

With its exposed brick walls and eclectic display of art from local artists, the café was cozy. Grams redecorated every ten years or so, and currently the decor was bright, vibrant colors. Soft music wafted out from speakers mounted strategically on the walls.

Grams was busy helping a customer. Lauren made her way toward her, with a quick stop at the large glass display case so she could drool over the baked goods. Everything was fresh. Everything looked delicious.

When she finished up with her customer, Grams checked her watch. "Why are you here?"

Lauren leaned on the counter. "Good to see you, too."

Grams chose a bag of tea and then added hot water to a mug. She handed it over to Lauren, who apparently had no choice in the beverage or the flavor.

"I meant that you didn't tell me you were coming in to do your work today. You normally give me a heads-up. Where's your little computer?"

"I'm not here to work. Brooke's loud mouth woke me up earlier than usual. And I don't want tea."

"You're getting tea. It's good for you."

Lauren pointed to the display case. "Can I have two of the berry muffins that Gabs made?"

"How are you going to fit into your too-tight jeans if you eat two muffins every day?" Grams asked, even as she moved to put two muffins in a bag.

Lauren accepted the muffins with a tight smile. "I'm taking one to Ethan, if you must know."

"The boy sings to you one time and now he's your boyfriend?" Grams said with a sneer.

Lauren gritted her teeth. "He's not my boyfriend." He was just her baby daddy. Oh God, Grams was going to kill her.

Grams grabbed a rag and wiped the counter. "Not your boyfriend? What the hell is wrong with you? He comes to my house and screams his lungs out for you. And brings you roses. And makes out with you on the porch."

"Grams—"

"Must be something."

Lauren clutched the bag of muffins tightly. "I don't know. I guess we're two people who are seeing each other."

"Boyfriend and girlfriend, then."

She shook her head. "Do we have to put labels on it? We're old friends, kind of, who are getting reacquainted." Realizing her words and how fast Grams usually was with a witty comeback, Lauren shot a warning glaze. "Don't say anything."

Grams's lips twitched. "I wasn't going to."

Yeah right. When it came to her, Grams never missed an opportunity to deliver a smart-ass comment or biting retort.

"Lauren Wallace, it's so good to see you."

Saved by the...*oh shit*.

Lauren had to hold in a grumble as she greeted Eleanor Davison, one of Grams's gardening friends. Well, frenemy was more like it. Grams and Eleanor had been having a silent competition over whose hydrangea were better for decades.

Eleanor had always been nice to Lauren and her sisters. At least, to their faces. Everyone in Seaside Cove knew she was one of the biggest gossips in town. Maybe on the entire Eastern seaboard. That was saying a lot, considering how everyone in Seaside Cove liked to get their gossip on.

Lauren could tell that Eleanor was currently bursting with some kind of news. She could practically feel her excited vibrations from where she was standing. From the look of her arched brow, Grams apparently knew it, too. But neither of them made to ask Eleanor.

Finally, the older woman ran out of patience. "You'll never guess what I heard."

Grams snorted. Lauren leaned back against the counter and sipped the tea that Grams had forced on her. She had to admit it was tasty, though not as good as a double shot, dark roast cappuccino would be.

"Is it about Ava and Tony? Because everyone has been talking about them this morning," Grams said, glancing through receipts as if she couldn't care less about Eleanor's gossip. Lauren knew she was dying to hear what Eleanor had to say, though.

Eleanor shook her hand and waved a hand. "That's old news. Came up at the church bazaar last week."

Grams began rearranging the items in front of the cash register. "Don't tell me it's about Lee. Because didn't I tell you?"

Eleanor nodded. "I'll give you that one. You were one hundred percent spot-on with that."

"With what?" Lauren asked, unable to keep her curiosity under wraps.

"Cross dressing," they said at the same time.

Lauren rolled her eyes. "Oh, who cares about what he wears?"

"His mother, that's who." Eleanor leaned in conspiratorially. "He's been stealing his mother's clothes and accessories. He sells them on some website, and then he goes and buys even more clothes."

"He was sticking to costume jewelry and such," Grams added. "But what he thought was a fake ring turned out to be a very real sapphire."

"Joyce is beside herself." Eleanor shook her head. "We all should have realized. Remember how he used to steal the other kids' supplies in elementary school? Mrs. Martin was forever sending him to the principal's office."

Lauren rolled her eyes again as Eleanor and Grams continued to talk about the criminal ways of young Lee. That was the thing with Seaside Cove. No one forgot anything. Stigmas never went away. God forbid you blew your nose wrong back in the 1990s.

Cher Reynolds would always be the woman who cheated on her husband less than a year after they were married. Sonny Percill would never live down the time he drank so much that he ran his fishing boat into the pier. Ernie Simpson was the mean guy who yelled at children.

And her mother had been the woman whose husband ran off on her and his three young daughters.

Lauren rubbed her temple, a headache forming. From being woken up early to dealing with Brooke, this day just wasn't for her.

"Anyway," Eleanor said dramatically. "What I came in to tell you is about Lucy Love. You know, Annette's granddaughter who was conceived out of wedlock."

"She still with that Simon?" Grams asked.

Eleanor huffed. "That's what I'm getting to. Lucy's mama, Janice, is so upset. Lucy and Simon are living together. Not married," she said with a shocked face to Lauren. "Anyway, Lucy told her mama who told Annette who spilled the beans to Lorraine, my very dear friend. Simon proposed, and Lucy said no."

Grams stopped wiping the counter and looked up, apparently interested in this tidbit of gossip. "That's surprising."

"Neither Annette nor Janice were thrilled about the...living in sin," she whispered. Lauren fought the urge to roll her eyes as Eleanor continued. "Now, Simon tried to make an honest woman out of her, and Lucy said no."

"To think, they have that cute little dog together," Grams said. "How can they not get married?"

"Apparently Lucy didn't take the dog into consideration. She gave a flat-out no when he tried to propose."

"Those two need to get married," Grams said with one definitive nod. Case closed. The boss had spoken.

Lauren's heart sank. If Grams thought two people sharing a little dog was enough of a reason for them to walk down the aisle, she was definitely going to push her knocked-up granddaughter toward the altar.

"Of course. My daughter's best friend from high school's niece was at The Thirsty Lobster last night." Eleanor leaned in with a wink. "That Ethan is quite the catch. Very attractive." She leveled a smug smile in Lauren's direction. "If you can keep him in one spot, that is."

Grams and Eleanor went back and forth for a few more minutes. Grams became intrigued with some story that Peggy was passing along about someone Lauren didn't know. Finally, Eleanor ran out of steam. With a grumbled goodbye, Lauren watched Eleanor leave the café. She turned to find Grams eyeing her.

"What did you expect? You know how she is," Grams said.

"You're just as bad."

Grams looked genuinely shocked. "I am nothing like Eleanor."

Lauren practically choked on her tea. "Uh, yeah, you are. You, Eleanor, and this entire town are a bunch of gossipmongers."

She rocked back on her heels, thinking about everything she'd just heard. Grams waited on two more customers. When she was free, Lauren asked, "Do you really think Lucy and Simon should get married?"

"Of course."

Ridiculous. Sure, marry two more people off so they can fight and snipe at each other and be miserable. That was going to end well.

"I gotta go," she said to Grams, who waved halfheartedly as she talked to another customer.

An unfamiliar feeling was starting to rise from the depths of her stomach up to her throat. Panic? Was this anxiety?

No. She felt hot and irritated. She was *mad*. And she needed someone to vent to before she burned herself up from the inside out.

Lauren pushed open the café door and made her way to the sidewalk, heading straight toward Ethan's house.

CHAPTER ELEVEN

Ethan hadn't slept well.

He would like to think it was because he'd gone to bed after two in the morning. After making up with Lauren, he'd returned to the bar to find it was still packed and going strong. Luckily, Joe had had everything under control. Ethan really needed to give him some kind of bonus for last night alone.

Kind of shocked to think it, but he was excited about having a baby. A *baby*. A teeny, tiny human being that would be dependent on him for everything. Diapers and bottles and cribs and all that crap that babies needed. His brain was swimming with possibilities.

When he'd returned home after work, mentally and physically exhausted, he'd grabbed a beer instead of heading to bed. Walking around the house, he noticed a lot of areas that needed work. Really, the entire house. Like so many things in his life, Ethan had bought the house on a whim. It had been a great price, super close to the bar, and he knew he wouldn't have any problems selling it when the time came. Plus, it had a little backyard perfect for barbeques.

But as he'd moved from room to room the night before, he'd wondered what Lauren would think. Of course, she'd been here already, but they'd been a little preoccupied with other...activities. What would she think of the comforter on his bed?

Would she like the way his kitchen was set up? Did she even cook?

The more he thought about it, the more interested he was to see her in his space.

He grabbed a second large cup of coffee from his Keurig and leaned back against the counter to enjoy it. No sooner had he taken his first sip than the doorbell rang. Ethan made his way to the front of the house and opened the door to find a flushed Lauren on his doorstep.

Her cheeks were red, her eyes were bright, and he couldn't miss the fact that her fingers were curled into tight fists.

"Good morning, sexy," he said.

She raised a brow. "Good? Good? It is not a *good* morning. It is a completely screwed-up morning. That's what it is." She shoved a bag into his arms. "Here, I brought muffins."

The scent of baked berry goodness hit his nose, and his mouth watered. Before he could ask what kind of berries were in the muffins, he noticed his elderly—yet still very active in the town's gossip chain—neighbors, Mr. and Mrs. Crawford, working in their yard. They were both watching Lauren openly with interested expressions on their faces. Ethan offered a wave and ushered Lauren inside.

"Let's get you away from eager ears," he said, nodding toward the Crawfords as he closed the door on their fascinated stares.

"What does it even matter?" she asked. "Everyone already knows our business. They all know we slept together my first night in town."

"Yes, so let's not give them anything else to get chatty about."

She sighed loudly and then collapsed onto his couch. She held out her hand. "Muffin. Stat."

He chuckled as he hopped into the kitchen to grab plates and napkins. "You want any coffee?" He paused, stuck his head around the corner. "Are you allowed to have coffee?"

He jumped when he found that she'd walked over and was right in the doorway.

"I've read that one mug a day is totally fine. But I've already had some today. I'm good with water." She snapped her fingers impatiently. "Seriously, I need those carbs like yesterday."

"Rough morning?" he asked, handing over the plate with the muffin.

She bit into it, closed her eyes, and moaned. His mouth watered again, only this time it had nothing to do with the baked goods.

She went to the tiny peninsula in the kitchen and pulled out the stool to sit. He put a tub of butter in front of her, just in case.

"Yes, butter. That's what I need. We should follow this up with ice cream sundaes."

Since he only had one stool for the peninsula, he stood across from her, content with his muffin, which he finished in three large bites. "Muffins, butter, and ice cream. Is this a weird pregnancy craving?"

"No. This is a *Seaside Cove hasn't changed at all* thing. It's a *Seaside Cove is the capital of gossip* thing." She swept her hands out dramatically. "It's a *having a dog does not equate to marriage* thing."

"I was with you until that last one. Care to elaborate?"

She sighed. "Grams thinks that Lucy Love and some guy named Simon should get married because they live together and have a dog. Also, do you know that people still use the phrases 'living in sin' and 'making an honest woman out of' someone around here? And not ironically."

He nodded, waiting for more. When she didn't continue, he spoke up. "What exactly is going on with Lucy and Simon? I just played poker with him the other night. He didn't mention anything about Lucy."

"Something about Simon proposing—"

"Simon asked Lucy to marry him?" Ethan interrupted. "That's awesome."

"She said no." With that, she flung her head down onto the counter yet managed to hold onto the last bite of her muffin.

"That's too bad. I thought they were heading in that direction."

"Not the point," she mumbled against the granite.

"What's the point? Lauren? Lauren?" he tried again, softer this time. "What is going on?"

She remained silent.

"If you don't finish that muffin, I will."

She reluctantly smiled and straightened. "Over my dead body." She shoved the muffin into her mouth.

"You've finished your muffin. Now you must spill the beans. Not that I mind seeing you all razzed up—"

"What does that even mean?"

Ethan kept going. "Your cheeks are all rosy, and your eyes are even bluer today. Whatever made you mad also made you more beautiful."

She stared at him, that perfect mouth opening and closing. He'd disarmed her.

"Thanks," she said almost shyly.

"You going to tell me what has you all riled up now?" He picked up his coffee, which wasn't quite as warm as before she showed up on his doorstep.

She scrunched up her nose. "I mean, I think I've been away from here for too long. I forgot what it was like."

"Good old Seaside Cove," he agreed. "Remember how they would go nuts and talk for days over the littlest crap? Who asked someone to prom? Did the local team win the hockey game? So and so was getting divorced."

"Yeah," she moaned.

"Well, we gave them something kinda huge to discuss when we left the bar together that first night. Imagine if they knew about that little peanut," he said with a nod toward her stomach.

She returned her head to the counter.

He leaned down, pressed a kiss to the top of her head. She rose again, met his gaze. "I want to be mad at you."

"Oh yeah?"

She nodded. "I want to say it's your fault that we clearly forgot protection at some point. Yell at you for letting me drink all those gin and tonics. I don't know, just take it out on you."

"But you can't?" he asked.

She shook her head. "I can't."

"Because I'm so loveable."

"Ethan..."

"And crazy hot."

She laughed.

"It's okay," he said. "People tell me all the time. You should have heard the gossip train when I first returned. All anyone in town could talk about was my hotness. My raw, animal sex appeal. It was overwhelming."

She threw her napkin at him. "Stop making me laugh. I'm trying to brood."

He squeezed her hand. "We're having a baby together! It only matters what you and I do from this point forward. Which brings me to something else."

She arched a brow.

"I've been doing some thinking. You could move in with me."

She blinked. Once, twice. Other than that, she didn't move a muscle.

Ethan pushed a hand through his hair. "We're having a baby. Doesn't it make sense that we live under the same roof?"

She blew out a long breath, laden with frustration. "Ethan, I thought we went over all of this yesterday. You said—"

"I know, I know." He put his hand up. "I'm not asking you to marry me."

She eyed him for a long time. "Explain yourself."

"We've known each other since elementary school. We were great friends in high school. At least, when you weren't annoying the crap out of me."

Her only response was a grumble.

"I don't think it should come as a shock that we have great chemistry together. In and out of bed."

She blew out a breath of air, her eyes darting everywhere. Everywhere but at him.

"I have this house all to myself. We should share it."

She pushed away from the counter, stood up. "I don't even know if I'm going to stay here, Ethan. More than likely, I won't."

"I understand that," he said, holding his hands up in a surrendering gesture. "But while you're here in Seaside Cove, why not stay with me? Don't you want to go through this whole process together? Wouldn't it be helpful?"

"I came here to help my sister, which I've been a real slacker about. Something is going on with Gabby, and I'm trying to get to the bottom of it. I want to make sure she's okay."

He got that. He did. "I guess I'm just excited we're having a baby. I'm going to be a dad. It's going to be fun."

"Fun?" She shook her head. "It's going to be a ton of work. There is research to do and protocols to follow."

Protocols? Wow.

"I know that," he said. "There are doctor's appointments and baby books to read. But if we do everything together, I'm sure there will be moments of fun."

He had visions of scrolling through a

baby-related blog while they snuggled on the couch. He could see backyard barbeques with her sisters and his friends. Shopping for baby clothes and supplies. Making dinner together before he went to the bar. Bingeing a new show while he rubbed her growing belly and felt little kicks.

Lauren pointed at her stomach. "Stop saying fun. Nothing about this is fun. It's a serious responsibility, Ethan."

He frowned. Her words gave him pause. "Just because I'm not making a to-do list every single day doesn't mean I'm not being serious."

"Right now, I feel like I'm going to throw up at any minute. I can't stay awake for more than six hours at a time. Everything's changing. And I haven't even told Grams yet."

He perked up. "Let's go tell her right now."

Lauren looked like he'd just slapped her. "We can't do that."

"Why not? Is she not home?"

"Ethan, we can't tell Grams because...because..."

"Because why?" he asked.

"Because she'll make us get married."

In all honesty, Ethan didn't know if he wanted to get married, either. But seeing the disgusted look on Lauren's face didn't make him feel too great. It wasn't like he was some troll living under a bridge.

He crossed his arms. "You don't want to move in here, even temporarily. You don't want to get married. You don't want me to help with anything. And you don't want to tell your grandmother who raised you that this baby even exists. Maybe, Lauren, *you* are the one who isn't taking this seriously."

Ethan knew it was immature, but he was happy to see that he'd stumped her.

. . .

After Lauren left Ethan's house so he could get ready for work, she decided to roam the quaint little town center of Seaside Cove. She needed the walk and the time alone, since her thoughts were racing in a million directions at once.

That hadn't gone well.

What had she expected? She'd been in a sour mood when she arrived at Ethan's house.

But he hadn't helped matters with his moving in together and "babies are fun" talk. Not to mention, telling Grams. What was he thinking?

She ran a hand over her flat stomach. They had created a baby. Now they had to figure out how to proceed.

Pausing, she took in a big whiff of fresh, salty air. The birds were singing, there was a nice breeze in the air, and the sun was shining.

Yet, Lauren still felt uneasy, and it wasn't only because of her visit with Ethan. Or the gossip she'd heard from Eleanor. Or the fight she'd had with Brooke.

She started walking again, turning the corner of Main Street onto Willow Avenue, spotting a whirl of energy with long brown hair wearing a beautiful, but completely out of place for this town, pale pink dress with nude wedges. Brooke had just left one of the businesses on Willow.

Lauren couldn't keep the sigh inside. She let it out and walked toward her sister. Brooke was the last person she wanted to see at this moment. Their little tiff this morning had gotten under her usually-much-thicker skin. Typically, whatever Brooke was going on about went in one ear and out the other. But today, she'd hit a nerve.

Still, Lauren was curious why her sister currently looked pissed. Lauren knew that pinched expression and clipped movement. Something wasn't going perfectly in Brooke's utopia.

"Hey, B," Lauren called.

Brooke stopped and craned her head. She put a hand over her eyes to shield her from the sun. "L? What are you doing here?"

"Just taking a walk. What about you?" she asked as she caught up to her sister. Together they began walking toward the water as if they'd silently agreed on the direction.

Brooke hitched a thumb over her shoulder. "I need a little help with the wedding I'm planning. The bride's parents added an extra hundred people to the guest list. One hundred." She pulled a disgusted face that caused Lauren to giggle. "I can't believe I need help. You think I want to admit that?"

"I'm shocked you did," Lauren said.

"Well, I don't want to tell Lucas or anyone else in the company. With a hundred extra guests, every count, every estimate is off. We need more of everything. I've been running around all morning."

Lauren halted briefly to pull her sunglasses out of her purse. "Have you ever thought about opening your own company?" Brooke was currently working for a huge event firm in Chicago, which just happened to be owned by her dear fiancé's parents.

"Come on, L. You know the prices in Chicago."

"I also know the prices here in Maine. Why not open something and run it out of Seaside Cove?"

"You and I, we don't belong in Seaside Cove anymore. We're fish out of water here."

Lauren shrugged. "I don't know. I kind of like being back." She found the admission somewhat startling. Even with the gossip and the rumors, she still thought her hometown was charming.

Brooke rolled her eyes. "Enough to move back here?" She waved a hand through the air. "There's no movie theater in town. You have to drive for an hour to do any decent clothes shopping. There's not even a Starbucks, for god's sake."

"Good thing, too," Lauren said with an exasperated voice. "Since our grandmother runs a café where most of the town picks up their morning lattes. And she's currently employing our little sister."

Ignoring the sarcasm, Brooke stopped at a spot next to the water with a nice view of all the ships in the harbor. "Speaking of Gabby—"

"Were we?"

"We should. How do you think she's doing? Really?"

Lauren leaned onto the railing. "Honestly? I'm not sure. She seems like her usual, happy-go-lucky, bubbly-Gabby self one minute, and then the next minute—"

"It's like a dark cloud is hovering over her," Brooke finished. "I see it, too. What's with all the phone calls she's ignoring?"

Lauren shook her head. "I wish I knew. If she's in trouble, I want to help her."

"Same." Brooke reached into her Kate Spade handbag and pulled out a lip gloss, which she applied expertly without a mirror. "You don't think she owes money, do you? I know she had that roommate who really screwed her over financially, but I thought she was past that."

"I did, too. I came up here to help her get back on track," Lauren said with a sigh. "I'm not doing a very good job so far. I tried to go over her finances the other day, and she clammed up. She won't even entertain my vision board. And I'm getting the distinct impression that she doesn't want to be an actress anymore."

Brooke's eyes widened. "But that's what she always wanted to do."

"It doesn't make any sense. I was thinking—"

Brooke's phone started playing "Chapel of Love."

"That's Lucas. I have to take this." She answered her phone while Lauren suppressed her eye roll.

"I'm working on it, honey. You don't have to check in on me every five minutes. I've been in the event planning industry for a lot longer than you." She listened for a moment. "No, I don't mean to insult you. I know your parents are counting on you. Yes, of course, I realize that you are trying to prove yourself so you can take over the business. But I just…well, yes, no. Everything is under control with the wedding here."

Brooke began pacing with her phone, completely distracted as she continued reassuring Lucas, who was really starting to grate on Lauren's nerves. She'd only met him a few times, and she'd never gotten a particularly warm-and-fuzzy feeling from him. But the more she heard Brooke talk about him and with him, the more worried she felt for her sister.

"Seriously, Lucas, come on. Don't you trust me?" Brooke did something very unusual for her. She ran a hand through her perfectly glossy and well-styled hair, mussing it up. She looked like she was about to punch someone.

Right at the moment when Brooke was about to change the course of her aggravated pacing, she turned, running smack into a very tall and built man. Lauren hadn't even had a chance to call out a warning. The man came out of nowhere.

Brooke stumbled backward, dropping her phone. The man reached out and steadied Brooke before she fell onto the ground like her cell.

Holy hell, Lauren thought. Who was this? She definitely didn't remember him from high school, and someone that tall and muscled would have no doubt left an impression.

Before Lauren could think on it anymore, a large, shaggy, black-and-white dog the size of a pony came barreling around the corner. With a lopping tongue, he targeted Brooke and jumped up, his muddy paws reaching the shoulders of Brooke's fancy pink dress.

Now covered in mud with a slobbering dog

trying to give her kisses, with a stranger sporting a man-bun holding her arms, Brooke looked like a deer in headlights. Tempted to snap a pic of the comical scene, Lauren ran over to her sister instead. She reached down and scooped up Brooke's phone, which was luckily not cracked or broken. She could hear Lucas shouting, so she gleefully ended the call.

"What the hell!" Brooke pushed away from the man. She tried to disengage with the dog-horse, but said dog-horse wasn't having it. She looked like he'd found his new best friend.

"No," he said to the dog. "Bad girl. Down," he commanded.

Lauren stifled a laugh. Brooke always claimed she didn't like dogs, yet they always seemed to gravitate toward her.

"You okay, B?" Lauren asked, handing the cell phone over.

"Yes. But my dress." She let out a little whine. Then Brooke turned narrowed eyes on the man. "Who in the hell are you? You just run into people and knock them over and then have your ferocious dog try to eat them?"

Lauren had to hand it to the guy. He seemed pretty unruffled. As for his "ferocious" dog, well, he was just happy as a clam with his tongue lolling to the side and tail wagging a million miles an hour.

"I'm Kai," he said. He took his time looking Brooke up and down. "I'm sorry about my dog. This pretty little lady," he said with a nod toward the mutt, "is Princess."

And "Princess" could pass for a small dinosaur.

Lauren spotted someone running toward them from the opposite direction. She recognized Ethan immediately and couldn't stop the smile from forming. It was automatic, a natural response to seeing him.

"Lauren, what's going on? Is everyone okay? Oh, hey, Kai," Ethan said.

"Ethan," Kai greeted. "The bar open yet?"

"Joe should be setting everything up for lunch now. I was just about to head over when I saw you guys. Are you okay?" he asked Lauren with a slight tilt of the chin toward her stomach. She nodded. "I see you've met two of the three Wallace sisters," Ethan said.

Kai whistled. "Two out of three? There's another one? Oh boy. Is she as beautiful as... What's your name?"

Brooke just stared at him.

"That's Brooke," Lauren said, "and I'm Lauren. The youngest is Gabby, and yes, she's beautiful, too." She thought both of her sisters were gorgeous in their own way.

"Can't wait to meet her." Kai stepped closer to Brooke. "And I'm really glad I met you. I hope we run into each other again."

Brooke's response was to gesture to the mud on her dress and sulk. With that, she abruptly turned on her designer shoes and stalked away from all of them.

They all watched her go, but Kai seemed especially interested. "Your sister is...special," he decided.

An apt word choice. "Yeah," Lauren agreed.

"We've been trying to give her back for years, but they won't take her."

Ethan, who wore an amused expression on his face, finally jumped in. "Why don't you and Princess head on over to The Thirsty Lobster? Have a beer on the house."

"Not gonna turn that down." Kai made a clicking sound, and the dog dutifully jumped to attention next to him. "Nice to meet you, Lauren. And nice to meet your sister, too."

Lauren grinned. Until she realized she and Ethan were alone again. She shivered, as the sun had decided to hide behind a cloud.

"I'm sorry, Lauren. About earlier at my house. When you said you didn't want to get married... well..."

She tilted her head. "What?"

"You don't want to get married, or you don't want to get married to *me*?"

She met his gaze and saw the vulnerability there. Not to mention the hurt. A lump formed in her throat.

"I get that it might be difficult to tell your grandmother that I knocked you up."

Lauren scrunched up her nose at the term he used. "Lovely."

Ethan let out a small chuckle. "You know what I mean, and I get that Grams isn't going to be thrilled with either of us. I've always been a little afraid of her."

Even if she thought his suggestions of moving in together and/or getting married were unfounded, she knew his heart was in the right place. He deserved more than she was giving him.

A few rays of sunshine started peeking out from behind the clouds as Lauren took Ethan's hand. "My parents got married because Mom got pregnant with me," she admitted out loud for the first time ever.

Lauren remembered the first time she'd heard her mom talk about this. Adults tended to think that kids didn't understand things. Maybe they didn't. All Lauren knew was that she remembered that comment into her own adulthood, when its meaning became clear.

She had been conceived out of wedlock, and her mom and dad had been forced to marry. Marry because of her. And they'd never been happy.

Ethan stiffened. "Ah."

"They had a horrible marriage, which ended, as I'm sure you and everyone else in town knows, with my dad walking out on us."

She didn't expect him to pull her toward him, but that's what happened. His arms made her feel warm and secure.

"I'm sorry," he whispered against the top of her head.

She leaned back. "It's okay. It was a long time ago." She chewed on her lip while she considered.

Ethan nodded slowly in understanding. "Your aversion to marriage is becoming a lot clearer. But you know that Grams *will* eventually find out about the baby."

"I know. That's why…" She paused for dramatic effect. "I came up with a plan."

Ethan raised an eyebrow. "A plan? Seriously?

You wrote out a plan?"

"Ha ha, very funny." She took a step back and whipped out her phone. "Yes, I've been putting considerable thought into this. And I made some notes." She shook her phone.

"Of course you have," he said drily.

Lauren sighed. "This is how I do things, Ethan. You know that."

He ran a hand over his face. "Sorry. Continue."

"Okay, the plan for telling Grams is pretty simple. First, I think it's important to wait until I'm at twelve weeks because it's safer for the baby at that point."

"Less risk of miscarriage after the first trimester," Ethan said, to her surprise. "What?" he asked. "I read some articles."

She smiled. "So, you get it."

"I should point out that your sisters already know."

Lauren looked up from her phone. "That's different. They were there when I realized I might be pregnant. Then, they went with me to buy the test and they were with me when I took it." She tapped her phone. "But speaking of my sisters, I think they should be there when we tell Grams."

"Why?" he asked.

"Gabby makes Grams smile, and Brooke is good with defusing a situation. All that experience dealing with bridezillas."

Ethan was rolling his neck back and forth as if he'd just had a really tough workout. "Not that I don't appreciate 'the plan,'" he said with air quotes, "but can't we just tell her now? I understand not making it public for a few months, but this is your grandmother who raised you."

She shoved her phone in her purse and stepped into his face. "Ethan! We have so much going on right now. Gabby is still getting situated, and Brooke needs to get through this wedding she's planning."

"That's why we should consider telling Grams with*out* your sisters."

Lauren was tempted to pull out her phone again so Ethan could review her notes. But she resisted. "We need to maximize the positive energy and Grams's good mood. That's why we need Gabby and Brooke. Now, I was thinking the first week of August would be an ideal time to tell her. Maybe August fifth."

"I don't know," Ethan said. "I think I have a dentist appointment."

Shoot. She bit her lip, considering what other dates in August would work—until she realized he was making fun of her.

"You suck," she said for lack of anything more intelligent.

"Sorry, I couldn't resist." He leaned over and kissed her lightly on the mouth. Even the brief kiss had the effect of wiping her mind clean. She sighed and slowly unscrambled her thoughts.

"I think the best way to do this is to make the whole thing about Grams."

"Oh, sure." Ethan rocked back on his heels. "Your pregnancy is totally about Grams. Why would it be about either of us, or, you know, a new person coming into the world?"

She ignored him. "Anyway, we need to make it less about the fact that I'm preggo and more about Grams becoming a great-grandmother. Gabby can make a cake, and I'll have Princess Brooke decorate with some balloons and streamers. Maybe a bouquet of flowers."

"You're telling me that we have to wait until August—"

"Fifth," she supplied.

"August fifth," he repeated. "We'll have cake and decorations and congratulate your grandmother on becoming a great-grandmother."

"Yes, exactly." She kissed the tip of his nose, and a smile spread on his face.

He sighed. "I don't agree completely because I think it's going to be really hard for all of us to keep this secret..."

"But?" she prompted.

"But I'll go along with it." He nodded, decision final. "August fifth it is."

CHAPTER TWELVE

It had started raining after all, and Lauren spent the afternoon in her bedroom. She did a little work and also a little reading. Currently, she was devouring an article in a magazine she picked up in town called *Pregnant Women Monthly*.

Today, she was learning about how her body was going to change over the coming months. She couldn't deny that there was a lot of gross stuff in here. Mucus plug? No thank you.

She flipped through the rest of the pages, stopping on a collage with sleeping newborns. She almost sighed as she took in the angelic little faces. She ran her fingers over the page, imagining that she would be having her own little bundle of joy.

"What's that?"

Lauren jumped a mile at Grams's voice. She quickly covered the magazine.

"Scare a person to death, Grams. Jeez."

Grams narrowed her eyes in that way she had. She was like a velociraptor trying to figure out her next meal choice. Not for the first time in her life, Lauren was thrilled that Grams couldn't read her mind. Because she definitely wouldn't take kindly to being compared to a ferocious dinosaur.

Actually, she probably would.

"Heard you and your sister had quite the morning," Grams said, leaning against the doorjamb.

"Mine wasn't too eventful, but Brooke's certainly was interesting," she said with a wry smile.

"Heard she got run down by an enormous dog."

Relaxing, Lauren laughed. "You heard right."

"I'm sure all of Maine heard, since she's been bitching about her dress since she got home. I believe she's at the drycleaners right now."

Lauren and Grams both rolled their eyes.

"A tragic day in the life of Brooke," Lauren said. "Getting dirt on her dress while an adorable dog named Princess licked her."

"Princess?" Grams closed her eyes while she thought about that. "That would be Kai's dog."

Interested, Lauren sat up. "You know him?"

Grams shook her head. "I haven't met him yet. But the whole town is abuzz with his arrival. You know how gossipy they are about a new person."

They weren't the only ones. Grams was probably the conductor on this gossip train.

"Peggy and Wendy told me he was hot."

"Oh yeah. He's definitely hot. Do you think…"

She trailed off, wondering if she should broach this subject with Grams. Especially when she didn't have all the information yet. Brooke would no doubt kill her for even thinking it. Despite how much Brooke annoyed the shit out of her, she was her sister, and there was no way she wanted to see her in a bad, unhealthy relationship.

"Spit it out, girl," Grams said, an impatient tone to her voice.

"Never mind," Lauren said, shaking her head.

"Do I think what?" Grams prodded.

Lauren scooted forward on the bed. "Do you

think Brooke and Lucas's relationship is healthy?"

"Of course it's not healthy," Grams said. "They met at work. I told her not to date a coworker, but did she listen? I swear, that one with her head in the clouds and romance on the brain. Not to mention that Lucas's snobby parents own the company. There's nothing healthy about that. It's dangerous."

Lauren hated when she and Grams agreed. It wasn't natural. "I told her the same thing."

"See?" Grams wagged a finger from the doorway. "Doesn't listen."

"Their relationship just seems so...unbalanced," Lauren decided. "I'm a little worried."

"Well, stop," Grams said, finally coming into the room. Immediately, she went to a pile of Lauren's laundry and started refolding a shirt on top.

"What are you doing? I just folded that."

"You folded it wrong."

Lauren growled under her breath. "There is nothing wrong with the way I do laundry. And anyway, they're my clothes." She reached for the shirt, but Grams ignored her.

"As I was saying," Grams continued, "you have your own shit to worry about."

Lauren froze. What was she talking about? Did Grams know about the baby? "What do you mean?" she asked cautiously.

"Everyone saw you and Ethan fighting near the docks this morning."

Lauren relaxed, but only a little. "We were not fighting. We were talking. There's a difference."

"What were you talking about?" Grams studied a pair of shorts in the laundry pile before putting it aside. Apparently, it was folded adequately now.

"We were discussing how nosy my grandmother is," Lauren said.

"Cute. Anyway, you should seriously consider not seeing that boy."

Lauren peered at her grandmother. "I'm thirty-three years old. Are you telling me I can't see someone?"

"It's not that you *can't* date Ethan. It's that you *shouldn't* date him."

"Grams!" Lauren fell back against her pillows. "You need to chill."

She snapped a finger in front of Lauren's face. "You are supposed to be here to help your sister. How are you doing that when you're so busy prancing around town with Ethan?"

"I don't prance." Lauren chewed on her lip. Grams had a point.

"Your sister is downstairs now. Why don't you go talk with her?"

Pregnancy brain must be a real thing. For the second time today, she agreed with Grams.

• • •

"I hate you," Gabby said. "You know that, right?"

Lauren tapped her pen against her laptop. "Insulting me will not end this session of 'help Gabby learn how to manage money.'"

"I know how to manage money." Gabby's face fell. "Just not well."

"Exactly. You've always been bad with money."

Gabby slumped down in her chair, which pulled

at something in Lauren's heart.

They'd been reviewing Gabby's personal finances for over an hour. Her criminal roommate had done a real number on her miniscule savings account. But Gabby wasn't helping matters with her lackadaisical spending.

They'd set up shop in the dining room, one of the rooms that was rarely used, since Grams always preferred to eat at the large, and much less formal, kitchen table. But Lauren had always liked this room, even though the wallpaper was old and there was a stuffy-looking Persian rug sitting on top of the wood floors.

Grams had a beautiful oak table that extended to fit twelve people. On one wall she had this really ornate China cabinet where she displayed her mother's dishes, which were a delicate pearl color with tiny rosebuds on the rim. Lauren had never eaten off them, and she didn't think she'd ever seen Grams use them, either.

On the other wall was an absolutely gorgeous stained-glass window. The center design had a trio of roses. When they were little, Lauren told her sisters that there was a rose for each of them and that's why there were three. That had been a lie, of course, since the window had been installed in the early twentieth century.

"Listen, Gabs, everyone goes through bad financial times at some point."

Gabby frowned. "I'm kind of at an all-time low."

"Which means there's nowhere to go but up." Lauren made a few more notes. "And you're doing something about it. We'll get you back on track."

"Maybe you should have been a financial advisor," Gabby said.

No, Lauren knew without a doubt she'd chosen the right career path. Not that she'd set out to be a social media strategist. How could she when that career hadn't existed when she was growing up?

She'd majored in communications in college, not really knowing what she was going to do with that degree. She liked to write and thought about different avenues in that area. But after falling into a low-level job in a large marketing firm after graduation, she ended up gaining experience and moving up the ladder into different positions until she found social media.

"I'm good where I am," she said, peering at the spreadsheet she'd created with Gabby's finances. She pointed at something on the screen. "What about this expense? If you're really leaving New York, it can go away."

"I'm definitely leaving." Gabby sat back in her seat, twisting a piece of hair around her finger as she stared at the computer screen.

"What about your taxes?" Lauren asked. "Did you do them this year? Turn them in on time?"

Gabby nodded, and Lauren tried not to make her relief too obvious. She didn't want to offend her.

"What about marriage?" Gabby asked.

Lauren turned. "What about it?"

"What if—hypothetically, mind you—you had to file taxes and you were married? You know, like, in the future? Don't you have to file jointly?"

"I think you can file separately. Why?"

"Just wondered. I, uh, had a friend who got married this year. I was thinking about her earlier." She coughed. "Anyway, maybe you and Ethan will get married someday. High school sweethearts."

Lauren rolled her eyes. "First of all, we weren't high school sweethearts. We could barely stand each other back then."

"You were together all the time. I remember." Gabby took a sip of the tall glass of iced tea Grams had brought in earlier.

"We were friends. But friends who didn't like each other. And anyway, I'm not going to marry Ethan or anyone else."

Gabby's eyes widened. "Why not?"

She shrugged. "I don't really want to get married."

"Stop," Gabby said dramatically. "You don't want to get married? Like, ever?"

"I don't know. I don't think so." She tapped the pen against her lips. "I want to be in a long-term, committed relationship. I guess I just don't think you need a piece of paper for that to happen."

Gabby let out a short laugh. "I have one sister who does nothing but think of weddings. My other sister doesn't want to get married at all. Where does that leave me?"

"Somewhere in the middle," Lauren suggested. "Speaking of, you haven't talked about a relationship in a while."

Gabby squirmed, suddenly very interested in the papers in front of her. Interesting. There must be someone in her life.

"Are you seeing someone?"

Gabby made a pained face. "Nothing like that. No. Definitely not."

She doth protest too much.

Lauren practically bounced in her seat. "Gabbykins. Who is it?"

Gabby pushed away from the table abruptly, making her glass of iced tea wobble. Lauren righted it before it could spill onto her laptop.

"Sorry," Gabby said. "I'm going to grab a snack. Want anything?"

Yes—answers. A look into what was going on in Gabby's life. "I'm good."

She watched Gabby walk into the kitchen, haunted by her reaction. Lauren had a feeling they were nearing the end of their session together. As she began to tidy up the space, her thoughts went from Gabby to relationships to marriage.

Was it weird that she wasn't into the idea? It didn't take a therapist to figure out that her issues were directly related to watching her mom and dad. Or maybe even something to do with control, which Lauren liked having at all times. Marriage seemed unpredictable to her. Another person was thrown into the mix, and you had to navigate things together. No thank you.

Even being a bride never appealed to her. Seemed like a lot of stress. She'd never really fantasized about a wedding like other people she knew. Sure, it would be cool to wear a fancy dress, and she'd definitely be into cake tasting. But she'd watched perfectly rational, levelheaded friends lose their cool while planning their weddings.

Lauren heard the sound of very heavy footsteps

on the old wooden floors right before Ethan appeared around the corner and asked, "Whatcha doin'?"

"How did you get in?"

He grinned. "The front door."

"Cute," she said. "What are you doing here?"

"Yes, what *are* you doing here?" Grams asked as she walked into the dining room, wearing an apron, with a towel also slung over her shoulder. She had a rolling pin, which she was hitting against her other hand. "Didn't you just see her this morning? Are the two of you that codependent already?"

"Honestly, Grams."

Ethan leaned over and swiped a quick kiss over Lauren's mouth, which fell open in shock. "I missed her," he said to Grams. "How are you doing, Mrs. Josephs?"

Grams peered at him for a full minute. "You want some iced tea?"

"Sure," Ethan said jovially. Grams went back into the kitchen and then returned with iced tea. Lauren noticed that Ethan's glass had a lemon wedge and a straw. Not to mention a little plate piled with homemade cookies. *Interesting.* Grams must like Ethan. The rest of them never got such treatment.

"What's your real reason for coming over?" she asked.

"I did miss you."

He looked around the room, and Lauren followed his gaze. They were alone. Good thing, too, since this time he framed her face with his hands and kissed the hell out of her.

"I brought your sunglasses back."

"Huh?" she asked, dazed from that kiss. Hands down, Ethan was the best kisser.

"The reason I'm here. I brought your sunglasses." He produced them from his back pocket. "You left them on the bench near the water."

"Oh my god. Thank you. I can't believe I did that. I tell you. My brain has been so muddled since—" Lauren cut herself off.

Of course, Grams chose that moment to reenter the room. "Since what?" she asked.

"Since, since..." Lauren stumbled.

"Since you had that big online conference thing for work." Ethan sat next to her. "I have to admit that I still don't get everything about your job, but I know you must have really worked your butt off."

She grinned at Ethan.

"Hey, Daddy!" Gabby said gleefully to Ethan as she sauntered back into the room. Lauren's heart fell as Grams perked up, looking over at Gabby.

"Oooo," Gabby dragged out. "Hey, Daddy-o. What's shakin'?"

"Are we in a movie from the fifties right now?" Grams asked. "I was already there once. I don't need to live it again." With that, Grams once again left the room.

Lauren let out a long breath of relief. "Daddy-o? Seriously?"

Gabby grimaced. "Sorry."

Ethan's smile had never faltered. He took a moment to look at everything laid out on the table. "What's all this?"

"Well," Gabby began, "my lovely sister here has

taken it upon herself to make me her next project."

Lauren shook her head. "You're way more than a project, Gabs."

"She's helping me get my life together," Gabby amended. "Now that I'm moving back here from New York. I just have to decide what I want to do. What I can actually do. Where I should live. Here with Grams or get my own place. How to afford my own place. Where I want to be in five years."

"So, just some light decisions," Ethan said.

"Exactly." Gabby pointed at him. "What do you think I should do, Ethan?"

He ran a hand over his chin. "Well, I know you're a really good actress."

"How do you know that?" Gabby asked. Lauren had to wonder the same thing.

"I remember some of your middle school plays. But also, people talk about it at the bar. Seaside Cove is proud of their very own Meryl Streep."

Gabby smiled shyly. "That's nice to hear."

"However," Ethan continued, "it seems like you've been there, tried that."

"Yes." Gabby sat up straighter.

"Ready to try something new and different?"

Lauren batted Ethan's arm. "Don't tell her that."

"Why not? Anyone can see it."

"You've talked to her for a whole thirty seconds. What do you know about what she wants to do?"

"In that thirty seconds, I was able to ascertain that she isn't happy with acting anymore. Mainly because she didn't mention it at all."

"She has years invested into her craft," Lauren countered. "Classes and workshops and headshots and an impressive résumé."

"And lions and tigers and bears," Gabby added.

"Plus, she was on Broadway," Ethan continued. "She did her thing. Now she wants something different."

"Do I get a say?" Gabby asked.

"Shh," Lauren said, staring daggers at Ethan.

"This is the time for you to try new things," Ethan said to Gabby. "Get out there and explore."

"Yes, exactly." Gabby was nodding.

"No, no, no," Lauren said, waving her hands. "She is not going to explore. She needs to repair her finances and her life. She could teach acting, singing, or dancing."

"I really don't want to teach."

Lauren ignored her sister. "She could talk to different agents up here. Get some local work. Maybe try out for a play at the community theater."

"You're not listening to me, Lauren," Gabby said.

"No, you're not listening to her," Ethan agreed. "It's easier to try new things when you're younger and have fewer responsibilities."

Lauren froze. She looked from Ethan to her stomach. "Is this about the baby?"

Ethan threw his hands up. "There's a big leap."

"You didn't answer the question."

"Because it's a ridiculous question."

She was going to puke. Ethan and his stupid adventures. Of course he thought Gabby should just wander off and go wherever the wind took her. Without a plan, without fear of consequences.

She opened her mouth to really give him a piece of her mind when she felt something. Oh no. It wasn't just figurative puke. It was very real nausea. She covered her mouth a second before she shot up and ran to the bathroom. She barely made it there before she emptied her stomach.

When she was done heaving, she sat back, realizing that Ethan was behind her, holding her hair away from her face.

"Feel better?" he asked softly.

"Ugh. Kill me now. I hate throwing up."

"Not on my list of favorites, either."

She stood up, a little wobbly. Ethan reached out to steady her. She held on to the sink for just a minute, gathering herself. "Thanks." She rinsed her mouth out before splashing water on her face.

"Why do they call it morning sickness when it can happen at any time of the day or night? That's some bad branding."

"Did you just get sick?" Grams said from the hallway.

"No. Yes. Just a little."

"How do you get a *little* sick? Either you threw up or you didn't."

Gabby joined them in the hallway as well. Her face was filled with panic.

"I did, but I'm fine now."

Grams stood back and crossed her arms. "Oh really. What made you sick in the first place?"

"It was probably…" Gabby began, but then looked off into the distance.

"Yes?" Grams asked.

"I think it was…" Ethan chimed in but also had

nothing to save her.

"Food poisoning," Lauren said as the thought popped into her mind.

"Food poisoning?" Grams repeated. "From what? You ate at my café this morning. Don't you tell me that I gave you food poisoning."

"No, you didn't. Of course not," she said, desperate to fix this.

Lauren thought back to high school. She remembered the time her friend Danielle, who was a vegetarian, had drank too much at a party and gotten sick. They told Danielle's mother that she'd eaten meat. Her mom bought it.

"I gave up red meat," she said, inspired by her memory.

"What?" Ethan and Grams asked at the same time.

"That's right. I don't eat red meat anymore. Earlier today, Ethan gave me a hamburger."

Grams hit Lauren in the arm. "Why in the hell would you eat a hamburger if you gave up red meat?"

"That's a good question. I guess because I didn't want Ethan to feel bad. Which was wrong. Because that's why I got sick."

"That is the dumbest thing I've ever heard. You expect me to believe that?" Grams put her hands on her hips.

This was it. They were done for. Their secret was about to be out.

Grams leaned forward and peered at her. "No one in their right mind would give up red meat. What is wrong with you?"

Lauren just shrugged.

As Grams turned and walked back into the kitchen with Gabby, Lauren heard her mumbling about vegetarians and "hippy-dippy, oaty-crunchy people who couldn't enjoy a damn burger."

Lauren and Ethan looked at each other.

"Crisis averted," he said.

"For now."

Lauren knew she wasn't going to have much time before Grams found out about the baby. Then, everything would change.

CHAPTER THIRTEEN

"I never thought about contacting a lawyer," Gabby said as she returned to the dining room, carrying a bag of chips and a bowl of dip.

"That's what I'm here for." Lauren hungrily reached for the chips. She'd been working with Gabby for the last couple of days. They'd gone through aptitude tests and combed a couple of job search sites. Now, Lauren was reviewing Gabby's past lease and making sure her sister wasn't liable for anything else.

Gabby slumped into the chair next to Lauren. "I don't exactly have the money for a lawyer, though." She tapped on a folder. "At least, not according to my new financial plan."

Lauren grinned. "Don't worry about that. I just want to make sure all of your bases are covered. Brooke and I decided to take care of it for you. Consider it an early birthday present."

"Gee, I was hoping for a new purse," she said with a laugh. "But a lawyer sounds good, too." She reached for a chip. "Thanks, Lauren. Thanks, Brooke."

A grumble came from the other end of the table, where Brooke was also "helping" Gabby. Apparently, Brooke's definition of help consisted of her working on her own crap. Not that Lauren was bitter.

"Hey, B, you gonna take a look at this or what?" Lauren tapped her laptop where a lengthy email from the lawyer they'd hired was pulled up on the screen.

"Yes, I'm just in the middle of something right now."

Lauren seethed. "What a coincidence. I'm in the middle of helping our sister."

This comment was answered with Brooke finally looking up long enough to throw a dirty look in Lauren's direction. Gabby jumped in.

"Want some chips?"

"Actually, do we have any veggies? I'm watching carbs."

Of course she was. Brooke had one of the best bodies in America, yet she'd always felt like she needed to lose weight. She'd been trying every diet under the sun for most of her life.

"There are some carrot sticks in the fridge. I'll grab them." Gabby walked to the kitchen.

"Brooke Elizabeth Wallace," Lauren said through clenched teeth. She was finished with being nice. "Stop dealing with your work and come help me."

Brooke pointed a perfectly shaped, French-manicured finger in Lauren's direction. "I can't help that I have work to do. I was lucky that my company took on the Mitchell-Chandler wedding in Kennebunkport. That's the only reason I was able to take this time in Seaside Cove."

Lauren blew a long breath out of her mouth. "I have work to do as well. But today was supposed to be about Gabby."

"I'm here; I'm listening. But you know how insanely important what I do is."

"You're a wedding planner," Lauren reminded her.

"Yes, weddings are joyful. I bring joy to the world."

The sad part was Brooke truly believed that. While she probably did bring joy to the couples she worked with, throwing in the rest of the world's population might be a bit of a stretch. Perhaps it was time to bring Brooke back down to Earth.

Unfortunately, her phone went off and she couldn't lay into her sister.

She perked up at the sight of Ethan's name on the screen. "Hey, you," she answered.

"I have some crabs with your name on them."

She paused. "I truly hope you're referring to the crabs you eat."

Ethan bellowed out a laugh, causing her to grin like she was back in high school on the phone with her boyfriend. She had to stop herself from winding a piece of hair around her finger.

"All crabs are purely edible."

"Thank goodness for that," she replied.

"Who are you talking to?" Brooke asked as Lauren walked to the other side of the room.

"None of your business," Lauren said, once again feeling like she was back in high school and her little sister was bugging her.

"Excuse me?" Ethan asked.

Lauren ducked out of the dining room, passing Gabby as she did. She heard Gabby say, "It's probably Ethan."

Lauren walked through the kitchen and out onto the porch. Happy to be out of the house, in the fresh air, she took a deep breath. She stayed under the safety of the porch roof as the rain that had been falling all day continued.

"Sorry," she said to Ethan. "That was my nosy sister."

He chuckled. "So, what do you say? To crab or not to crab? I checked, and crabs are perfectly safe for pregnant women."

She was touched he even thought to check. Lauren glanced back at the house, spying Gabby peeking out from the dining room window. She shook a finger at her sister, who blew a kiss to her before turning her nebby self away from the window.

"That sounds amazing, but…"

"Uh-oh," Ethan said.

"Brooke and I are working with Gabby, and we're on a roll today. This is the whole reason I'm back in town."

Ethan didn't miss a beat. "No, I get it. Helping your sister is important."

Lauren bit her lip. "Rain check?"

"Definitely."

He didn't say anything else, but Lauren heard the disappointment in that one, single word. She got it. She felt the same way. Suddenly inspired, she glanced over her shoulder, making sure no one was listening.

"I'm bummed about the crabs," Lauren said. "But how would you feel about a late-night rendezvous?"

• • •

At ten o'clock on the dot, Lauren made her way quietly out of the house. She'd snuck out a few times during her teen years, and she knew all the creaky spots to avoid and the best way to slip out unnoticed.

She wasn't sure why she was sneaking out, though. She was a grown woman, a single, grown woman meeting another single adult. She didn't have to hide anything.

Only, it was kind of fun this way, she thought with a laugh.

She descended the path at the far end of the garden that brought her down to the beach below the house. She walked to the left where there was an alcove in the cliffs. It was the perfect spot for a late-night get-together.

Immediately, Lauren removed her shoes. She loved the feel of sand between her toes.

From the light of a large full moon, she could see the waves beating against the beach. A breeze blew her hair around her face. Even though it had stopped raining a few hours ago, the ocean still seemed restless.

She understood the feeling.

She grinned when she saw Ethan waiting for her on a large blanket in the sand. He was watching the ocean, a calm expression on his face. He was peaceful. Meanwhile, she had enough inner turmoil to fuel the entire Atlantic Ocean.

"Hey there," she called out.

He turned and hit her with the most charming smile on the East Coast. She actually paused to catch her breath.

"You know," she said as she closed the distance between them, "we really shouldn't meet up like this."

He raised one eyebrow. "I believe this was your idea."

He had her there.

"I know. But I truly think we need to set some rules."

Ethan popped a grape into his mouth. "We already have rules."

She eyed him for a long moment. "Do you even remember those rules?"

He didn't meet her eyes. "I don't know. Something about having as much sex as humanly possible."

"Be serious." She took a deep, fortifying breath. "I did want to see you tonight."

He grinned and reached for her. But she managed to sidestep him. "Butttttt," she drew out, "we need to define this." She gestured between them.

"Why?" he asked with all seriousness. It would have been comical if she wasn't in her most resolute mood.

Lauren tossed her shoes onto the sand and plopped down on the blanket. "You're exactly the same as you were in high school. You know that?"

He offered her a glass of wine, which had her raising an eyebrow. "Did you forget I'm alcohol-free right now?"

"It's seltzer. You're the same as you were in high school, too, by the way," he said. "You need to just let go and have some fun."

"I'm pregnant. I kind of already had my fun—

hence, this situation."

She watched a wave forming, cresting higher and higher, gathering speed and strength, rushing closer and closer to the shoreline, until it finally gave in and tumbled to the earth.

"I have no idea how long I'm going to stay here. What if we get attached and then I leave? What then? Do we stay together? Is it even smart to continue this knowing I'm going to leave? Of course, we have a baby now. We're going to be connected forever."

Ethan watched her from his side of the blanket for a long time. He had a thoughtful expression on his face as he nodded his head slightly. Finally, he opened his mouth, and she waited to hear his solution to their predicament.

"Chillax."

Lauren blinked. "Are you kidding me?"

"No."

"Ethan McAllister, you don't take anything seriously. I can't believe I started any of this with you."

She twisted, pushing up to her knees, preparing to leave, but Ethan reached for her hand and pulled her back down.

Laughing, he said, "You have got to calm down."

"I hate when people tell me to calm down. And I really despise being told to 'chillax.'"

"People or me in particular?" he asked.

She narrowed her eyes. Again, he laughed. Damn him and his appealing laugh and his amused eyes and those sexy laugh lines around his mouth. Most of all, damn the fact that she couldn't stay mad. Against every fiber in her being, she started laughing, too.

"I could always make you laugh back in high school. Glad to see that hasn't changed," he said.

"Shut up."

He touched his glass to hers. "Cheers, friend."

"Cheers," she said on a sigh. "Anyway, I hope I didn't take you away from the bar," she said.

He stood, holding out a hand to her. "Nah, it was my night off. I also have a phenomenal staff that I trust implicitly."

She allowed him to pull her to a standing position. "That's good."

He brought her to him for a long, comforting hug. He gave the best hugs. With his strong, muscular arms wrapped tightly around her, she felt blissful and safe. Lauren took a moment to inhale his cologne, something crisp and clean that was mixing with the salty scent from the ocean. She could stand like this with him for hours.

Only, he pulled back and kissed her. If she thought he gave great hugs, that was nothing compared to his kisses. It was clear that Ethan was quite experienced in this particular area, and Lauren couldn't be more grateful.

The way he took control of the kiss made her knees weak. He framed her face with his hands, brushing his thumbs over her cheeks before tilting his head and changing the angle. He moved his lips over hers with such skill that she was helpless to do anything but melt into his embrace.

"Breathe," he said when they came up for air.

"Huh?" she said.

"You need to let go and breathe, relax. For you

and the baby. Let's take an hour or two and forget everything."

Lauren sighed. "I have a hard time forgetting anything."

"No kidding," he said, crossing his eyes and making a funny face. Ethan leaned down and grabbed a brownie.

"You thought of everything," she said, taking a bite and savoring the chocolate goodness. "Hm, dark chocolate."

"I know the way to your heart."

He said it jokingly, but what she feared was that he actually did know.

They sat on the blanket together. "I think we're making some good progress with Gabby. At least, I hope we are."

"That's good. I like the kid."

Lauren took a sip of her seltzer. "She wouldn't like that you called her kid. But she likes you, too. In fact, she told me she had a crush on you in high school."

Ethan raised an eyebrow. "Yeah? Two out of three Wallace sisters were into me."

She batted his shoulder. "Don't make me regret telling you things, McAllister."

He ignored her jibe. "Now, we have to get Brooke on board with my hotness."

Lauren let out a loud laugh. "If you're not her awful fiancé, she's not paying attention. Which sucks for me because I need her to dive into this plan I have for Gabby."

"Speaking of diving in," Ethan said, putting his glass down in the sand. He rose and stripped off his shirt.

Lauren choked on her wine. "What are you doing?"

"I'm going swimming." He unfastened his belt, unzipped his jeans, and began to pull them down his legs.

He was wearing boxers. In the light of the moon, he looked amazingly hot. Ethan had a good body: strong shoulders, defined muscles, and that tapering of his waist that made her mouth water.

"You're going swimming? Out there?" She pointed at the ocean, and Ethan nodded casually. "You do realize how cold that water is right now?"

While a lot of other beach areas in the U.S. were warming up in June, Maine wasn't one of them.

Ethan removed his shoes and socks.

"Ethan, you are naked."

He looked down at himself. "Holy shit, I am. Well, not completely. But I'm working on it."

She laughed in spite of the fact that she was standing on the beach with a naked man.

"I'm going swimming. Care to join me?"

He reached for the waistband of his boxers, her eyes following suit, locking onto the sight.

She looked toward the water and then back to Ethan. "I can't just go skinny dipping."

"Why not?"

"I don't know. I didn't prepare for that." She'd shaved that morning, but not as carefully as she usually did when she wore a bathing suit. Plus, she liked to tie her hair back when she went into the water. Not to mention there were laws against this sort of thing.

"Do you prepare for everything?" Ethan asked.

"Pretty much."

He chuckled. "Now that you and I are involved, you have to get used to doing some things on the fly. It makes life so much more interesting. Just think what your Instagram followers would think of this story." He pointed at himself and then at the ocean.

"I don't think my Instagram followers—or my followers on any other platform, for that matter—are ever going to see photos of this night."

"But look at that." He walked behind her, placed his hands on her shoulders, forcing her to take a couple steps forward. "Check out the way that full moon is reflecting off the ocean. How cool is that?"

Very cool, she agreed silently.

"I would hate to miss out on such a beautiful night. Unless you're scared of skinny dipping with me." With that, Ethan took off running.

Damn, his body looked amazing. She was so transfixed by it, she almost didn't let his dare sink in.

"Wait a minute," she called. She wasn't afraid of skinny dipping. Although, she'd never actually done it before.

Lauren bit her lip, considering. Cold water. Dark water. Cold, dark water. Or naked Ethan. Wet, naked Ethan.

Ethan let out a *yahoo* as he dove into a wave.

It really wasn't a fair comparison.

She quickly removed her clothes and ran toward the ocean.

She frolicked—there was no other term for

it—into the cold water of the Atlantic Ocean. They splashed and chased each other until she got used to the temperature.

Then they ran out of the ocean and into the warmth of the towels Ethan brought with him. He wrapped a towel around her, rubbing her arms.

It was easy to tilt her face up and take his lips with hers. His arms came around her, and they kissed each other passionately until they tumbled onto the blanket on the sand.

They made love. Slowly, sweetly, bringing each other pleasure amongst the sounds of the waves and the salty sea air.

This wasn't like their first time together. That had been all frenzy and lust. This time it was an exploration of each other. Both times had brought enjoyment, but tonight was sweet and unrushed. A connection was forming with each touch, each kiss, each sound of pleasure.

She definitely would never take a photo of something like this. She shared personal aspects of her life on social media, but in a very controlled way.

But if she did share this, if she truly captured the night with the massive ocean sending waves back and forth against the sand, the moon shining down, and their naked bodies intertwined, Lauren would have tagged it #Happiness.

CHAPTER FOURTEEN

In the blink of an eye, almost an entire month had flown by. At least everything in Ethan's world was going great.

Mostly.

No, life was good. Better than good.

So why did he have a constant nagging feeling of uneasiness? It didn't make any sense when his life was moving along nicely.

The bar had been packed most nights. Now that they were getting into the height of the summer, the traffic was nonstop. Ethan wasn't complaining. Neither was his bottom line.

Plus, he was seeing Lauren, whom he'd not only had a crush on since high school but he was insanely attracted to now. And they were having a baby together. A baby that she didn't want to tell anyone about yet.

Ethan understood that a lot of women chose to keep their pregnancies close to the chest for the first twelve weeks. There was concern for health and other complications. But with Lauren, that wasn't the only reason she was staying silent.

She insisted that Grams would want her to get married. Knowing Lauren for most of his life, he couldn't imagine why she was so concerned about this. It's not like Grams could force her. Ethan chuckled. The idea of someone, anyone, "forcing" Lauren Wallace to do anything was beyond comical.

She was far too independent-minded.

His smile faded. After learning about her parents' marriage, Ethan realized the real issue ran deeper. He just hoped that he could help Lauren come around to his way of thinking, which was that a baby, planned or otherwise, was a happy event. Something to be shared with your loved ones.

But he tried to push all of that out of his mind because Lauren was on her way over to his house. He'd picked up a couple of BLTs from the bar, with a large side of fries for them to split. Lauren claimed she was craving bacon. Ethan was also craving bacon, and he wasn't even pregnant.

He heard a light knock on the front door followed by Lauren immediately entering the house. "Ethan?" she called.

"Back here," he said.

Just like that, his kitchen lit up when she walked in. So did his mood.

She looked like a ray of sunshine in a bright yellow sundress, with a pair of short black leggings underneath. Her hair was pushed back from her face with a large orange headband, and long matching earrings dangled from her ears.

He didn't miss that her lips were painted a bright pink a second before she planted a big, smacking kiss on his lips. Said lipstick was probably on him now, and he couldn't care less. He was proud to show the town that he had been kissed by Lauren Wallace.

"You look delish," she said with a wink when she pulled back.

"You take my breath away," he said quietly.

A small sigh escaped her lips right before he took them again. This time he took his time moving his lips over hers, enjoying her taste.

When he finished the kiss, he looked deeply into her blue eyes.

"Wow," she said. "That was some welcome."

"How are you feeling?" he asked. "Any more queasiness, nausea, vomiting?"

"No, Dad," she said dramatically. "I feel fine today. Just tired."

He'd read that exhaustion was common in the first trimester. "Good. Then you are allowed to have this."

He revealed the BLTs and fries, and Lauren grinned. They brought their food into the living room and set up on the couch. As they began eating, he asked, "When do we get one of those pictures?"

She glanced up with a blank look on her face. "Huh?"

"You know. The black-and-white picture with the baby."

She smiled. "You mean a sonogram? Not until week eight. That's my next scheduled appointment."

"I can't wait to see the little peanut."

She popped a fry in her mouth. "You do realize it's not going to be a great pic. They are going to probably look like a little blob."

"But we can tell if it's a girl or boy, right?"

"Sorry, but no."

His hand froze, holding his sandwich halfway to his mouth. "Seriously? I need something."

Lauren laughed. "Patience, young Jedi. My doctor said we don't find out the sex until around week twenty. But, as luck would have it, I do happen to have something for you. It's not a sonogram or the sex of our baby, but I think you'll like it." She produced a white paper bag from her purse and shook it. "Brought you some cookies from the café."

"Did Gabby make them?"

Lauren blinked. "As a matter of fact, she did. Why?"

"Gabby's cookies are amazing. Everyone has been talking about them at the bar."

Tilting her head, Lauren stopped eating her sandwich as she took him in. "Really?"

He nodded. "In fact, so many people had mentioned them that I bought a whole tray and put them out on the bar." He snapped his fingers. "They were gone in about five seconds."

"I knew Gabby liked to bake, but I had no idea she was actually good at it." Lauren shook her head. "What else is happening at the bar?"

Popping a chewy chocolate chip cookie into his mouth, Ethan sat back and savored the taste. Gabby had definitely gone down the wrong career path with acting.

"Ethan? You still with me?" Lauren asked, amusement in her voice.

"Sorry, but this is so freaking good. Anyway, the bar. You will be interested to know that someone has been asking questions about your sister."

"Which one?"

"See if you can guess." He ate another half of a cookie. "New Seaside Cove resident, Kai

Blackwater, who's usually the silent type, has asked me a couple of questions."

"Hm," Lauren considered. "There's no way Kai could have missed Brooke's engagement ring, since it's the size of Rhode Island. He must have been asking about Gabby."

Ethan shook his head.

"Seriously?" she asked, scooting closer and her eyes lighting up. "Kai was asking about Brooke?"

"Bingo."

Lauren's face fell. "Too bad Brooke is engaged to her ultra-boring fiancé."

He laughed at the pained expression on her face. "Not a fan of your soon-to-be brother-in-law?"

"That's putting it mildly," she said drily.

As Lauren filled him in on all the reasons why she wasn't a fan of her sister's relationship, it dawned on him that the two of them really hadn't had a conversation about *their* relationship. A DTR, Determine The Relationship talk, he learned from one of his waitresses. They never got back to that conversation after she brought it up on the beach weeks ago. Maybe now was the time. "...but Brooke was always the type to have a serious boyfriend. One date and they were a legit couple," Lauren was saying.

Ethan seized his opportunity. "What about you?"

"What about me?"

"What does it take for you to become serious with a guy? One date?"

She rolled her eyes.

"Five dates?" he asked.

She snagged a cookie, broke a piece off, and popped it in her mouth. "Ethan," she groaned.

"A handful of dates plus a surprise baby with a devastatingly hot guy who is the envy of men everywhere and the desire of all women?" He winked at her for good measure.

"I don't know. I'm only having a surprise baby with you."

"Cute," he said.

"Thanks," she said with a grin.

"But seriously. What are we?"

She sighed, then stared at the other half of the cookie as if it held all the answers to life's great mysteries. After a long moment, she looked up and met his eyes. "What do you want to be?"

"I think we are dating."

She nodded. "I agree."

"I know you don't live here. But I'm about living in the moment. As of this moment, I think we should be officially dating."

Her only response was an arched eyebrow.

"Boyfriend and girlfriend." He gestured back and forth between them.

"Interesting," she said.

"That's all you have to say?"

She tapped a nail, painted the same shade of pink as her lips, against her mouth. "I feel that we need to have some ground rules if we're *officially* moving in this direction."

It wasn't a no. That's all Ethan could think. "You go ahead and make those rules and fill me in later."

"But, Ethan, we need to do that."

He pushed her plate aside and scooped her up. "There's something else we need to do right now."

"What about my rules?"

Ethan kissed her as he walked them to the stairs. "I really want to hear all of your rules, but first, I have to make love to my *girlfriend*."

And saying the word "girlfriend" had all of his anxiety flying out the window.

• • •

Lauren was still reeling from her midday, impromptu, sexy-time romp with Ethan.

She bit her lip and eyed him as he steered the car to an unknown destination. He was so attractive. She shook her head. What had been wrong with her in high school? She so clearly should have gone out with him instead of what's-his-name.

He'd been so freaking cute asking her to be his girlfriend earlier. When he said they were officially dating, she felt butterflies in her stomach. She liked the idea of putting a label on their relationship, even if their future wasn't completely set in stone yet. And she was still planning on making some rules. Ethan may have thought she was joking, but rules were important to make sure they were on the same page.

"Excited?" he asked.

"Excited and curious." After they'd fallen in bed together—and, okay, taken a shower together, too—Ethan told her he was taking her to a special place. A secret, surprise, late-afternoon date.

She was into it, and her mind was guessing all

kinds of different locations. Restaurants and other fun spots on the coast. There was a fabulous place that looked like a tiny shack from the outside but served the most amazing crab on the planet. Or a third-generation Italian-run restaurant that was about an hour inland from Seaside Cove.

Maybe they were heading to a movie or something to distract them for a couple hours. In any case, her mind was ripe with possibilities, and she felt herself getting more eager the longer they drove.

Then they pulled into the parking lot of one of those massive shopping complexes that held every store possible: home goods, home improvement, clothing stores, coffee shop, Target, an electronics store, and even a gym. When Ethan pulled the car into a spot in front of a baby store, she shifted to face him.

"What are we doing here?"

He met her question with a look of confusion, then said, "This is your surprise outing."

"It's a baby store."

"Rumor has it, we're having one of those."

Her dreams of a romantic dinner or some entertaining adventure drifted away as she watched two super-pregnant women enter the store.

"Might as well get started on a registry," he said nonchalantly.

It was his natural ease that set her off. Somewhere, deep inside her, she knew it was completely irrational.

"We don't have anything for the baby yet," she said.

He sat back and took her in. "That's where the store comes in. I sense they will be able to assist us with any questions we may have. I bet they even have lists for us to look at."

"I already have lists. I've been researching car seats and strollers. I have a whole spreadsheet comparing breast pumps."

He reached for the door handle. "Great. Let's go, then."

"I don't have it with me, Ethan. It's on my iPad. I knew I should have brought that," she said to herself.

He frowned. "What's the problem?"

She pointed at the store. When no recognition passed over his face, she explained. "You want to just go into a baby store and start buying, without any kind of plan or list or sense of what we might need. Hell, Ethan, we don't even know where I'm going to be."

His shoulders dropped, and he broke eye contact. "I thought you would like shopping for the baby."

Now she felt like the biggest jerk on the planet. "I would. I mean, I do like the idea of shopping. I'm just not prepared."

He tapped his fingers against the steering wheel. "You have to prepare to shop?"

"For this kind, yes. It's not like we're buying a pair of shoes."

"We could buy a pair of baby shoes," he joked. "Sorry, just trying to lighten the mood." He squeezed her hand. "Come on. Let's at least take a look. Maybe we can get one thing. Like a crib."

Thoughts of consumers' reports and lists and research on the best and safest cribs flitted through her mind. She was so not equipped for this. She'd wanted to be way more organized before she stepped foot into any kind of baby store. She'd only begun her initial research into cribs. There were still a few blogs she'd wanted to check out because she'd heard they had great ratings on baby furniture.

Lauren stifled the large sigh that desperately wanted to rip out of her body. Her anxiety wasn't only due to not having her iPad. This situation was so indicative of her and Ethan's personalities, and maybe a telltale sign that this might not work out between them.

"Just a crib," he whispered to her.

As she exited the car and started walking toward the store with its cute little baby displays in the window, she realized this was an outing for the two of them. Maybe there were no candles or flowers or yummy lobster dishes. But, in his way, Ethan had tried to do something special for her.

She shook off her concerns—mostly—and followed Ethan into the store. She couldn't stop the smile when he reached for her hand and led her to the customer service station.

They spoke to a really knowledgeable woman named Jenny, who explained registries. And thank all that was holy, she had a really thorough list for Lauren to peruse. As Ethan checked out some glider chairs, Jenny even shared some of her favorite websites for comparing baby products.

Then Ethan, Lauren, and Lauren's new best

friend, Jenny, made their way to the back of the store, where the cribs were located. Jenny took the lead, explaining the pros and cons of each crib.

That's when the tables turned. Ethan started to seem a little overwhelmed, but Lauren was suddenly in her glory. Pros-and-cons lists—that was something she understood, something she could get behind.

After what felt like a brief period of time but, Ethan told her had been almost one hour, Lauren picked her favorite crib.

"Wonderful," Jenny said. "I try to keep my personal feelings out of it and let the customer make their own choices. But I was going to point you in this direction. I just had my daughter six months ago, and this is the crib we got. My husband and I love it."

That gave Lauren peace of mind. She grinned up at Ethan, who handed over a credit card. "Ring it up," he said.

"I can get it," Lauren said, reaching for the denim satchel purse she'd brought along today.

Ethan put his hand over it. "No, I want to do this."

Lauren didn't feel it was fair to Ethan for him to cover 100 percent of the cost of the crib, but she sensed that it meant a lot to him. And besides, there were plenty of other things she needed to buy yet. She nodded and let him handle all the details. As she walked around the rocking chairs and gliders, she decided it was actually kind of nice to have someone else take care of her for a change. Not that she didn't delight in being the provider for her family and friends.

Ethan returned from the checkout station when his phone rang. His face lit up. "Oh man, I haven't talked to him in forever."

"Take the call."

"But…" He gestured toward Jenny, who was still clicking keys on her computer.

"Seriously, I got this if she has any questions. Go talk to your friend."

Since Jenny didn't appear to be in any hurry to ring up their transaction, she settled back on one of the gliders, put her feet up, and watched Ethan. He was gesturing excitedly as he paced around the stroller section, smiling and laughing.

Lauren sat back and closed her eyes. She loved the crib they picked. It would look really cute in… Lauren's eyes flew open as she put a hand to her mouth. Where would this crib go? Her condo was in Virginia. Ethan's house was in Maine.

Once again, she looked to Ethan, still on the phone. Their locations weren't the only difference between them. Take today, coming to this store. Ethan brought her here on a whim, while Lauren would have preferred to prepare for something like crib shopping. It was mere luck that they got a knowledgeable salesperson.

She really needed to start putting some concerted thought into where she was going to live and how sharing a baby with Ethan would work. They couldn't just raise a baby on a whim.

She gulped as anxiety flooded her. *Breathe*, she told herself. They'd just decided they were in a relationship. That was a positive step forward for

Ethan. He wasn't going anywhere.

"Alaska! Oh man, I've wanted to live in Alaska for a long time."

Her mouth fell open. Alaska, what now?

She dropped her legs off the accompanying stool and sat up straight. Ethan was running his hand along one of the receiving blankets near her. She couldn't help but overhear.

"No, I'd be perfect for that job. In fact, I've been managing this bar, so I have a ton of experience to bring to the table."

Managing a bar? More like owning a bar. Being responsible for employees, vendors, patrons. Responsible, in general. Stable. Stationary—as in living in Seaside Cove and buying cribs and asking women to be his girlfriend. Not running around the world with a serious case of wanderlust.

She could feel her pulse picking up. Panic was starting to grip her tightly, and her breathing was becoming labored. As she usually did to calm herself, she whipped out her phone and started making a list. She glanced around the store for an idea. Other nursery accessories. Perfect.

But she couldn't concentrate as Ethan waltzed by her, laughing again with whoever that was. This person who was offering him a way out of Maine. A way to abandon her and leave all the baby research firmly in her hands.

"I'll think about it," he said. "I'm really glad you reached out."

He was? Her heart dropped.

• • •

Ethan ended the call and shoved his phone into his pocket. When he turned, he found Lauren watching him with a horrified expression on her face. She'd gone pale, and it looked like her hand was shaking.

He was at her side in a split second. He pushed her hair off her face. "Hey, what's going on? Are you feeling okay?" He gulped, his heart rate quickly climbing. "The baby?"

Lightly, she shook her head. "I feel fine. The baby's fine."

"Are you hungry? Did your blood sugar drop? You're so pale. We've been here a long time. We need to get you something to eat. Or are you nauseous? You've been doing better with the morning sickness. Do you need to run to the bathroom?"

"I feel fine, Ethan," she snapped.

He stood quickly. What was going on?

"What's wrong?" he asked.

"Alaska," she said with great emphasis and wide eyes.

And that's when it dawned on him. She'd overheard his call. He pushed a hand through his hair. From her vantage point, it would have sounded like he was making plans to move to the Last Frontier.

Bobby had presented an intriguing opportunity, though. Ethan couldn't deny that. But there was more to the story.

He sat down on the stool in front of her. "That was my friend, Bobby. He's starting a chain of restaurants and bars."

"In Alaska," she repeated.

"In Alaska," he confirmed.

She rested back on the glider, her gaze trending

downward toward her clenched hands.

"Listen, Lauren, I'm more than likely never going to work in Alaska."

She didn't meet his eyes. "More than likely." Her face was set. "But maybe."

"My friend Bobby is amazing. A great guy. But most of his ideas and ventures never come to fruition."

"But some do?"

He leaned toward her so that he could get her to actually look him in the eyes. "Some do, yes."

"If this Alaska idea actually worked out, you would go." It wasn't a question.

"I would…" He trailed off because he honestly didn't know.

He was currently in a baby store with a woman he'd wanted for at least half of his life, shopping for a crib for *their* baby.

No way would he abandon her with their child. At the same time, it was a very real option that she would return to Virginia, despite the fact that he had the feeling she was starting to enjoy being in Maine near her family.

If she did leave Seaside Cove, they would be coparenting from different states anyway.

She sat forward, her sad eyes suddenly turning determined and direct. "Ethan, you own a bar. If some other job opportunity comes up and tickles your fancy, what are you planning on doing with The Thirsty Lobster?"

"My goal is to set The Thirsty Lobster up for success. I would never leave it in poor hands with someone who didn't see its awesome qualities.

Someone who wouldn't take care of it."

"You would sell it?" she asked.

He couldn't say for sure. He didn't like the idea of someone else taking control of The Thirsty Lobster. He was attached. More than he wanted to admit. "I might just hire a great manager. Someone trustworthy and knowledgeable."

The small amount of color that had returned to her face disappeared again. "You really would up and leave, wouldn't you?"

He didn't answer her because he didn't know what to say. Or even what he felt. He'd liked shopping for the crib with her. He liked getting to see her all the time. His favorite part of the day was when they told each other what they'd done that day.

Still, there was another part of him that feared staying in one place too long. Dreaded the idea of making decisions based on the wants of another person, rather than his own desires. He'd learned the hard way how wrong that could go.

He realized there was nothing he could say to assuage her anxiety. For once, his usual laid-back attitude was being tested. He'd wanted to live in Alaska for a long time. But he'd also wanted Lauren for a long time.

He loved the bar. Even if it wasn't the forty-ninth state, he loved Maine, too. Seaside Cove would always be home. After being away from it for so many years, he was truly enjoying being back in town, interacting with the community, and catching up with old friends.

But deep down, there was a tingling that always

reminded him of his desire to travel, experience new things, make the most of life.

"Hey," he said softly, trying his best to comfort. "Why don't we get out of here and get something to eat?"

"But—" she began.

"Lauren, I'm not moving to Alaska any time soon." At least, he didn't think he was. "This is nothing for you to worry about today. I promise."

Although, he didn't know that. As they walked out of the store, he knew the bliss they'd been experiencing for the last couple weeks may have come to an end. The honeymoon period was over. In its place were the hard decisions of life.

Unfortunately, Ethan had no idea what was going to happen. Usually, he thrived on that. But today, for the first time, the unknown made him feel extremely uneasy.

CHAPTER FIFTEEN

Lauren finished working and closed the lid of her laptop. She gathered all of the glasses and mugs she'd used throughout the day and brought them to the sink in Ethan's kitchen.

She'd started working from Grams's café earlier in the morning, but there had been too many interruptions to concentrate on work. Not to mention, Grams was on a kick about Lauren's eating habits, which had changed since she'd become pregnant. Currently she was too nauseous for a lot of her usual favorites, so she stuck to bland foods and lots of carbs. Grams took the liberty of reminding her that too many carbs weren't going to allow her to wear her too-skinny jeans.

Gabby also kept stopping by Lauren's table in the back corner to chat. Lauren suspected that Grams had been persistently asking for some cookie recipe that Gabby claimed was secret. Unlike Lauren, Gabby would rather hide than tell Grams to back off.

After not one, but two, former classmates stopped to say hi and catch up—a welcome distraction but still a distraction—Lauren had realized she needed to get out of there.

Ethan's house had turned out to be perfect, since he was working at the bar in the morning and afternoon. Nothing to get in her way or take her away from work. Plus, it smelled like Ethan.

Especially when she'd gotten cold and put one of his shirts on.

She'd breathed in his scent, a unique musky aroma mixed with fresh soap. It was comforting, and she snuggled into the flannel.

"Pathetic," she said aloud.

Here she was, cuddling with Ethan's clothes while she hadn't gotten any closure from the other day at the baby store. Her emotions were all over the place when it came to her "boyfriend" who may or may not consider moving to Alaska.

That emotional turmoil mixed with her job and her pregnancy left her absolutely exhausted. She toddled over to Ethan's big, comfy couch and curled up with a soft blanket.

If she closed her eyes and allowed herself, she could pretend that this was her everyday life. Ethan and her living together. Lauren would work from the comfort of their house while Ethan was at the bar.

Her eyes popped open. *Whoa.* She needed to dial it way back. This had to be a hormone thing. She was still upset about the other night and feeling way too vulnerable.

What she needed was to focus on something else.

She quickly composed a text to her sisters. Asked if they wanted to order pizza and have a girls' night.

Lauren decided to change into a new outfit that she may or may not have bought at a little shop on Main Street called The Sparkly Mermaid.

One of her biggest rules was never buy an

outfit without also buying accessories that may be needed for said outfit. That's why she'd also picked up dangly pink earrings and a metallic silver belt to go with the cute summery jumpsuit in a pretty turquoise color. She was just touching up her makeup in Ethan's bedroom when he walked in, immediately stripping out of his shirt.

Lauren couldn't help but watch him in the mirror. Things had been a little strained since the Alaska conversation, but still. The man had a killer body, and she was only human.

"I see you ogling me," he called over his shoulder as he grabbed a shirt from the closet.

"Please. I'm far too busy looking at myself to be concerned with your hotness."

"Sorry I couldn't be here today."

She applied a thick coat of mascara. "No problem. I needed the quiet to work, and I got a ton accomplished."

"Good. Looks like you're getting ready for something. Where are you heading?"

"I asked my sisters to hang out this evening." She applied lipstick that was a deep shade of pink. One of her favorites. "I'm craving a little sister time."

"I thought you fought with your sisters."

Lauren blotted her lips. "All sisters fight."

"I was going to see if you wanted to come by the bar for dinner. Hang out a little."

"Oh."

Ethan paused with one arm in his shirt and one arm out. "Is everything okay?" He finished putting the shirt on. "Are we okay?"

"Oh. Yeah."

"Because, about the other day—"

She shook her head, cutting him off. "It's fine. I'm not trying to avoid you. Nothing like that."

He crossed to her, placed a kiss on the top of her head. "I'm going to be working late tonight. I need to put some quality time in with the bar."

"No worries. Let me know if you need anything."

"Shoot me a text if you want to…" He finished the sentence by wiggling his eyebrows.

She laughed and batted him in the arm. With one last, long, sweltering look, Ethan left the room. Lauren finished getting ready and slipped out the front door, heading to her car.

As she drove to Grams's house, she didn't know how to feel. She was starting to fall for Ethan—a strange thought, for sure. She was having incredibly strong feelings for the man whose baby she was carrying.

On the other hand, she was terrified to let herself fully go with Ethan. That damn job offer had shaken her to her core. Sure, Ethan hadn't accepted it, claiming it probably wouldn't pan out anyway. *Probably.*

He'd also tried to reassure her that he was here for her and the baby. But was he?

Maybe if the job in Alaska did come through, he would say no this time. But what about the next time?

What about the time after that?

She knew without a doubt that he would continue to get offers. Enticing, exciting opportunities to do fun things that didn't involve a screaming baby far, far away from here.

Here. Seaside Cove. Lauren couldn't believe it, but she really was starting to consider this home again. She could work anywhere that had an internet connection. Gabby was staying for the foreseeable future, and she really did want to make sure her sister was okay. She was far from getting to the bottom of what was happening with Gabby.

All of these thoughts and feelings were swirling around her as she walked from her car to the house. Lauren hated not being able to sort through things, make sense of a situation. So, by the time she reached the beautiful house by the sea, she felt agitated.

She breezed through the door, calling out for her sisters. Almost immediately, the delightful sound of Gabby stomping down the stairs met her ears. She smiled. Just like when they were growing up. For someone who was graceful and an amazing dancer, Gabby could really clomp around.

"You're here," Gabby said as she jumped off the last step in front of Lauren.

"I'm here."

"Cute jumpsuit. New?"

Lauren nodded. "From The Sparkly Mermaid."

"Oooh, I went in there. Grams said it's new. Great stuff." She stuck her tongue out when Lauren elicited a little *ahem*. "I didn't buy anything. I am fully aware that I am flat broke."

"Is Grams still out for the next couple hours?"

Gabby wrapped one of her curls around her finger. "She is. Playing poker with her friends." She laughed. "That's right. Rose Josephs plays poker once a month. Did you know?"

Lauren followed Gabby into the kitchen, where they both grabbed drinks. "I didn't know about her little gambling meetup, although it doesn't surprise me. I bet she's a hustler, too."

"Totally," Gabby agreed. "I ordered pizza, by the way. Should be here in sixty to ninety minutes."

"That long?" Lauren raised an eyebrow. "How many did you order?"

"Welcome to Seaside Cove," Gabby answered. "Where we have one pizza shop that serves the whole town. The Sox are playing the Yankees tonight, too."

That meant Ethan's bar should be busy. She wondered if anyone would use the coupon she put on Instagram in one of her attempts to help his social media and marketing.

They made their way up the back stairs. Before they could turn into Gabby's room, Brooke came barreling out of her bedroom, headset on, gesturing wildly with her arms.

"Because, Lucas, that's how it's done. I'm not saying you're incompetent. I'm simply trying to explain the industry." She noticed her sisters. "Just give me a minute here. Did you order the pizza?"

Gabby nodded.

"No, I was talking to my sisters. No, Lucas, I did not. Yes, I realize that pizza is full of carbs…"

Lauren and Gabby exchanged a look that clearly showed their disdain for the continued daily arguments between their sister and her supposed soulmate.

"He really sucks, doesn't he?" Gabby asked as she flopped down on her unmade bed.

"At first I thought he was boring. Then I upgraded him to jerk. But after hearing Brooke's side of their conversations, I have to change his status once again to asshole."

"Cheers to that." Gabby raised her soda in Lauren's general direction.

Lauren would have toasted to the assholery of Lucas, but she was too busy taking in her sister's bedroom. There was stuff everywhere. Clothes exploded out of the closet. Drawers were hanging open. There were scarves and necklaces hanging from multiple locations. A semi-wet towel was on the floor.

Her fingers itched to tidy up the space. Not for the first time in her life, she wished for that Mary Poppins power of snapping her fingers to clear everything up.

"You want to clean, don't you?" Gabby asked with a grin and apparent glee in her voice.

"No, I don't want to… Yes! Hell yes. I mean, seriously, Gabs. I know you had to move all your stuff back home, but what the hell. How do you find anything in here?"

"I know where every single thing is located, thank you very much."

"You're a liar," Brooke said, breezing into the room. There was no sign of her phone or headset now, thank God. "You couldn't find your pink flip-flops this morning."

"How's your beloved?" Gabby said in way of a reply.

Brooke narrowed her eyes. "Fine," she said through gritted teeth. "Just fabulous." She stopped in front of Gabby's full-length mirror, removed a sock that was hanging off the corner, and checked out her reflection, turning in each direction. "Did you order veggie pizza?"

"No. I ordered extra cheese and lots of meat. And screw Lucas for making you worry."

"He didn't…" Brooke trailed off, clearly unable to finish the statement.

Lauren watched the exchange with sadness. Was Lucas telling Brooke she needed to lose weight? Brooke was absolutely freaking gorgeous and in perfect shape. She ran almost every day and took really good care of herself.

She might have to change her Lucas status to straight-up asshat now.

Taking pity on her sister, she decided to try and change the subject. She put her bag on Gabby's bed. "Thanks for the impromptu girls' night."

Brooke pushed a pile of clothes on the floor and sat on the trunk at the end of the bed. "No problem. What's the occasion?"

"Who cares? We're having pizza and junk food. By the way, how's it going with the hubby?" Gabby asked Lauren with a mischievous smile.

"Not my husband."

"Your life partner?" Brooke suggested.

Lauren leveled a stare at her. "He's my old friend."

"How about your old friend with benefits?" Gabby offered.

"Kind of," she teased. "And maybe boyfriend, too."

Brooke and Gabby both grinned. "It's sweet," Brooke said.

"It's irresponsible, considering we don't know where our future is going," Lauren conceded with a big sigh.

Brooke stopped studying her nails. "Trouble in paradise?"

Yes. "No. Just... I don't know." She pushed a hand through her hair, pretending to fluff the strands when really it was pure frustration. "Ethan is..." She couldn't decide.

"Hot," Gabby said.

"Funny," Brooke added.

"Your friend from high school and the father of your unborn child."

Lauren waved a hand in the air. "He's all of those things. Especially hot." They all grinned at that comment. "But he's also spontaneous and impulsive and rash."

Brooke faked a shocked expression. "Oh no. Not rash."

"Shut up." But Lauren didn't put any real feelings behind the words. Thinking about what Ethan may or may not do in life was really making her exhausted.

Brooke leaned forward. "I know that an impetuous, reckless person is pretty much akin to a serial killer to you. But Ethan has some great qualities that should more than make up for that."

It was true. Ethan was kind. She liked watching him at the bar, the way he interacted with people. He was so comfortable with any type of personality. And he was always himself.

He also made her laugh. Or, at least, when he wasn't considering moving to the North Pole or wherever.

"Let's not forget his hotness," Gabby said.

"Anyway, I don't feel like talking about Ethan right now." Or herself. And she really didn't want to talk about her feelings.

"Well, good," Brooke said. "Because I have something better for this girls' night." She waited dramatically until she knew she had everyone's attention. "I think we should go play in the attic."

Lauren and Gabby both squealed as if they were little girls again.

Grams's attic was an amazing place. An antique collector would definitely have a field day. There were clothes from the 1950s, records from the 1960s, an old phonograph, Grams's wedding dress, various vases, pillows, and other knickknacks from over the years. There was a cello in one corner and an antique baby stroller in another. There was even a large spinning wheel. Lauren and her sisters used to play Sleeping Beauty with it when they were little.

The three of them ran up the stairs to the fourth floor. The dust hit them pretty hard when they first entered the room, but they didn't care. Immediately, they started rummaging through items.

Lauren found a box with old photo albums, most of which she'd looked through countless times before. But at the bottom of the pile sat an album with a white cloth cover. As she removed it from the box, she realized it was her parents' wedding album.

She smiled and her heart sped up, which was silly, since her parents' marriage hadn't been the best union. But she'd never seen this before and knew very little about it. Only that it had been a small affair here at the house.

She opened the cover to find an eight-by-ten photo of her mother in her wedding dress. Lauren's breath caught. She had been devastated by her mother's death, but she'd made her peace with it. Still, there were times when all those emotions came flooding back. Seeing her mom in a long ivory gown with a lace veil, wearing a hopeful smile, bright blue eyes sparkling, definitely affected her.

The gown was simple, classic. Her mother had liked nice clothes but never anything flashy.

The more Lauren studied the image, the more she saw Brooke. Out of the three of them, Brooke was the one with their mother's elegant features.

The other thing that struck her was how young her mom looked. She had been young, Lauren reminded herself. Only nineteen years old when she'd walked down the aisle. Lauren couldn't even imagine becoming a wife at that age. She'd always known if she ever married it would be much later in life.

Of course, her mom and dad's circumstances had been very different. Lauren couldn't remember how old she was exactly when she'd done the math. Her parents' anniversary and her birthday weren't nine or more months apart. They were only six.

One time, after her dad had left, Lauren asked

her mom why she'd married him in the first place. She would never forget that her mother's answer hadn't been love or desire. Instead, she'd said, "I'd been urged to marry him." At eight years old, she'd thought it was an odd answer. At thirty-three, she understood that her mom had been pregnant with her and that's why a wedding had occurred.

Because of Grams. Grams had urged her mother to get married. She knew Grams had also "urged" her parents to get divorced.

Lauren sat back with a scowl on her face. There wouldn't have been a divorce if Grams had stayed out of it to begin with. All the fights and the hurt could have been avoided if Grams hadn't interfered.

She loved Grams, but she didn't agree with what she'd done.

"What's that?" Gabby asked, plopping down next to Lauren. She was wearing a large black hat with a huge purple feather and strings of pearls attached. To complement it, she was also wearing long gloves.

"Mom and Dad's wedding album," Lauren said.

Brooke came over, carrying an old baby doll that Lauren remembered had been Brooke's favorite.

"Wow," Gabby said. "Look at them."

"Mom was so beautiful," Brooke said softly.

Lauren pushed a lump down her throat. "You look just like her," she told Brooke. The two of them exchanged a long glance, understanding between them.

"I wonder if Grams kept Mom's wedding dress," Gabby said, unaware of the moment between her sisters.

Lauren sat back, her gaze again on the album, drinking in the sight of her parents alive and seemingly happy. "Do you ever wonder if things between Mom and Dad would have been different if—"

Before she could say anything else, "Chapel of Love" burst out of Brooke's phone. Lauren swallowed. The moment was over. She closed the album, Gabby removed the ugly hat and gloves, and Brooke was back to arguing with Lucas as she trudged down the stairs.

Later that night, after they'd eaten pizza and decimated Grams's "secret" stash of ice cream, Gabby hung back. She watched Lauren with those big blue eyes of hers.

"What?" Lauren finally asked.

"Everything okay with you and Ethan?"

"Yeah, of course." Her shoulders slumped. "I don't know."

Gabby nodded. "That's what I thought. Do I need to kick his ass?"

The juxtaposition of the question with Gabby's bouncy curls falling around her face was enough to make Lauren laugh. "You think you could take him?"

Gabby snorted. "Easy peasy. He'd go down like that." She snapped her fingers. "I was in a play once where I had to learn karate for the part. I was a natural."

"I have no doubt. But I don't think I'm ready to

resort to violence just yet."

They walked onto the porch. Lauren loved being on the porch at nighttime. Fireflies flitted around the garden and trees, bringing their light to the otherwise dark yard. The sound of the ocean pounding against the beach below the cliffs roared into the wind. Some might think it was scary, but it had always soothed Lauren. She loved sleeping with her windows open, the sound of the waves lulling her to sleep.

Wind blew her hair around her face, causing a chill to creep up her spine. Lauren wrapped her arms around herself.

Gabby took it as an invitation and also wrapped an arm around Lauren. "Everything's going to be fine, L," she said, her voice merging with the wind and flying off into the breeze.

"I hope so."

"I know so," Gabby said with a squeeze.

"So many things are changing right now," Lauren admitted. She hated not feeling in control, but a baby was a whole other level of worry. It didn't seem to matter how many lists she made or books she read or websites she visited; she wasn't going to be in control.

Throw in Ethan's lackadaisical attitude, and it was enough to make her severely question everything in her life. How was she going to manage all of this? She had no doubt she could raise a child on her own. It would be hard, but she could do it. Luckily, she made a good living and had a hearty nest egg saved. She could hire help—another assistant, a nanny, a cleaning lady.

But that wasn't the same as another parent. A partner. A dad for her child.

She could do it herself. But, for the first time, she didn't think she wanted to.

What she really knew in her heart was that if the baby was born and she stayed in Seaside Cove, stayed with Ethan, and started a life with him, and then he up and left, she wouldn't recover. Her mother never had. Maybe Lauren was starting to finally understand how she'd felt all those years ago.

"I'm not sure Ethan is taking this seriously. I don't know if he's going to be in my life or if he's going to leave," she whispered into the night air as much as she did to her sister.

"If you could choose for him, would you want him to stay, be a part of your life and the baby's?"

"Yes." The answer came fast and hard. She felt her knees weaken and was glad Gabby's arm was still around her.

"I know you," Gabby said. "You want what you want, when and how you want it. I always liked that about you. Plus, you didn't screw up your life the way I did."

"Gabs!" Lauren exclaimed.

"It's true. I made so many mistakes, so many bad decisions. The wrong roommates, the wrong career choices, the wrong romances, the wrong people to trust." Gabby drew her arm away and walked to the railing. She turned back to face Lauren. "Yet, I still believe things will work out for me. I don't know how they will, or when. But some-day, it will all be fine."

While Gabby might admire Lauren's determination in life, Lauren would always be envious of Gabby's optimism.

"Do me a favor, L."

"Anything."

"Give Ethan a chance," she said gently, giving her a hug. "He might just surprise you."

CHAPTER SIXTEEN

Two days later, Lauren woke up to a cacophony of sounds. Without even opening her eyes, she smiled as she listened to the birds singing outside the window. Far in the distance, she also made out a lawn mower.

Then came the roar of a ferocious dinosaur. A tyrannosaurus rex, to be precise. Otherwise known as the sound she'd assigned to Grams's text messages.

Rolling over, she grabbed her phone off Ethan's bedside table.

Grams: *Are you trying to give me a heart attack?*

She groaned into the pillow before typing back.

Lauren: *Always. What specifically are you referring to?*

Grams: *Your car is parked outside Ethan's house. Everyone in town knows you spent the night.*

Lauren rolled her eyes.

Lauren: *Am 33. Get over it.*

She may have sounded confident in her text message, but she started having heart palpitations at the thought of going home later.

Grams: *Am 80. Watch it!*

Lauren gulped. Luckily, her nerves were interrupted by yet another sound. She couldn't quite distinguish it. Maybe something moving across the floor. Then a small bang, followed by a curse.

Curious, she pushed the covers back and got out of bed. After a quick bathroom stop, she walked down the short hallway to find Ethan in one of the two spare bedrooms. He was facing the wall, hands on his hips, surveying something. She saw he wore wireless earbuds, as well as a backward baseball hat, jeans, and a T-shirt. He looked hot as hell.

She was surprised to see him awake, though. It wasn't the crack of dawn, but it was early, and he hadn't returned from work until well after two in the morning. She'd decided to surprise him by waiting in his bed. Naked.

When she dragged her gaze away from his arm muscles, she realized the room was in complete disarray. He'd been using this room for...well, she wasn't quite sure. A junk room, maybe. There was everything from clothes to lamps to books and suitcases scattered throughout.

Now, added to all of that were about a million boxes, a tape gun, and a ladder.

"Ethan," she said. He didn't budge. She remembered the earbuds and crossed the room, tapping on his shoulder. "Ethan," she repeated, louder this time.

He jumped before eyeing her with a slow grin. "Morning, darling." He removed his earbuds. "Hope I didn't wake you. I couldn't sleep, so I thought I'd start getting things ready."

She glanced around the room again. "Ready for what, exactly?"

He hit her with an odd stare before gently patting her stomach. "The baby."

She sat in an old director's chair in the corner,

wondering for a moment why he had it. "Well, we have quite a bit of time before the baby gets here."

"We already have a crib on the way," he pointed out.

True. "What specifically are you preparing in here?"

He pointed at her. "I think you need some coffee. I have some downstairs." He spread his arm out to encompass the room. "I thought this would be a good room for the nursery."

The nursery. The room where the baby slept. She felt her eyebrows drawing together. She hadn't thought about a nursery here in Ethan's house. When she first discovered she was pregnant, she'd briefly considered converting her second bedroom in her condo to a nursery and then debated if it would be better to buy a bigger place.

Also, hearing the word *nursery* made something inside of her stomach flutter. A nursery for a baby—a real, live baby. That she was carrying. This was real. If the crib shopping didn't prove it, talk of a nursery certainly did.

Good thing she was already sitting down.

Her reaction was ridiculous. As Ethan correctly pointed out, they'd already bought a crib. Where did she assume that was going to go? The bathroom? Of course they needed a nursery.

"Hey, you okay?" Ethan asked. "You went a little pale." He crouched in front of her.

She tried to laugh, but it came out as more of an unsteady exhale. "I think I really do need that coffee."

He rubbed her legs and stared at her for a moment.

"You know, you look pretty, even in the morning."

"I...what?" This time she did let out a little chuckle.

"Just sayin'." Ethan rose. "I liked having you waiting in my bed last night. But I loved waking up to you even more."

She was glad she was sitting, because if she hadn't been, she would have melted into a gooey puddle of sparkling hearts.

Unaware of what his sweet words did to her, Ethan continued. "If you don't like this room, I can always switch and use the other bedroom. I just figured, since I hadn't set this room up as anything practical yet, it would be good. Plus, it has two windows, and it's closest to my bedroom."

"This room is fine. It's great." She remembered her promise to Gabby from the other night. She needed to give this a try. After all, Ethan appeared to be trying. Gabby may have been right, too. He was surprising her.

He narrowed his eyes. "You said that like you were talking about a root canal."

She sighed. "I'm sorry. I just hadn't thought about where the baby would sleep yet. Or really, anything about the baby actually being here. Like, in human form."

This time, Ethan laughed. "Come on."

She followed him to the kitchen, and he served her coffee and toast.

He sat down at the table opposite her. "Did I freak you out?"

She bit into her toast, relishing the burst of apricot jam he'd smeared onto it. "You didn't freak me out. I think the baby freaked me out. Nine months really isn't a lot of time when you think about it."

He pushed a tablet across the table. "Need to make a list?"

"Never hurts." She ate more toast and thought about the room upstairs. "You know," she began, "I'm surprised you have all that stuff up there. I would have thought with all of your world travels you wouldn't have accumulated much."

Ethan nodded. "I definitely traveled light. But I managed to pick up some cool stuff here and there. Usually, I would ship it back to my parents' house. Unfortunately, they retired to Florida and dumped all of those belongings, along with all of my childhood crap, on me."

"That explains all the boxes."

Ethan whipped out his phone and also pushed it across the table. "I googled some nurseries."

That surprised her. "Oh yeah?"

He nodded and bit into a banana. "My Google search led me to Pinterest." He ran a hand over his face. "You could spend months, maybe years on that site."

She laughed silently, well aware of the rabbit hole that was Pinterest. "I teach a class on Pinterest," she said.

"Of course you do. Well, you should have done me a solid and warned me about its time-sucking power."

Ethan poured another mug of coffee for himself and continued. "Besides the crib we already picked out, I think we should get a changing table, a bookshelf, and a rocking chair. I just want to ask again. Do you want to find out the sex of the baby early?"

"I'm still okay with waiting."

"I was only asking because we could obviously tailor the nursery if we did find out. But no worries," he said with a shake of his hand. "We can either get neutral bedding and decorations or just wait until we have the baby and then pick things that are more specific."

Fascinated, she sat back in her chair. "Be honest. Do you have a preference?"

He cocked his head. "I don't think so. A son would be fun to take to baseball games and teach him how to catch and hit in the backyard. Of course, you can do those things with a girl, too."

She folded her hands together and rested her chin on them as she watched him.

"A boy could be a little mini-me. But a girl…a daughter. Wow. That would be crazy." He pounded his fist on the table. "She's not dating until she's thirty-five."

Lauren grinned. "Is that so? I don't think she will like that very much." She gestured toward the window. "Also, you don't have much of a backyard here to teach either our son or daughter how to play baseball."

He nodded. "I'm sure we'll move into a bigger place by the time they're old enough to learn."

We? She took a big gulp, and her heart rate sped up. All of this was surprising her. Did he mean they would move into a bigger place in Alaska? Or Nepal or Mars or wherever the fancy took him? She felt herself shutting down. The need to curl into a protective ball and guard her heart was overwhelming.

You promised Gabby. Try.

Lauren called on her inner reserves to gather courage. "Yeah," she said slowly.

A line formed on Ethan's forehead as he shot a concerned look across the table. "I know that Alaska threw you for a loop, Lauren."

"No, it didn't…" There was no good that would come from lying. If she wanted Ethan to be straight up and honest with her, she needed to do the same with him. "It really did. The truth is, I don't know where your head is or what you really want."

"I know it's hard for you, but I like to live my life in the present. I want you and the baby to feel comfortable here in this house. That's my current objective."

She glanced down at the nursery pictures on his phone. How she truly wanted to trust him.

"Even if you don't stay in Seaside Cove, I am going to have the nursery here for when you and the baby visit."

She sat back in her chair, put his phone back on the table. "What if you're the one not staying in Seaside Cove?"

He sighed. "Live in the present, Lauren. I live in Seaside Cove right now."

More than anything in the world, she wanted to let her guard down. She wanted to push all those worries and anxieties and questions far away. However, it just wasn't in her nature to do that.

Ethan's warm brown eyes implored her to believe him. To have faith in him. But she had a baby in her tummy who needed her to protect and defend.

She was torn between her innate personality and her desire to be with the man she was falling for. And she had no idea which side would win.

But maybe for now, just for right now, she could let go a little bit.

Picking the phone back up, she scrolled through the pictures. One nursery caught her eye and kind of melted her heart. Baby stuff was pretty adorable.

She held the phone out. "This is cute."

He grinned. "I liked that one, too. The wall color is nice." His eyes rolled upward, as if he could see through the ceiling into the bedroom. "We should paint the walls in that room. They're just blah-white right now."

"Painting walls is a very couple-y thing to do." Again, she thought of her sister and that promise to try. "But it would be fun."

Ethan relaxed. "Then let's do it."

. . .

They'd gone with a beautiful sky blue that would be great for any gender. Lauren couldn't wait to see it on the walls.

Ethan got called into the bar, so she took the opportunity to spend more time with her sisters. She shot them a text message to see if anyone was up for dinner.

Brooke, who was working in Kennebunkport for the day, declined. But Lauren and Gabby made their way into town.

Toward the end of Main Street, Lauren spotted Coopers, a family-run ice cream parlor that had been in Seaside Cove for as long as anyone remembered. Her heart gave a little leap at the fact it was still around. Her dad used to take her here after Brooke was born.

"Coopers is still here," she said, grasping Gabby's hand.

"I mean, I love ice cream as much as the next girl, but I don't think I've ever teared up about it."

Lauren rubbed at her eyes. "I'm not tearing up. I'm just...happy to see that it's still around. Come on, let's ditch dinner and get ice cream instead."

"You're going to be the best mom ever." Gabby laughed but allowed Lauren to drag her to Coopers, where they each got a double-scoop cone.

Cones in tow, they jogged across the street, walked through the park, and made their way down to the beach.

"Ice cream and a walk on the beach," Gabby said. "I could get used to this."

"Now that you're back in town, you could do this every day if you wanted," Lauren pointed out.

"The walk is a plus, but my hips might not love the ice cream portion of this plan."

They walked along in silence, finishing their ice cream cones. After they passed a couple walking with a toddler in tow, Gabby turned to Lauren.

"Seriously, L, when are you going to tell Grams that you're preggo?"

Lauren pursed her lips. "Well..."

Gabby pulled her hair back into a ponytail. "You are going to tell her, right?"

"Of course I'm going to tell her." Lauren looked down and pretended to examine a seashell. "It's not time yet. "

Gabby pinned her with a stare. "When is the right time? At the kid's high school graduation?"

"August 5th, that's when we're telling her. In fact, I've already set into motion plans for a small, but fun, party. I want it to be a celebratory night with lots of Grams's favorite foods and music and flowers. I don't want this to be something I just drop on her out of nowhere."

"What gives?"

"Nothing. I'm just being cautious and taking everyone's feelings into consideration. Anyway, we really need to discuss some options for possible savings accounts for you. Or we could talk about you enrolling in some classes I found."

Gabby groaned, just like Lauren knew she would.

"You don't play fair," Gabby said. "Let's call a truce. For the rest of this walk, I won't bug you about telling Grams and you won't badger me about my career. Or my lack of savings account."

Lauren plastered her most innocent smile on her face. "Deal."

Not surprisingly, their walk was quite pleasant.

When they finished, they slowly walked back to Main Street. Lauren paused in front of The Thirsty Lobster.

"Thanks for dinner," Gabby said. "I think rocky road might be my new favorite."

"My pleasure," Lauren replied, but Gabby didn't move. "What?" she asked.

"How are things with Ethan since we talked?"

Lauren thought about the day. About how Ethan took the initiative to start getting the nursery ready. It meant a lot to her.

She only wished she could trust that he was here to stay.

"Better," she told her sister.

"Ethan seems happy," Gabby said, looking over toward the bar. "I'm glad. I heard that his divorce really did him in."

She snapped her head around. "Yeah?"

Gabby nodded. "I was hanging out with some friends from high school last night. They told me he was pretty despondent when he returned to Seaside Cove. I think his ex-wife really messed with his head."

Lauren got the gist of what had gone down in his divorce, but she wouldn't mind hearing more details. Obviously, Ethan would be upset about his divorce. He'd conveyed as much. But she hadn't realized the level of emotion.

"I wonder if there's more to the story than he told me."

"Why don't you ask him?"

"I will."

"Coming home?" Gabby asked.

She looked toward the door as it opened. She spotted Ethan behind the bar. Her body filled with warmth as she took in everything about him from his solid shoulders to his strong arms to that kissable mouth.

"I take that as a no." Gabby was laughing as she turned and started to make her way home.

Lauren went into the bar and talked with some high school classmates for a while. Even though Ethan kept sneaking her glances, she realized he was really swamped. With a wave and a wink, she left him to his work, walking back to his house, where she watched some bad reality television, took a bath, and painted her nails.

Ethan ended up staying at the bar through closing. He'd texted around nine to tell her everything was going well, just busy.

When he finally returned, Lauren had been in bed for hours. She'd read a little. She'd surfed around on her iPad for a while. Finally, she'd lost the battle to stay awake and drifted off.

She hadn't heard Ethan arrive home. But when he got into bed, he'd paused and placed a soft kiss on her forehead. She opened her eyes and smiled at him.

"Hi," she said.

"Hey, you," he said. "I didn't mean to wake you."

"That's okay."

His nose twitched. "You smell really good. Like a garden of fresh flowers."

She smiled. "I took a luxurious bubble bath and then slathered copious amounts of lotion all over. It was quite indulgent." She rolled onto her side to face him. "How was the bar?"

"Definitely not luxurious or indulgent. But good."

He told her about everything that had happened that night. Sounded like it had been busy. Not surprising for a Saturday night. Naturally, he'd dealt with a million questions about the two of them. The entire place had been disappointed over a Red Sox loss. He thought he was going to have to break up a fight between two guys, which started as a debate over the future of the Patriots. Luckily, after some yelling, they'd worked it out on their own.

He pushed the hair off her face. "I like telling you about my day, er, night."

"I liked everything about today," she said.

Maybe she was half asleep. Maybe she was more awake than she'd ever been in her entire life. But for some reason, it felt like the lights dimmed around everything else except Ethan. He was in the spotlight now. He was becoming her world.

That thought should have scared her. But it didn't. Instead, she felt…happy.

Lightly, she ran her fingers up and down his arm. She noticed he'd removed his shirt and pants. The only article of clothing he wore was a pair of blue boxer shorts with bright red lobsters on them.

She traced one of the lobsters on his upper thigh with a light and flirty finger. Ethan inhaled sharply.

"Ethan," she said.

"Mmm," he replied.

"Make love to me."

CHAPTER SEVENTEEN

She didn't have to ask him twice.

He brought her to him and kissed her thoroughly. Their lips met and fit perfectly together. So did their bodies.

She was wearing a tank top and lounge pants. She'd tried to put her hair up in a ponytail, only it was too short, so most of it had fallen and was splayed out on the pillow in a very sexy way.

This was how he liked her best, all casual and comfy. Not that her usual parade of cute outfits and accessories wasn't adorable. But her laying in his bed, her face clean of makeup and her hair messy, made his body react more strongly than if she was wearing some red-carpet glamour outfit.

He shifted back. "You are beautiful. Do you know that?"

Her only reply was a smile. She ran a finger over his cheek. He took that same hand and brought it to his lips. Kissed each finger before turning it over to nuzzle her palm.

"I'm so lucky you came back into my life." He grazed his teeth playfully over her wrist. "Took you long enough to realize how awesome I am."

She laughed. "Impatient much? We slept together my first night back in town."

"But I've been crushing on you for almost twenty years now."

That's when Ethan realized that for more than

half of his life, Lauren had been the woman he'd been measuring all other women against. He hadn't even been aware that she'd stayed firmly rooted in his mind after they'd both left town.

It wasn't only her beauty that attracted him. She was the whole package. Smart, with a quick wit, determined and strong. He was in awe of her ability to start a successful business. His heart melted at the fact that she dropped her life in Virginia so she could be with her family, check on them and make sure everyone was okay.

Something shifted in him at that moment. Not a different feeling. More, a realization of what he *was* feeling at this moment. What he had been feeling probably for a couple weeks now. Or since she'd returned to Seaside Cove two months ago.

Maybe even since high school.

He was in love with her. The recognition of that fact slammed into him like the waves crashing into the beach: strong, hard, and steady.

A deep understanding that he'd never been in love before washed over him. He'd thought he'd been. But holding Lauren in his arms as the light from the moon shone into his bedroom, taking in her sweet, rosy scent, watching her magnetic blue eyes roam over his face, made him sure that this was his first foray into love.

Gently, he pushed her back against the pillows, covered her mouth with his. His hand went to her breast, softly kneading. She moaned against his mouth, and it was the sexiest sound he'd ever heard.

His lips roamed along her jawline and down the

column of her neck. She obligingly shifted so he could reach the spot that she really liked. Because he knew that nuzzling that spot got her all kinds of excited, he spent a little extra time and attention there.

Tonight, he was going to shower attention and adoration on her body. Tonight was going to be for her.

He spent time removing first her clothes and then his. He ran fingertips over every inch of her soft, supple skin. Then he followed each touch, each caress, with his mouth. From her brightly painted toes to the top of her head with all that thick, dark hair, he made sure he discovered every single inch of her.

This wasn't like the other times they'd made love. This was more intimate somehow. He felt connected to her on every level: physically, emotionally, spiritually.

Somehow Lauren had gone from that untouchable crush in high school to a superhot, super-sexy fling to mother of his child. It felt like everything in his life was changing. He'd picked out paint for a nursery today.

But somehow, the thought of a permanent change didn't bother him the way it usually did. Right now, with Lauren in his arms, he felt content.

For once, he didn't have thoughts of running off to another location. In fact, he couldn't imagine ever being anywhere else other than right here. With her.

• • •

Ethan decided he was going to have to stay in this bed with his limbs wrapped around Lauren for the rest of his life. Not only because it felt so amazingly good, but also because he didn't think he would ever be able to move again.

"Mmm," she murmured sexily against his chest.

"Happy?"

"Very. My body feels…sated," she decided. "I never truly understood that word before. Now I totally get it."

As did he. He ran a hand along her back, eliciting a delicate shiver from her.

"I don't know where that came from, McAllister, but anytime you want to do that again, I'm game."

He snuggled her closer, wishing he could tell her about his feelings. They'd shared everything tonight. It seemed appropriate. Only, Ethan wasn't sure that he was ready to tell Lauren he was in love with her. More, he didn't think she was quite ready to hear it.

Although, what better time than right now?

"Can I ask you something?" she said, interrupting his musing.

"Anything," he said simply and meant it.

She pushed up and off his chest. He watched as she chewed on her lip for a moment. "It's kinda personal."

He pushed an errant hair behind her ear. "I think I can handle it. I'm tough."

"How badly were you hurt by your ex-wife?"

Maybe not tough enough for that. He wondered if she felt the same change in the air as he did. If this were a movie, it would be when the soundtrack changed and the wind started blowing maniacally. Or maybe the sound of thunder would echo loudly, rattling the glass of the window.

He shifted, untangling his limbs from hers. But her hand shot out and wrapped around his, entwining their fingers. The small gesture was not lost on him. In fact, it offered great comfort.

"Long version or short?" he asked.

"Long. You've already given me the short version."

"You know how I met Veronica."

She smiled against her pillow. "Wearing a tuxedo and swirling a fancy drink while winning everyone's money in a swanky poker game in some fancy-pants casino with leather couches and crystal chandeliers."

He let out a sound that was somewhere between a laugh and what his mother called a guffaw. "I think I was wearing jeans. I know I was drinking a beer. And the poker house I liked smelled like smoke and cabbage."

Her smile got even bigger, her dimples winked at him, and there was a certain sparkle in her pretty blue eyes.

"Go ahead," he said. "Laugh it out."

She squeezed his hand. "I'm not laughing. I want to hear about you and Veronica," she prodded.

"Right." He exhaled a long breath. "What can I say? She was gorgeous. She had that sun-kissed California look. Tall, with long, shiny blond hair and gorgeous eyes."

"Ahem." Lauren quirked an eyebrow.

He chuckled. "Sorry. She was beautiful, but she had nothing on you."

Lauren settled back into the blankets and pillows. "That's better."

"What I did not know was…well, everything."

"Young love is very intense," Lauren said wisely. "And very impatient."

He let out a mirthless laugh. "You can say that again. In any case, she talked me into marriage, but it didn't feel like that. At the time, I was convinced it was totally my idea. And there was a layer of excitement there, too. I'd been living a very spontaneous life for a long time. Impulsive, making decisions as I went along. Felt natural."

She rapped on his chest. "No good comes from not planning. I'm telling you."

He grabbed her knuckles and placed a chaste kiss on them. "I think there's probably a happy medium."

She narrowed her eyes but remained quiet.

"Veronica and I never took the time to ask questions or get to know each other. We both assumed things. She assumed that because she met me on the night of a very big poker win that I had a ton of money."

"And you?" she asked.

He swallowed. "I assumed she loved me."

She rubbed a hand over his hand. Ethan didn't want to meet her eyes because he didn't want to see sympathy there. Or pity. But when he finally locked eyes with Lauren, he found a silent comfort.

"I won the first couple of games when we got to

South America. We took those winnings and cele-
brated by traveling around, staying in these
amazing beach locales. Private villas and champagne and moonlight swims in infinity pools that
overlooked the ocean. The prices are much different in the southern hemisphere, and my dollar was
going way further. Looking back, I can see how she
would have thought otherwise. But then…" He ran
a hand over his face.

"You stopped winning," she supplied.

"That's when I lost big. It was almost two years
into our marriage." His legs were restless. He kept
swishing them through the tangled sheets, trying to
smooth them out. "Two whole years I was with this
person, and I didn't know her at all. That still kills
me."

He felt a familiar tightening in his chest—one
he'd come to associate with any thoughts about
that time in his life. The truth was, Veronica wasn't
the only one to blame. He'd been too caught up in
the moment to open his eyes and see what was really going on.

"In the meantime, I kept telling Veronica how I
wanted her to meet my family. I wanted to bring
her home to Seaside Cove and see where I was
from. And I was dying to go visit her family in
California. Only, she never talked about her family."

"Why was that?" Lauren asked.

"I didn't learn this part for a very long time.
While she was in Europe, Veronica's very wealthy
father cut her off financially. That happened right
before she made it to Budapest."

"Oh, Ethan," Lauren said softly.

Ethan twisted the sheet around his hand. "You know me. You know where I'm from." He gestured around the room. "I'm not some wealthy, James Bond, card-playing millionaire. I had just hit a lucky streak."

"You hit a lucky streak right when a woman needing money walked into your life." Lauren nodded, as if she understood everything he'd been telling her.

He ran a hand through Lauren's thick hair, giving himself the moment he desperately needed. "After the money was gone, I took odd jobs where I could find them. A lot of tourism and food service jobs."

"And your wife?"

His answer was a raised brow followed by a slow head shake back and forth.

"Things continued to go downhill. Veronica wanted to go back to different beach towns we'd visited. She wanted a bigger apartment, more clothes, more stuff. I was making enough for us to get by, but with little left over. She suggested we return to the U.S."

He'd actually been excited at the prospect.

Lauren scratched at her cheek. "I didn't realize Veronica had been here in Seaside Cove."

That news would have certainly reached her, Ethan thought. He shook his head. "No, we never made it here. I think Veronica was doing some research on her own. She wasn't into cold weather."

He noticed a wrinkle in her brow. "Interesting," she said.

"She wanted to go somewhere a little more glamorous like Miami or Vegas. She even mentioned San Diego."

"Beautiful locations," Lauren added.

"Expensive locations." He rubbed a hand over his jaw. He needed to shave. "I came up with a—wait for it—plan."

She grinned.

"My parents were still living here at the time. I thought we could move into their basement and have this whole apartment set up for us with our own entrance, a kitchenette, bathroom, and all that."

"What happened?"

"My well-thought-out suggestion was the final nail in the coffin, apparently. Veronica had had enough. She threw her wedding ring at my head, called me all kinds of fun names, and used my credit card to book a return trip to the States."

Telling this story exhausted him. He laid back against the pillows, letting out a long sigh. He hadn't talked about Veronica out loud in a long time. It was actually kind of nice to get all of that out in the open.

Lauren popped up, placing her head on his chest. "Thank you."

"For what?" he asked.

"For telling me all of that. I know it wasn't easy."

No, it wasn't easy. But it was part of his story. "Think differently of me now?" He asked the question with as much nonchalance as he could inflect in his voice, but his stomach twisted in knots, waiting for her answer.

Lauren narrowed her eyes, peering at him. "Of course I don't," she said.

He let out a breath.

"Ethan," she said, shaking his shoulders. "We've all been through crappy situations."

He pulled her back down so she was nestled against his chest again. "I still can't believe how ignorant I was. How could I not see Veronica's true intentions?"

"You were in love. That often comes with blinders." A shadow passed over her face at the comment.

He had been in lust. He'd realized tonight what real love was, and it wasn't the relationship he'd had with his ex.

"I'm not proud of how long it took me to realize that she was using me."

"But you did finally realize it," she said.

He took in a long breath. "The truth is, she wasn't the only one to blame."

"It usually takes two people. But, from what you're telling me, you fell in love, and she was using you as a means to fund the lifestyle she wanted."

"I definitely fell... I fell fast and hard," he said. "I jumped into that relationship as if my life depended on it." Ethan knew he was impulsive. He had liked living that way. Sometimes, he still craved it. The ability to get up and go whenever you felt like it.

His biggest regret with Veronica was that he hadn't taken the time to get to know her. Maybe if he had, he wouldn't have ended up divorced. He would have seen he was being used. That she didn't have the same feelings for him.

Lauren propped her head up on her hand. "Do you think she loved you?"

He was surprised at her intuitive question. She was reading his mind.

"What?" she asked. "What's with the funny look?"

He chuckled. "I was just thinking that same thing." He took a long moment. "No, she didn't love me," he said with certainty. That confession stung more than anything else. "I think she liked me, and she was attracted to me physically. Overall, though, I was a means to an end."

"That's awful, Ethan," Lauren whispered. "I'm so sorry."

They had a wonderful night together. Now, they were sharing confidences under the light of the moon streaming through his bedroom window.

They talked for a while longer, veering away from Veronica and sharing stories of travel, interests, books, and more mundane, less emotional things. He could tell Lauren was exhausted as her words began to blend together and her eyelids started to flutter.

As it always did, thinking about Veronica left him feeling alone and empty. A lapse in judgment that he was desperate to learn from, but his biggest fear was that he would repeat the same mistake.

He eyed Lauren lying next to him on her side. He took in the outline of her curves. Watched as her breathing began to slow and she drifted off to sleep. He ran his hand lightly over her dark hair, pulled the blanket up.

He loved her. He probably always had. But back

in high school, it was a teenage crush, more superficial than anything. Now, though…well, being with her physically and sharing secrets brought their relationship to a whole new level.

He liked the way she was passionate about her work. He liked how loyal she was to her family. He liked the way she listened to him with attentive eyes and focused energy, as if he was the only person in the world.

He even liked her stupid lists of rules. Well… mostly, he thought with a silent laugh.

Ethan supposed what he liked was her organized side. Hard to take fault with that, even if he personally did not alphabetize his condiments or hang his clothes based on color and occasion.

Lauren was here in his bed. That left him with a question that he didn't want to ask. Even more, he'd give anything not to answer.

If she wasn't pregnant, would she be with him?

CHAPTER EIGHTEEN

Lauren woke up with a smile, then stretched, feeling satisfied and complete.

She turned to thank the source of that pleasure only to find Ethan's side of the bed empty. Her chest tightened as she rolled onto her back and stared at the ceiling. After last night, she would have loved to wake up next to him, feel the heat from his body, the sound of his deep breathing.

And if her hand just happened to fall and land on his rock-hard pecs, well, she would just have to live with that.

Pushing those thoughts away, she reached for her cell phone. Her mood lifted once again at the text message from Ethan. He had to run to the bar for some pre-brunch emergency.

Just like that, her mood went back to happy and content. She dressed, had her one cup of coffee and some toast, and left the house.

She wanted to check in on Gabby.

When she opened the door of Rose's Café and stepped inside, she was welcomed with the fresh scent of lemon.

"Hey, Gabbykins," she said, sidling up to the display counter. "I smell a whole bunch of lemon."

Gabby grinned. "I may have gone a tad overboard this morning."

"Imagine that."

Gabby shrugged. "Grams said I could make

some new things for the menu. Anything I wanted. I started with lemon-poppy muffins. Then, I moved on to lemon-blueberry scones. And for dessert, lemon bars."

"I'll take one of everything," Lauren said as Grams pushed through the door that led to the kitchen. "Hi, Grams."

"Look what the cat dragged in. I forgot what you looked like."

Grams had made it known that she wasn't happy Lauren was spending so much time with Ethan. And to be fair, Lauren hadn't really meant to stay over at his house so many nights in a row.

Grams leaned on the counter and eyed her. "That tank top a size too small?" She arched an eyebrow.

Lauren looked down. She had to admit that it was a tad tight. Or maybe her boobs had started to grow. She'd definitely put on a couple pounds already. She ran a hand over the bright turquoise tank, which had previously been one of her favorite tops to wear with her corresponding ankle-length skirt. "I, uh, think I've put on a little weight."

"I've noticed."

She had? Lauren pulled on the bottom of her top, willing it to stretch.

"Maybe if you weren't eating ice cream for dinner, you would be able to maintain your figure."

Of course Grams knew that she and Gabby went into town last night.

"Although," Grams continued, "I am happy that you spent some time with your sister, since you're supposed to be helping her get her life in order."

"She has been helping me, Grams," Gabby said.

"Shh. Go help Mrs. Watzel," Grams said to Gabby, who rolled her eyes but made her way to the cash register.

"Grams, I am doing—"

Grams stopped her with a simple hand in the air. "You've been spending a lot of time with Ethan."

"We're dating." Lauren waited for that comment to feel weird. Only, it felt completely natural coming out of her mouth.

"For how long? Are you staying in Seaside Cove longer than you planned? Because I believe you were going to go back to Virginia at the end of September."

Lauren crossed her arms over her chest. "My plans were never set in stone."

"It's like you and Ethan are cooking up some kind of surprise."

Lauren froze. She met Grams's eyes. This would be the perfect time to tell her about the baby. She spotted Gabby watching her from the other end of the café.

Her heart started beating in overtime. She'd picked August fifth to reveal her news to Grams. That was the plan.

Yet, here she was, feeling the words traveling up her throat, ready to jump out of her mouth. Wouldn't it be easier? She'd have it done and over with, even if Grams wasn't going to like that her first great-grandchild was conceived out of wedlock, just like her first grandchild had been.

"Once I found out I was pregnant with Lauren, I had *to get married."*

Her mother's words from all those years ago

sounded in her ears so clearly, Lauren almost looked around to see if her mother was standing there.

She wasn't ready to be pushed into marriage. To even hear that suggestion.

She swallowed hard.

"We, um…that is…Ethan and I…"

"You're what?" Grams thrust her chin into the air and peered at Lauren.

"We're getting reacquainted." She'd chickened out. Inside, Lauren deflated. *You're sticking to the plan*, she said to herself. Then why didn't she feel as good as she normally did when she followed her own agenda?

Grams waved a hand in the air. "You've known him your whole life. How much more do you need to know? You need to be home with your sisters."

Lauren had had it. She grabbed the bag of treats her sister had put together for her. "I'm leaving. I have errands to run."

Grams gave a sharp nod as Lauren made to leave. "Fine, leave. But don't think you're fooling me."

Lauren turned back around. "What is that supposed to mean?"

"Things between you and Ethan are a lot more serious than you are letting on." Grams began wiping the counter. "Just don't fall in love with him."

Lauren watched as Grams went back to her work. She stood in place for a few moments, letting those words sink in.

Don't fall in love with him.

When a gaggle of teenagers burst through the door, Lauren took her leave. Fall in love with

Ethan? Please. Grams was just trying to get under her skin.

Before heading home, Lauren took a walk around town, snapping some photos for Instagram, and ran some errands. But she forgot to pick up more shampoo from the drug store. Then she misplaced her car keys, which took a whole half hour to find. After that, she bought the wrong kind of coffee for the house.

Despite the mistakes, she had a certain pep in her step. Lauren hated the sound of whistling, but if she didn't, she would have been whistling quite the tune. She just felt happy. And that had everything to do with Ethan McAllister.

Don't fall in love with him.

Lauren shook her head. She wasn't going to fall in love. That's not what this was about. She'd simply had a few lovely days with Ethan. That's all.

However, as she walked from her car to the house, she started thinking about Ethan's ex-wife. She shook her head again. She'd love to meet Veronica, who sounded just super charming. She could think of quite a few things to say to her.

Ethan said he'd felt ignorant for not realizing Veronica's true intentions. But when you were in love with someone, it was hard to keep a clear head.

She froze in the middle of the driveway.

In essence, she'd just checked out of her life for the last two days, eschewing her normal responsibilities to play house with Ethan. She was forgetting things, too, because her head was stuck in the clouds. As she waltzed around town daydreaming about Ethan instead of staying focused on her goals.

Was she...in love with Ethan? A better question: was she losing all sense of logic and good judgment?

She loved being with Ethan. She loved when they did things for the baby together. She loved the way he actually took an interest in her job.

Don't fall in love with him.

She bit her lip hard. No, she couldn't love him. She needed to keep her wits about her. Look at what love did to people. Take her mother, for example, or even Brooke. Brooke loved Lucas, and she was completely losing herself to him, constantly apologizing and deferring to his every whim and giving up perfectly good carbs.

Hadn't Ethan just given her the greatest warning story last night about the perils of falling in love? His relationship with Veronica had derailed his entire life and he'd ended up divorced and broke and hurt.

No, she would not allow herself to fall in love with him. She would retain her independence. She would not get hurt.

Quickly, she dashed into the house and up to her room, where she dropped off her stuff. Then, she ran back to her car. Without thinking, she drove straight to The Thirsty Lobster.

She pushed through the front door with force, just like she had her first night back in town when she ran straight into Ethan. She would have taken a moment to laugh about that, but she was on a mission.

"Hey, Lauren," Joe called from behind the bar.

She mumbled a hello. At least, she thought she had. Hard to tell when she was too busy looking for Ethan. Her gaze darted around the room.

Finally, she went straight to the bar. "Ethan?" she asked.

Joe gave her a funny look. "He's in his office. Go on back."

Without delay, she crossed the bar. She'd been in Ethan's office once before. As far as offices went, it wasn't a particularly inviting one. It was a dark, tiny space that held a desk, a filing cabinet, and little else.

She rapped her knuckles against the door right before entering. Ethan sat behind the desk, his eyes glued to something on the computer. A mound of papers was scattered across his desk, and there were two empty glasses next to him. Her fingers shook with the desire to organize everything.

"Well, hey," he said with a genuine smile when he looked up. "You look gorgeous. I love that blue."

Lauren knew that blue was his favorite color and maybe, perhaps—it may just have been possible—that she chose this outfit based on that preference.

Just like you would do for someone you loved, she thought. *Dammit.*

Unaware of what was happening in her head, Ethan continued. "I didn't expect to see you, but I'm so glad you're here."

"Hi."

Now what? She hadn't gotten that far in her mind. As she tried to figure out what to say—especially when she had no idea how she even felt, she said, "I just saw Grams at the café."

"I heard," he said, coming out from behind the desk and propping a hip on the front.

"You heard? How… Oh, right. Seaside Cove."

"Seaside Cove," he agreed. "Wendy came over to tell me that you and Grams were fighting this morning. What was that about?"

She waved her hand nonchalantly through the air. "I'm fat now, apparently."

Ethan tilted his head to one side and then the other as he took her in. He wiggled his eyebrows. "You're looking good from this angle. But maybe you should come closer so I can give you a more thorough exam."

She batted him in the chest. "Shut up. Anyway, Grams has never been particularly tactful when it comes to me, but I kind of got the distinct impression that she's starting to get suspicious."

Ethan raised one brow. "Then maybe it's time to tell her you're pregnant. I mean, I know it's not August—"

"Fifth," she supplied.

"Right, whatever."

"Oh, PS," Lauren continued. "I actually have gained a little weight."

Lauren was trying to steer the conversation away from telling Grams. She wasn't sure how she expected Ethan to react, but it certainly wasn't with a huge grin.

"What?" she asked, amusement in her voice.

"Are you telling me that you're showing?" He closed the gap between them and reached for the bottom of her tank top. "Let me see. Let me see."

Again, she batted his hand away. "No, get out of here. I'm not showing, per se. I just look like I ate an entire Thanksgiving dinner. All by myself."

"I want to see our little baby turkey."

She couldn't deny Ethan's extreme excitement. She wasn't that mean. Lauren pulled up her top and rolled her eyes. "I told you. Nothing to see."

Ethan placed a hand over her stomach, lightly rubbing.

"No bump," she said. "At least, not yet."

One hand remained on her stomach. The other came up to capture the back of her neck. He pulled her to him and pressed his lips to hers. Softly, slowly, he kissed her as if she was the most delicate flower that he didn't want to blow away in the wind.

"It's amazing," he said when he pulled back.

She met his eyes and felt herself tumbling fast down some imaginary hill. She knew what was at the bottom, too. Love City.

Her palms began to sweat. She wondered if Ethan noticed. "Is it hot in here?" she asked.

"Not particularly."

Great. It was just her feeling like the walls were closing in on them. She couldn't even meet Ethan's eyes as her anxiety began to climb.

As usual, she did the opposite of what Grams said. It had always been that way between the two of them. Grams said to go right; Lauren went left. Grams said not to fall in love and...

Shit.

She'd fallen in love.

What was worse was that she'd fallen in love

without a plan. There was a baby to consider. There was a whole geography situation to figure out. There was childcare and maternity leave and navigating a romantic relationship with a former friend.

She hadn't set any rules, any boundaries.

Ethan put a finger under her chin, lifting her face so he could look into her eyes. "I feel like that brain of yours just went into overdrive. What's going on in there?" He tapped the side of her head.

"Nothing. It's just—" Something caught her attention out of the corner of her eye.

A blue overnight bag rested on the floor. It looked like it was filled to the brim. Ethan's jacket was thrown across the top of it, along with his sunglasses, wallet, and iPad.

His eyebrows drew together as he studied her. "What's wrong?"

"Uh...nothing."

He put a finger under her chin, raising her head so she was forced to meet his worried gaze. "Are you okay?"

She pointed toward the bag. "Is that..." Was he leaving? Had he planned on telling her?

"Huh?" He looked confused for a moment. "Oh, my bag."

"Are you going somewhere?" she asked, her voice sounding small and weak.

He sat back on the edge of the desk. "That's why I'm so glad you're here. I didn't think I'd get to see you before I leave."

Just like that? He was taking off.

"Remember my friend Bobby?" Ethan began. He was interrupted by the ringing of his phone.

"Hang on one sec."

Of course Lauren remembered Ethan's friend who wanted him to move to Alaska. How could she forget? So, Bobby was in on this. What a shock. He must have convinced Ethan to move to Alaska.

Lauren stepped toward the file cabinet and put a hand there to steady herself as her legs had suddenly started feeling weak. She couldn't believe what was happening. She realized she was in love, and Ethan was leaving.

Her chest felt so tight, yet at the same time, her pulse was racing. How could this be happening? Maybe if she'd figured out her own wayward feelings a day earlier and told Ethan, he wouldn't... No, she couldn't think that way. Besides, she didn't want him to stay because he felt obligated. She wanted him to stay because...because...

She loved him. She wanted him to love her, too.

"Sorry about that."

Her head snapped up at the sound of Ethan's voice.

He put his phone in his back pocket. "It's been a wild, unexpected morning."

Since she didn't know how else to respond, she simply nodded.

"I ran home to throw some stuff in a bag," he said, gesturing toward the bag on the floor. "I was bummed you weren't there."

"Yeah, well, I went to the café." She couldn't believe her voice was coming out so calmly when she felt like she was a second away from hyperventilating. "To once again be ridiculed by Grams." She offered a smile but knew it didn't stretch across her face.

"Hey, Ethan," Joe said, popping his head in the door. "Sorry to interrupt, but you wanted me to remind you." Joe tapped his watch.

"Right, thanks, Joe. You sure you can handle everything here?"

"Not a problem. We all have your back."

Lauren couldn't believe it. Ethan wasn't only leaving her, he was leaving his staff, this bar. She felt the air leave her lungs. He'd told her that he had hired trustworthy people who were good workers. She supposed that was as good a play as Ethan could make.

He ran a hand through his hair. "I told you. It's been nuts." He leaned over and shut his computer down. Then he came to stand in front of her again.

Here it came. The excuse. The platitudes.

It's been great, Lauren, but I gotta go.

My inner traveling child has been restless.

Nothing to keep me here.

Well, she'd be damned if she stood here and listened to any of it.

"Let me tell you—"

She took a quick step back and bumped into the wall. "No, don't worry about it." She chucked a thumb toward the door where Joe had just been. "Seems like you're late."

"Lauren," Ethan began, crossing his arms over his chest.

She shook her head. "You don't have to tell me anything. You should go." She reached down and grabbed his wallet and keys, handed them to him. "I have things to do as well."

Love was scary. Love was unpredictable. Love didn't always turn out the way you thought it would.

She didn't want to lose Ethan. That was her biggest fear right now. She didn't want him to take off on her. She didn't want to go back to Virginia. She wanted the two of them to be together with the baby. With each other.

But Ethan was leaving. Because that's what Ethan did.

"But I want to tell you. Bobby called with the coolest offer. I couldn't believe it."

She really didn't want to listen to this. Suddenly, she felt exhausted, and all she wanted was to go back home and curl up in her bed.

She'd been the one protecting herself for most of her life. She'd been in charge. For the last couple of weeks, it had been so nice to have Ethan make her feel like she was finally part of something. But she shouldn't have believed. She let her guard down.

There was another quick knock at the door, and Joe once again stuck his head in. "Sorry again, guys. Ethan, I have one question about the inventory before you leave."

"Of course." Ethan started walking out of the office. He held out an arm for Lauren to follow, which she did. Only, when Ethan went behind the bar to talk with Joe, Lauren kept walking until she was out on the sidewalk in front of The Thirsty Lobster.

Slowly, as sadness filled her entire body, she made her way back home. Alone.

CHAPTER NINETEEN

Ethan couldn't believe his luck.

He hadn't been thrilled to be woken with a frantic phone call from the bar. But after he'd made his way into The Thirsty Lobster and fixed everything in his power, he'd calmed down. Or maybe it was the amazing eggs benedict that Samantha whipped up for him in the kitchen.

In either case, he was about to head back home and talk Lauren into returning to bed with him when he'd received a call from his friend Bobby. Bobby, whom he now owed a free drink, a big meal, and some kind of favor.

After months of searching, Ethan had nearly given up on trying to find the old arcade game. Did the bar truly need a Ms. Pac-Man machine? Maybe not. But it had been Ethan's favorite as a kid, and he'd been determined to track one down.

His friend Bobby always knew a guy who knew another guy, and *that* guy owned one. After some back and forth, they agreed on a price. The only catch? Ethan had to pick it up today. No sweat off his back. He had an SUV, and he was more than willing to make the four-plus hour drive to get it.

"That was weird," Joe said.

Ethan looked over as they sorted through the lists for inventory. "What was weird?"

Joe leaned back, jutted his chin toward the front door. "Lauren."

Ethan put the clipboard down. "Huh?"

"Lauren just left without saying goodbye."

After a quick glance around the bar, Ethan turned toward the door. Lauren was gone? "Maybe she's in the restroom."

Joe shook his head. "I saw her leave."

It wasn't like the hair on the back of his neck stood up, but Ethan definitely felt some kind of uneasy feeling. "That is weird," he agreed.

"You guys have a fight or something?" He held his hands up in front of him. "It's none of my business, but she looked a little off when she came in here. Plus, she was kind of pale in your office."

Pale? His pulse picked up. The very last thing he wanted was for Lauren to get sick. She had enough on her plate as it was.

"Listen, we haven't really talked about it, but I obviously know Lauren is pregnant," Joe said quietly.

Ethan let out a deep sigh. He wasn't upset that Joe knew his business, but he was annoyed at himself for not discussing it before now. "She is. We're having a baby."

A grin spread across Joe's face, and he held out a hand for a healthy shake. "Congrats, man. That's really great news."

"Thanks. We're excited. And surprised. And still a little shocked. And maybe a little anxious."

They both chuckled.

"I can imagine," Joe said. "I like Lauren a lot. I just wanted to make sure she was okay."

"You know, I'm sure she's fine. You know how Lauren is—a social butterfly. She probably just saw someone she knew outside and got caught up in a conversation."

"Maybe," Joe said with a shrug.

"I'm sure she'll call or text shortly. Actually, I'll call her from the road. I didn't even get a chance to tell her about Ms. Pac-Man."

"Your other girlfriend," Joe said as he threw a rag at Ethan.

Ethan tossed the rag back. "My first girlfriend. Get it right. I'm a one-woman man."

Even as they joked around, something still felt off. Ethan gathered his belongings, said his good-byes, and headed out to his car.

If Lauren hadn't been feeling well, she would have told him, he assured himself. In fact, he would be the first person she'd tell. He was the father of her baby. That put him at the very top of her list of important people.

He was her person. And she was his.

That thought made him grin. Finally, after years of going it solo, after a crappy marriage, he'd found someone who respected and cared for him.

He started up the car, fixed his GPS, and pulled onto the street. Then he punched Lauren's contact. He didn't sweat it when she didn't answer.

But when she let it go to voicemail the next time he called, that uneasy feeling crept back up.

Seemed like "his person" was avoiding him.

• • •

Lauren spent the rest of the day driving up and down the coast, stopping at spots she used to love when she was younger.

There were a couple of scenic overlooks with out-of-this-world views. She went to Serenity Beach, a local favorite because tourists never flocked there. With large stretches of beautiful golden sand, there was nothing to do except walk and meditate.

Her last stop was a community garden. The hometown gardeners had really stepped up their game since the last time she'd been there. Rows of gorgeous flowers in an array of colors blew in the gentle breeze. The fresh scents of tomatoes, peppers, zucchini, and other vegetables reminded her that she needed to stop and eat at some point.

After a quick internet search, she let out a relieved breath that one of her favorite foods was still okay to eat while pregnant. So, she grabbed a lobster roll at a roadside food truck.

It was a perfect day. At least, in terms of the weather. She took pictures, sent some of them to social media, and even did a couple of videos. But mostly, she thought.

She knew she shouldn't have just left the bar like that. Ethan had called earlier in the day, but for the most part she'd been able to ignore him. She sent him a quick text saying she was working. That had held him off for a couple hours.

When she got sick of walking down memory lane—or maybe it was when she got sick of thinking—she headed back to Grams's house. She pulled into the driveway, shut off her car, and emerged into the quiet night. It was colder than usual for a summer evening. Unlike the lighter, friendly breeze from earlier in the day, the ocean was now whipping a chilly wind around, and Lauren shivered.

Then her phone let out a ping and she saw another text message from Ethan. Immediately, she shoved her phone in her purse and let out a different kind of shiver.

She didn't want to deal with Ethan right now. What was the point? He'd proven today that he was still the same Ethan. The person who could pick up on a whim and leave. Hadn't she been with him the night before, snuggled up next to him in his bed, dreaming of the life they were going to start together? Not twelve hours later, he was packing a bag and heading out to parts unknown. If she hadn't stopped at the bar, would he have even told her?

Irritated and pissed off and…sad, she stormed into the house. She could hear Gabby and Grams back in the kitchen, the sounds of pots and pans clanking and cabinets opening.

Turning in the opposite direction, she saw Brooke had once again taken over the living room with an explosion of wedding samples. A large swath of ivory tulle was hanging over a lampshade, and a dozen cake toppers dotted the coffee table, both end tables, and the couch.

"Can't a girl get any privacy in this damn house?" she muttered under her breath.

"Something you want to share with the class?" Brooke asked, holding two different candles in her hands, clearly deciding between them.

Her sister had the best hearing in the world at the worst possible moments. She ignored Brooke and went directly to the cabinet built into the base of the stairs. They used it for storing luggage.

Lauren started rifling through the bags until she found her purple suitcase. She yanked until it began to move.

"What are you doing?" Brooke asked, causing Lauren to jump a mile.

"Jesus, B. Scare a person to death."

Undeterred, Brooke leaned against the stairs. "Taking a trip?" She jutted her chin out toward the luggage.

Lauren straightened, blowing out a big breath in an attempt to get her now-messy hair out of her face. "Yes. I'm going back to the place where I belong."

With that, she grabbed her suitcase and made her way up the stairs and into her room. She was aware of Brooke's feet on the staircase because her sister was wearing heels—of course she was—and the *click-clack* of the Jimmy Choos annoyed her.

She ran up to her bedroom and immediately went to the closet and started pulling clothes out and throwing them onto the bed. All she could think about was her condo, her friends, her life back in Virginia waiting for her.

Only, her life would be a tad different when she returned. She'd have to swap early happy hours for gyno appointments and her spin class for prenatal yoga.

"What are you doing?" Brooke asked again.

Lauren paused for a second to take in her sister standing in the doorway. Brooke's eyes were drawn together as she took in the scene.

"What does it look like I'm doing? I'm packing."

Brooke sighed. "That's not what I meant. What are you doing with Ethan?"

"Don't start with me, Brooke." Lauren walked to the bed, began to hastily fold clothes. "He doesn't owe me anything." She looked up at her sister as the words tumbled out of her mouth. She wasn't even sure if she was saying them to Brooke or to herself.

"What the hell do you mean he doesn't owe you? Of course he does. He's the father of your child. The two of you are connected now for life."

A life full of not knowing where he was or what he was doing. Years and years of hoping to hear from him. *How fun*, she thought with a bitter taste in her mouth. She swallowed hard.

"What's going on, L?"

Lauren turned her back and focused on the suitcase. "Ethan is leaving."

"Where's he going?"

She threw a shirt into her suitcase. "I don't know."

"When's he coming back?"

She reached for her pajamas, which were in a ball on her pillow. "I don't know."

"So, you don't know where he went or when he's returning?"

Brooke was really starting to irritate her. "No. All I know is that he has left Seaside Cove. Probably forever," she finished with a pout.

Brooke's eyes widened. "Did he say he was leaving forever?"

"No. But I know him. He had a bag packed and, and...he's gone."

"Come on, L. He could be on a guys' trip or visiting his folks."

"That's not the point." Brooke leveled a look that Lauren couldn't ignore. "It's not."

"Tell me, then, oh wise one: what's the point of this little tantrum?"

Tantrum? Her sister, queen of dramatic, over-the-top outbursts was lecturing her?

"The point is that Ethan is Ethan."

Brooke waited, hands held out in a questioning pose. "What the hell does that mean?"

"He's unpredictable and spontaneous."

Brooke let out a fake gasp. "The horror."

"Shut up. It's not funny. It's, it's...terrifying. He can just pick up on a whim and move to Alaska."

"Is he planning on moving to Alaska?" Brooke asked with a head tilt.

"He isn't *planning* anything. Because Ethan doesn't plan. Or think ahead. Or take into consideration anyone around him and how his capricious actions will affect them."

It was true. Ethan had that desire to travel. That need to drop everything and try something new on a whim. "He's all, look at me as I jump on my Harley and ride off into the sunset without a plan or, or...GPS or anything."

Brooke narrowed her eyes. "Does Ethan even have a motorcycle?"

"No. Fine. So, he jumps in his Honda. Same thing."

"I think we might need to dial it back here."

Lauren grabbed her cell phone cord and started winding it around her hand. She shook her head vigorously.

Brooke leaned against the wall. "This has to be some kind of pregnancy hormone thing, because you are not usually this irrational."

Could it be hormones? Or was it the fact that she was in love with him? She loved Ethan, and before she could even tell him, he'd left town. Lauren felt tears welling up in her eyes, but she was quick to cough and suck them back down. She would not cry over him. She refused.

Brooke walked farther into the room, stood on the other side of the bed. "You're going to fuck this all up."

Lauren's head snapped up. Brooke rarely swore, and when she did, she stuck to the less offensive words.

"Did I get your attention?" Brooke asked. "Good."

Lauren swallowed hard. "I appreciate your concern, but I don't need a lecture."

Brooke swept out a hand to take in the pile of clothes on the bed. "Obviously, you do. I've called you a lot of names over the years. But I never took you for a coward."

Again, Lauren came to full attention. "You think I'm scared?"

"I think you're terrified." Brooke narrowed her eyes. "I'm just not sure what you're scared of exactly."

She threw a shoe into her suitcase. "I had a realization this morning."

Curiosity dawned on Brooke's face. "What kind of realization?"

"None of your business," Lauren said defensively.

Brooke rolled her eyes. "Just tell me already. I'm going to figure it out anyway."

She wanted to pace. She always thought better that way, but there simply wasn't enough space in the room. Instead, she'd have to settle for sniping at Brooke. "Why do you even care?"

"Hell if I know," Brooke snapped. "I mean, what with you being so super sweet to me all the time."

Rolling her shoulders back, Lauren eyed her sister. "I'd be a lot nicer to you if you ever took a moment to think of anyone but yourself."

Brooke's hand went straight to her hips. "I can sense you're about to call me selfish. Which is really comical, considering I just dropped work to follow your sorry butt up here and make sure you're okay."

Dang it. She was right. Didn't that just irritate Lauren more.

The fight started seeping out of her, leaving Lauren tired and defenseless. She picked up a headband and threw it in the suitcase with the strength of a mouse before collapsing onto the soft cushion that covered her window seat.

"I love him," she whispered to her sister.

"Okayyyy," Brooke dragged out. "Now we're getting to the heart of the matter."

Lauren didn't like this one bit. She was the oldest sister, and she was used to being the one that helped pick up the pieces. She dried the tears. She pointed out when one of her sisters was being irrational.

"Yeah, well," Lauren began. "I love someone who has no problem picking up and taking off for parts unknown. I don't even know how he feels about me."

Lips pursed, Brooke gave a definitive head nod. "You're incredible. You know that?"

Lauren didn't know what her sister meant, but she rolled her eyes out of habit.

"Of course he loves you. He's been in love with you since high school. Why do you think he was third wheeling it all the time?"

Sometimes she really underestimated Brooke.

"Ethan is a real stand-up guy, Lauren. Not just a great man but the father of your child. So, he went somewhere. You didn't even ask him where he was going. Instead, you're pouting like a child and running away."

"Shut up, Brooke. I really don't want to hear this right now." She grabbed a handful of bracelets and threw them into the suitcase without even taking the time to properly pack them.

"I don't particularly want to say it. But since you're too thick to get it yourself, I feel like it's my sisterly duty."

When Lauren wouldn't respond and wouldn't look up, Brooke took matters into her own hands. She grabbed the top of Lauren's purple suitcase and slammed it shut. Then she slapped her hands on top of it.

"Do you have any idea how lucky you are? I mean, what the hell? Do you know how many people would kill to have someone look at them the way Ethan looks at you?"

"Brooke—"

"Do you know how many women want to have children? Do you have any idea what it's like to think you might never get a chance to carry your own baby?" Tears filled Brooke's eyes.

Whoa. Lauren froze. This conversation had taken a sharp turn, and she wasn't sure she was following the new route.

Brooke pointed at her. "You're getting everything that so many people want. A baby with a man who adores you. A man who actually listens to you. A man who doesn't belittle your efforts and question every single thing you do and say."

Lauren sat down on the edge of the bed and took in her sister with her flushed cheeks and bright eyes. "Are we still talking about me and Ethan?"

Brooke took a deep gulp. "You're scared, and it doesn't have anything to do with the baby or Ethan going somewhere for a couple days."

"What does it have to do with?" Lauren asked.

"Love."

She groaned. "Come on, Brooke."

"I know you make fun of me for being a hopeless romantic. But I don't care. Love is real. It's strong and sweet and confusing and amazing and horrible and wonderful, all at the same time. And you have it, Lauren. Damn you, you found real love."

Lauren looked at her sister. Really looked. Brooke presented a good front. But there was a crack. Something that hadn't been there before. And that crack gave Lauren access to see into the inner workings of her sister.

"What's happened?"

Brooke shook her head. "Nothing. Listen, you would be such a fool to give up on Ethan."

"I'm not giving up on him. I'm claiming my independence. I'm keeping it intact while he's off doing god knows what with god knows who."

"You're running scared. That's not something a worldly, successful, self-sufficient, independent woman would do." Brooke tugged on a piece of Lauren's hair as she walked by.

Just as Brooke was about to step out of the room, Lauren stopped her.

"Mom threw everything away for Dad, and look what that got her."

The look on Brooke's face could be described as nothing short of pitying. "That's not true."

"What do you even know about love, Brooke?"

"Way more than you, apparently."

"You've been engaged to the supposed 'love of your life' for how long?" She used air quotes to emphasis the ridiculousness of Lucas being Brooke's true love.

"What's your point?"

"You plan weddings for a living. Why haven't you started planning yours?"

Brooke froze, cast her eyes to the floor. "You're clever, L. And you've always been good at turning our arguments around. But this isn't about me right now. It's about you and how you're a chickenshit."

She jumped up. "Shut—"

Brooke snapped to attention. "Don't tell me to shut up again. You're going to mess up your life and the life of that beautiful unborn baby because you're what? Scared? Cowardly? Stubborn? Well, I have three words for you. Get. Over. Yourself." She turned on her heels and started for the door. Before she crossed the threshold, she stopped, faced Lauren again. "You know, for being the oldest of us, you have a lot of growing up to do."

With that, Brooke finally took her leave. Lauren lowered herself to her window seat again and sat unmoving for a long while. Brooke's words reverberated through her head over and over until she couldn't take it anymore.

Without looking back, she grabbed her purse and hightailed it out of the house. She hurried down the long driveway, ignoring her car. She needed to walk.

When she got into the center of town, she didn't stop for any of the people she passed who called out greetings. She just kept going, walking in circles, going down dead-end streets and turning abruptly around, until she reached an area in the town's park that overlooked the ocean.

Suddenly exhausted, she slowed down to a near crawl. The breeze coming off the water brought a barrage of fishy aromas. Wasn't it strange how some days the ocean smelled fishier than others?

Her stomach did a little turn. The ocean smelled gross, and she loved Ethan.

She dropped down onto a bench.

Maybe he did love her. So what? Why did that bother her?

Her parents.

It always seemed to come back to them. Her mom had loved her dad, even when he'd been mean to her. Even when he'd left her.

She loved her mom, and she still thought about her every single day. Ellie Wallace had been amazingly sweet. She cared deeply about everyone in her world. She was the type of person who would drop everything if someone needed her. She'd be there at three in the morning if someone called.

And Lauren knew rationally that it had been cancer that killed her. Yet, she'd always suspected her mother had really died of a broken heart.

Because her husband had left. Because she'd allowed herself to fall in love.

Feeling beyond angsty, Lauren popped off the bench. And that's when the shooting pain hit her right in the lower stomach. It was like something on the inside was ripping away, and she felt a sharp, stabbing pain in her abdomen.

She crumpled to the ground as terror filled her. *The baby!*

CHAPTER TWENTY

Lauren immediately reached for her phone. Thank goodness it was never far from her.

She wanted to call Ethan. She knew she should call him—but he'd left. She didn't even know where he was. Brooke was right. She should have asked. But she couldn't deal with both that emotional roller coaster and whatever was happening in her body right now.

She debated between Brooke and Gabby, her finger hovering over their contacts in her favorites. But ultimately, she went with her gut.

"Hello?"

"Grams, I need you," she said, her voice hiccuping.

"Where are you?"

"At the oceanside lookout in Seaside Park. I need to go to the hospital."

Lauren pressed a hand to her stomach. *Please be okay. Please be okay.* Lauren breathed deeply as she repeated her plea over and over. It only took a minute for the pain to subside. By the time Grams arrived—which was in record time—she'd managed to get herself back on the bench.

"Lauren," she called as she neared. Lauren was pretty sure she'd never seen Grams move so fast in her life.

When she reached her, Lauren's hand shot out, and Grams took it between both of hers. She looked over Lauren long and hard, searching for something Lauren wasn't sure of.

"Maybe I overreacted," Lauren said. "The pain is already subsiding."

"Is it the baby?" Grams asked, sitting next to her on the bench.

Lauren almost choked. Did Grams just say… Maybe she'd misheard.

"You heard me," Grams said as if she was a mind reader. "Is everything okay with the baby?"

"But, how do you know? I mean, when did you figure out? How?" she stuttered.

Grams smirked, even as she flipped Lauren's wrist over and took her pulse. "When did I figure out that you're pregnant? I've known for quite some time."

Lauren's mouth dropped. "But the party— I had a plan—"

"What party?"

A party that was definitely not happening now. She shook her head. "It doesn't matter anymore. Just tell me how you knew?"

"You're no James Bond." Grams pushed Lauren's hair off her face. "Neither are your sisters. Or Ethan, for that matter."

Lauren's stomach clenched, and this time it had nothing to do with the baby. She didn't want to do this. Not here. Not now. At the same time, she felt lighter just knowing that Grams knew everything.

Maybe not everything. After all, she had no idea that Lauren was a big chickenshit who'd probably just ruined things with the father of her child.

"When did you find out?" Grams asked.

She owed her that much. "About a month ago. I took four pregnancy tests," she admitted.

Grams snorted. "Pregnancy tests. You're lucky they even have those. Back in my time, we had to wait for a rabbit to die. That was our pregnancy test."

"What the hell does that even mean?" Lauren asked.

"True story. But one for another time. Let's get you to the hospital. Can you walk?" Grams started to rise, putting an arm around Lauren.

"Actually, I'm feeling better. I had this really sharp pain, and it scared the hell out of me." She pointed to the area where she'd felt the pain.

"Hm," Grams said. "It might just be your uterus growing. It's getting ready for the baby."

As they walked to the car, Lauren took a big breath and asked the question that she really didn't want to hear the answer to.

"Are you mad?" she said softly.

"No."

She frowned. "Really? You're not mad that I'm pregnant out of wedlock?"

"I'm mad you didn't tell me. But we can discuss that later. Right now, let's concentrate on getting you to the hospital." She opened the passenger door and helped Lauren in. "Do you want me to call Ethan?"

Lauren shook her head. Grams stared at her for a long moment. Then she closed Lauren's door, circled the car, and got in on the other side.

They drove the first five minutes in silence. Lauren could feel Grams's questions even if she wasn't asking them out loud.

"Why don't you want me to call Ethan?"

Lauren put her head back against the seat and closed her eyes. "I just don't."

Grams made a right-hand turn. "You two get into a fight or something?"

Lauren opened her eyes and trained them on Grams. "You tell me, because I'm sure you know."

"I don't know a thing." She made a big show of fixing her rearview mirror. Finally, she said, "All I heard was that you went into the bar earlier today, looking upset. You talked to Ethan back in his office for a little bit, and then you ran out of the bar, looking even more upset. Oh, and Gabby and I heard you fighting with your sister. At first, I didn't think anything of it. The two of you always fight. But something about your tones was off. More serious than usual."

Lauren rolled her eyes. "That's pretty much the gist of today."

"What happened with Ethan?"

"Nothing," Lauren said, glancing out the window at the passing scenery. The hospital came into view, and she exhaled a long, relieved sigh.

"Lauren Rose," Grams said in her scolding voice. "Tell me why I'm driving my knocked-up granddaughter to the hospital. Did Ethan do something to upset you?"

"No, Grams. Ethan left for a trip or a...something; that's all. I think...well, I'm not really sure. He's gone at the moment, so it's just me."

Grams gave one single head nod. "Pushing him away, are you?"

Seriously, was the woman a psychic, because holy cow. How did she know that?

Lauren swiveled in her seat to find Grams with a smile on her face.

"I know you, and I've seen you push other men away. That's what you do," she said. "Another thing to blame on your father," she said under her breath, which of course Lauren didn't miss.

She was still stunned as they pulled into the parking lot of the hospital. Before they exited the car, Lauren put her hand on Grams to stop her.

"Thanks for bringing me. I think I owe you a long conversation."

"You think?" Grams said sarcastically. But her face softened. "First, let's make sure one of my favorite granddaughters and my favorite great-grandchild are okay."

Lauren's heart melted. She knew a very tough conversation was in her future. But for the moment, she needed to make sure everything was okay with her baby.

As Grams got out of the car, Lauren whispered, "I love you."

When Grams came around to her side to help her, she looked Lauren deep in her eyes. "I know. I love you, too."

. . .

Earlier that day, Ethan had been in the best mood.

It wasn't only that call from his friend Bobby, who found the arcade game he'd been dying to acquire for The Thirsty Lobster. But the night before with Lauren…wow, just wow. It wasn't only about the sex, which had once again been mind-blowing. But they'd really connected. The bond between them was growing, and he couldn't be happier.

So why, then, was he feeling so anxious and restless?

It just didn't make sense. Not only had his morning gone well, but he was currently cruising up the Maine coast, where he would shortly get on one of his favorite roads of all time, the Bold Coast Scenic Byway. Great views, a nice open road…and a lump in his stomach.

He glanced down at his cell phone to see if he had any messages or texts. Rather, he checked to see if he'd heard from Lauren. For the twentieth time, his screen was blank.

He'd been attempting to get in touch with her this entire ride. If he didn't know better, he would say that she was blowing him off.

Was she blowing him off?

He tapped his fingers against the steering wheel, which was a nice relief from the death grip he'd had on it.

Ethan pulled over onto the shoulder. He let the car idle as his brain replayed the events of the morning. It didn't take long for his aha moment to arrive.

"Well, shit," he said into the car.

It all came together like a bunch of puzzle pieces working themselves into one solid picture. Lauren had spotted his bags. She hadn't even asked where he was going or when he was coming back. Then she'd left the bar without a goodbye, and now she was avoiding him.

She thought he'd been taking off. Just like that. Leaving her and the baby without so much as a backward glance.

Ethan threw the car in drive and started down the road again. He made a quick pit stop. He grabbed some coffee, dashed to the men's room, then returned to his car, where he made a quick call before pulling out of the parking lot. Instead of continuing his journey north, he hightailed it back toward Seaside Cove.

Three hours later, Ethan was about thirty minutes outside of Seaside Cove when he received a text message. He pushed a button for the message to play through the speakers of his car. His phone's voice automation system began speaking in the British accent he'd programmed it to talk.

"Ethan, this is Brooke Wallace, Lauren's sister. Um, do you happen to know which hospital Lauren went to?"

He shot straight up in his seat. *Hospital? What the hell?*

As he pulled up at a red light at a large intersection, he stopped breathing. Suddenly, he couldn't remember how to work his phone. He fumbled with it as he tried to also keep an eye on the stoplight.

He called Brooke. "What are you talking about?" he barked into the phone instead of a normal greeting.

"Ethan." Brooke's breath whooshed out. "I don't know what's happening. Grams called Gabby, who called me. We thought you would know what's going on."

Ethan's mouth was suddenly bone dry. "I don't know anything," he eked out. "I was heading up north to pick up something for the bar."

The light turned green, and Ethan gunned the engine.

"Gabby said that Grams said something about a shooting pain and the baby."

His heart dropped. A shooting pain? Oh god, he needed to get to Lauren.

He heard Gabby in the background. Brooke made a disgusted noise. "I don't know, Gabs. That's what I'm trying to find out."

"Brooke," Ethan ground out between clenched teeth as he made it through a yellow light at the last second.

"Sorry," Brooke said. "Are there any new hospitals in the area? Any new medical centers? Where would Grams have taken her?"

Hospital, baby, Lauren, pain. His heart was going a million miles an hour as fear shot through him at the possibilities. Too many possibilities. None of them good.

He pressed the gas as he tested the speed limit. "Maine General," he said. "I think that's where she would probably go. It's still the closest hospital."

"We're on our way," Brooke said. "Turn left, Gabs. We'll meet you there." With that, Brooke hung up, leaving Ethan to concentrate on driving and squashing all of the horrible images in his mind.

Had he caused this? He began absentmindedly rubbing his eyebrow back and forth as he made his way to the hospital in record time.

He'd been so excited about the prospect of finding that damn arcade game that he hadn't opened his eyes to what had been happening right around him. Of course it would freak Lauren out. If only he'd stopped to explain to her what was happening. That he was merely taking a day-long road trip. He wasn't leaving her.

He didn't want to leave her.

The idea slammed into him with force. Once he got over the initial shock, he could admit that it felt right. Really right.

He wanted to be with Lauren. Not just for the summer. Not only because of the life they'd created.

The grin spread fast. He loved her and he never wanted to leave her. If he moved somewhere, she was coming too. Where she went, he followed.

His smile faded as fast as it had started. The woman he loved was in some hospital, probably because he'd freaked her out so much that morning.

He cursed himself the rest of the way to the hospital. He parked his car, unsure if he was parking in a spot he was allowed to be in. He didn't care. He dashed from the car and ran into the emergency entrance.

Ethan paused, trying to figure out what to do next. The waiting room was mostly empty. A few people were lounging in the area. One was drinking coffee, another riffling through a magazine.

A nurse walked by at a fast clip. Was she going to Lauren?

Finally, he spotted a desk with another nurse

behind it, tapping away on a computer. He rushed to her.

"How can I help you?" she asked with a kind smile.

"Lauren? Oh, um, my, uh, my girlfriend, she uh—"

Thank all that was holy that Brooke and Gabby showed up at that very moment. He was not handling this well.

They ran up to Ethan, one on either side. Brooke squeezed his arm while Gabby took charge. "We're looking for Lauren Wallace, our sister. She may have been brought in here recently."

The nurse looked over at Gabby. "Gabs, hi. Do you remember me?"

Gabby let out a breath of relief. "Susie?" she asked. "Ohmigod. Good to see you again. We graduated together," she explained to Ethan before turning back to the nurse. "Can you help us?"

Susie nodded. "Of course. Yes, Lauren and your grandmother came in half an hour ago. Lauren is getting an ultrasound right now. Unfortunately, I can't let you guys back there. But I'll do my best to keep you as updated as possible."

Ultrasound? The baby. Ethan thought he was going to be sick.

Brooke pushed him from behind. "What about him? He's the father. Can he go back?"

When this was all over, he was going to do something really nice for Brooke. He turned toward Susie.

"Of course. Follow me." She quickly tapped on the keyboard, nodded when she found whatever she was looking for, and then jumped up and came around the counter.

He had to hop to in order to keep up with Susie's clipped gait. She was short but quick. She took him through a set of double doors and back to an area that was partitioned off.

When he entered the small space and saw Grams holding Lauren's hand and a doctor moving a wand over her stomach, he felt like he was going to lose it.

All three women turned to him. The doctor smiled. "The father?" she asked.

He nodded. At least, he thought he did. All he could do was stare at Lauren. Her pale face was making her big blue eyes look even bigger, more vulnerable.

"Come in, come in. We have the baby up on the screen." The doctor gestured toward a monitor with a black-and-white image on it.

Ethan took a step closer and peered at the monitor. He felt his eyes widen. "The baby?" he asked with a dry throat.

"Yes, and looking nice and normal for this age. See?" She pointed at the monitor.

Ethan watched as the black-and-white blurs shifted on the screen. He had no idea what he was seeing, but he would take the doctor at her word.

He wanted to scream. Out of fear, out of anxiety. But then he heard something that had him freezing, those negative feelings slipping away.

It was the small and steady *thump thump* of the baby's heartbeat.

He looked to Lauren, whose eyes had gone

wide, a small smile on her face.

His child's heartbeat. Their child. It was amazing. Such a fast, little beat. He couldn't believe it.

Then, he glanced at Lauren again, who looked even smaller than usual on that hospital bed. He wanted to go to her. Scoop her up in his arms and never let go.

The baby was okay. Good. But what about Lauren? Was she fine, too?

"And Lauren?" he croaked out.

The doctor smiled. "She's going to be fine."

Ethan felt the air return to his lungs. Lauren was okay. The baby was okay. Now, he just had to work on the two of them being okay.

· · ·

Ethan was here. How was he here? How did he know?

Actually, she didn't really care. Despite it all, she really needed him here. Even if he was staying as far from her as possible in the small room.

"Good news. Your ultrasound looks good; the baby's heartbeat is healthy."

"Then why are you here?" Ethan asked.

Grams squeezed her hand, almost like she was saying, *I got this*. "Lauren had some sharp pains earlier."

Ethan's eyes went wide. She felt horrible. This wasn't how he should have found out about this.

Tearing her eyes away from Ethan, Lauren looked up at the doctor. "What were the pains I felt?"

"I feel confident that what you're experiencing is round ligament pains."

Lauren was at a loss. "What is that?"

"Basically, what it means is that the uterus is growing and expanding for the baby. Perfectly normal. As the uterus expands, it can cause sharp pains like the one you experienced earlier. Sometimes it lasts a couple of seconds. Other times, it's even longer. It's a little early in your pregnancy, but it's nothing I'm worried about."

Lauren felt like she could breathe again. Her whole body softened, and she felt like she could melt into a pile of happy glitter.

"I am worried about your blood pressure," the doctor continued. "Do you have a history of high blood pressure? Does anyone in your family?"

She looked to Grams, who wore a worried expression. She shook her head.

"No."

"Have you been under any stress lately?"

This time, she glanced at Ethan. He met her gaze with a serious one of his own. She quickly focused on the doctor again.

"Like emotional stress? A little."

"Well, I'd like to monitor your blood pressure. Let's have you buy a machine—you can get one at any pharmacy or online. I want you to test your blood pressure in the morning, as soon as you wake up. Then test again before bed. Keep a log."

A list. Finally, something she understood. Something that made her feel calm.

The doctor checked her chart. "You're seeing Dr. Raquel. I'll let her know what's going on and forward her the information from this visit. Make a follow-up appointment with her once you're home."

Lauren rested her head against the hospital pillow and took a deep breath. Relief filled her. The baby was okay.

"Any questions?"

So many, she thought. Would she have to go on blood pressure medication? Should she be concerned about the baby? What were Ethan's future plans? Were they going to be okay?

The doctor put a reassuring hand on her arm. "I know this is scary. But I don't want you to worry. It's all normal. I had round ligament pains during my pregnancy, too."

"You did?"

She nodded and smiled kindly. "They'll come and go. They usually occur when you change positions quickly, so try and get up slowly. Be aware of your movements. If you have any spotting or cramping, let your doctor know immediately."

"I can do that."

"Just try to relax and get that stress down." She smiled at Ethan, who was still standing completely still. His face remained devoid of color. "I'm sure your husband here will make sure you take it easy."

Husband. The word hung in the air, more potent than any mix of medications available in this hospital.

No one said anything. No one corrected the doctor's assumption. The doctor appeared oblivious to the tension in the small space. Grams, who didn't know all of the details of what had gone down between her and Ethan, had to know something big was up. She was perceptive.

And Grams. Oh man. Lauren wanted to hide when she thought about the fact that Grams had known all along she was pregnant. She was so obtuse. Of course Grams had known. She must have thought all of Lauren's random excuses were completely ridiculous.

The doctor left the room, and Grams stood. "Do you want to go back to Ethan's house?"

"Actually," Lauren said, scooting up on the bed. "I'd like to go home with you, Grams."

Ethan's face fell, but he remained silent.

If Grams was surprised by the request, she didn't show it. "That's fine." She moved to the door. "I'll go let your sisters know you're okay." She leaned toward Ethan, her eyes strong and direct. "Talk it out."

Ethan nodded at Grams before taking a step toward her.

"Listen, Lauren—"

But she cut him off with a hand. "No, don't." She shook her head. "You don't need to go into anything right now."

He sat on the side of the bed. It seemed like he was moving to hold her hand, but in the end, he let his hand fall onto his leg.

"Lauren, I wasn't leaving you this morning. I mean, I was." He jammed a hand through his hair. "But not in the way you thought."

She waved a hand through the air. "It doesn't matter."

He frowned. "Yes, it does. I was only leaving for

a day. I packed a bag because I wasn't sure if I would be too tired to drive all the way back home."

Curiosity overtook her. "Where were you going? To see your friend Bobby?" She couldn't keep the bitterness from her voice.

"Bobby? No." Ethan rubbed his chin. "I've been wanting this old arcade game for the bar. Bobby found a seller who lives way north. I was heading there to get the machine." He took her hand, rubbed a thumb over the back of it. "I wasn't leaving you."

She snatched her hand away. "You can do whatever you want. You're not tied down to me."

Ethan stood abruptly, knocking into a small table in the curtained-off area. "Not tied down to you? I would be, if you'd let me."

She swallowed hard. Was that true? Did Ethan want to be with her? Lauren closed her eyes as way too many thoughts began swirling around.

She heard Ethan take a steadying breath.

"I love you, Lauren. Maybe I have since high school. At least, when you weren't driving me crazy. I don't know. It started…I don't know," he repeated. "But I know I love you now."

He loved her. Lauren wanted to be happy. She wanted to reach for him. She wanted him to wrap her up in one of his amazing hugs.

Only, she couldn't allow herself to do that.

What would even happen if they took the next step? What was the next step? Living together, marriage? A marriage like her parents', where her dad eventually left anyway? Did she even want that?

Ethan shoved his hands into his pockets, looking helpless.

"You didn't call me," he said, hurt coating his voice. "I'm the father of that baby," he said, pointing toward her stomach. "Don't you think I'd want to know if—" He ran a hand through his hair again.

She didn't respond. Couldn't. What could she possibly say to wipe the pain off his face?

"That's it, then?"

Lauren held her breath even as her heartbeat raced. "It's not like that."

"Oh, yeah? Seems like it." He rubbed a hand over his face. "Do you have any idea how terrified I was when Brooke called me?"

Brooke. Ah, that's how he'd found out. She silently berated herself. She should have called Ethan. She knew that.

"I was going to call you," she said, trying her best to rationalize.

"When?"

"Once I knew everything was okay." She hated that she was doing this to him. He was so right to be mad.

"Now you're going to go back to your Grams's house? Why?"

"I need Grams tonight, Ethan. Please don't make me explain it." She cast her gaze down at her clenched hands.

He looked around at the machines in the room. "I don't want to cause you or the baby any more stress tonight. Go."

"What?"

"Go with your grandmother and your sisters.

When you're ready for me to be back in your life and the life of our child, give me a call."

He fled the room quickly, and Lauren stayed on the bed, too stunned to move. She was used to making people mad. Her entire relationship with Brooke was based on each of them pissing the other one off.

But Ethan wasn't mad. Not really. He was hurt. And she was the cause.

She closed her eyes as the tears threatened. She hadn't handled anything right today. She placed her hands over her belly and gave herself some time to get it together before she left the hospital.

And didn't go home with Ethan.

CHAPTER TWENTY-ONE

By the next morning, Lauren felt completely fine.

She hadn't experienced the round ligament pains again. Everything with the baby and her uterus seemed to be doing A-OK.

Her heart? That was another matter entirely.

Still, she stayed in bed most of the day, allowing Gabby to fuss over her. Grams brought her tea twice. She decided to make Lauren's favorite blueberry pie, and that's how Lauren knew she'd given her grandmother a real scare.

After a full day and a half of pampering, she got back to work that evening, throwing herself into a presentation she was going to give the next month. She scheduled social media for the next two weeks. She compiled a job listing for a new assistant. She submitted a proposal to be on a popular podcast.

Basically, she did everything but go to Ethan's house. Or call him. Or run into his arms.

And he didn't contact her, either.

That thought did bad things to her heart. Why hadn't he called? As if she didn't know. But still.

Her hurt morphed into anger as the day went on. How dare he not even check on her?

As the sun began to set that night, she'd worked herself up to a proper mad. Probably not the best time to talk to her sister, but when Brooke popped her head into Lauren's bedroom, she didn't really have a choice.

"How are you feeling? How's the baby?" she'd asked.

"I think we're both okay." Physically, at least.

Brooke hovered by the doorway. "Do you need anything? I can run to the store if you want."

Lauren shook her head.

Chewing on her lip, Brooke inched into the room. "Do you want to watch a movie or something?"

"You're being really nice to me," Lauren said.

One of Brooke's perfectly shaped brows arched. "You think I would be mean to my sister who just had a pretty big scare?"

Lauren shifted. "It's just, the last time we talked—"

"The last time we argued, you mean?"

Lauren let out a long breath. "Right."

"I'm happy that my future niece or nephew is going to be okay."

"Me too."

Brooke stepped back toward the hallway. "And I'm really glad that you're okay." She paused for a long moment. "Even if I'm still mad at you."

"It wouldn't be a day of the week if one of us wasn't pissed at the other."

Brooke smiled before leaving the room. Lauren couldn't deny her own grin. It was as close to an "I love you" as she and Brooke could give.

After that sisterly moment, Lauren dove back into work. Only, she couldn't concentrate. Not even close.

Irritated, frustrated, angry, sad—feeling all the emotions, really—Lauren made her way through the house until she pushed through the kitchen door and out onto the porch. She walked to the north side of the house. She sat on the banister with her back against one of the columns, like she used to do in high school, and took in the lighthouse that sat off in the distance. The water was beating against the large rocks at the base of the structure. A perfect complement to her mood.

She closed her eyes, trying to block out all of the things she and Ethan had said. An overwhelming sense of sadness filled her.

"You and your sister have been behaving like that since you were children," Grams said. "Yelling, screaming one minute, then ignoring each other for a while, plus a little bit of passive-aggressiveness thrown in."

"Yeah, well," Lauren began, picking at an invisible fuzzy on her shirt, not at all surprised that Grams had snuck up on her. Or that she'd heard her fight with Brooke. "She usually starts it."

Grams nodded. "She does. But she isn't usually right."

Lauren's head snapped up.

"She is this time," Grams finished.

Right? Brooke? What was happening in the world? Was she suddenly in some alternate universe?

Grams sat down on a rocking chair, facing her. She rocked for a few minutes, not saying anything. Lauren noticed she was holding a really old-looking box. Even though Lauren came out for the quiet, Grams's silence began grating on her nerves.

Finally, she couldn't take it any longer. "Say

something already."

"You're too self-reliant."

Lauren was getting just a tad bit irritated with people using what she considered her best quality against her.

"You're independent," she said as she pointed at her grandmother, almost like she was accusing her of some kind of crime.

"I am."

"What's wrong with me being the same way?"

Grams sighed, long and loud. "Lauren Rose, you've never really understood. Maybe because I haven't told you everything," she said softly. Lauren wondered if that statement was meant to be said more to herself than out loud.

"Told me what?"

Grams continued rocking. "I am independent because I had to be. You are *choosing* to live that way."

Lauren froze, took in the words, their meaning. It was two different ways to live.

"There's a big difference there." Sometimes Grams said exactly what she was thinking.

Lauren leaned forward. "I've seen what happens when you let someone in. It's rarely good."

Grams tapped the old box in her lap. "I was in love with someone who was not your grandfather."

Lauren almost fell off the banister. Only Grams could drop a bomb on her like that. She gulped, wondering what to say in response. Grams was focused on something in the distance, her blue eyes glazing over with memories.

Lauren turned in that direction. She spotted the

lighthouse. Grams had always seemed to like it. She'd even rearranged the furniture in her bedroom so she could sit in her rocking chair and view the lighthouse from her window.

"I was in love with a man. We courted. That's what you called it back then," she said with a little smile.

Lauren shook her head, attempting to clear it. She couldn't believe what she was hearing.

"What was he like?" Lauren asked.

"Strong but very patient. He loved the water and anything that had to do with it." Her smile faded into a frown. "He was very handsome. And a phenomenal kisser."

"Grams!" Lauren said, surprised.

She waved a hand. "Hush. I'm having a moment here."

"I can see that." Lauren chewed on her lip.

"He worked on a boat. They went off to sea. There was a series of horrible storms. Most of the boats that had been away at that time never returned. Many people in this town lost sons, brothers, uncles, husbands. I lost Cap."

"Cap?"

"That's what I called him. He wasn't a captain, but it was my little nickname for him. It always made him smile."

She ran her hand over the lid of the box. "I didn't want to think he was dead, but after a few months, I…" She trailed off, putting her arms in the air until they slowly fell back to her sides. "No one else from that crew showed up, either."

"You married Grandpa?"

"I did. After about a year. My parents urged me. He was from a good family. They had this house." She shifted. "I didn't love him. But I knew I would never love another man. Only Cap. That was it for me. He was it."

Lauren's heart swelled.

"My parents were right. Byron had a good job, he came from money, his family was well established, and, of course, there was this gorgeous house. Who didn't want to live here back then?"

Lauren glanced over at the wraparound porch, the baskets of beautiful flowers, the stained-glass windows. "Who doesn't want to live here now? It's still incredible."

Grams shrugged. "The week after I got back from my honeymoon, Cap turned up."

Lauren gasped.

"He'd been shipwrecked. But somehow, he'd managed to survive. He said it was the thought of returning to me that kept him going." Grams blushed, something Lauren had never seen her do before. It was endearing.

"Anyway, I was a married woman by that time. Your grandfather was not a warm man. He wasn't mean. He never lifted a finger to me or anyone else. Hell, he never even raised his voice. Not refined," she said with an eye roll. "It was just that he was aloof. He did his thing, and I did mine."

She took a moment before continuing. "I don't want to disparage your grandfather, especially not to one of his granddaughters."

"Honestly, Grams, I barely remember him."

"Mm, you were just in nursery school when he

passed." She sighed. "Still, I don't know what kind of grandfather he would have been. Maybe better than he was as a father. He did like to watch you sleep in your bassinet when you were an infant."

"He wasn't a good father?"

"He wasn't present. He left all parenting to me. Just like he left all cooking, cleaning, and house things to me. I started Rose's Café because I was bored. I didn't get pregnant right away like most of my friends. I needed something in my life. At that time, it was a very rare thing for a woman to start a business. Byron didn't really seem to care. I think he was happy to have me out of his hair."

That sucked. Lauren was reminded of how Ethan liked to hear about her business. How he didn't always understand what she was talking about, but he listened and asked questions anyway. It meant a lot to her.

"You share my independence," Grams said. "I've always been proud to see that in you. But you also inherited my stubbornness. That's always worried me."

"I don't understand."

"The two traits are very similar." She paused. "I could have left your grandfather and been with the man I loved. I was so pigheaded about it. I thought I was doing my duty."

"Well, to be fair, you did take vows. You were honoring them."

"Maybe. Foolishly, I mistook stubbornness for independence. Look at me, I thought. Being my own woman. Making decisions." She shook her head. "Decisions that would haunt me for the rest of my life."

Lauren wished she had the type of relationship in which she and Grams hugged. But it wasn't them.

Grams pinned her with an intense stare. "What I don't want is for you to hide behind this wonderful, amazing quality that you have. Your independence. I can't stomach the thought of you missing out on the best thing in the world. Love."

"But, Grams—"

"I didn't get to live my life with the man I loved. I didn't get to marry him. I didn't get to raise children with him. I didn't get to share all the little mundane eccentricities of life with him." She grabbed Lauren's hands and squeezed hard. "You have the chance to be with the one you love."

"Mom and Dad—"

Grams shot her a look. "No, you can't blame them. You can't compare yourself to them. You can't even really pretend to understand what their relationship was about."

Lauren sat quiet for a long while, going back and forth on whether she should ask the question. She wasn't afraid to ask, but she was beyond terrified of the answer.

Finally, curiosity won out. "Did she die of a broken heart?"

Grams's face softened. She stood and crossed to Lauren, took her hands. "Oh, honey. No, your mom died because of cancer."

Hearing that answer from Grams, a woman she loved to fight with but whom she also respected more than anyone else on the planet, left her feeling at a loss.

"They fought a lot, but she really seemed to love him," she whispered.

"She did. I don't get it. I never did. But I know this. Despite the fighting and the arguing, she was devoted to him. You and I, sharing the same sensibilities, will never understand it. But she did love your father. She got to live with her love. And after he left, she had the three of you, and I know she considered that love even better."

Lauren had a lump in her throat the size of Maine.

"You're not going to repeat your mother's mistakes."

She looked to the ground. "What if I do?"

"You're not the same person, so why would you make the same choices? But you can't let her actions and her decisions guide you."

"What about you?" Lauren asked. "Didn't you guide her? Er, force her." Lauren bit her lip, hardly believing she'd just said that out loud but desperately waiting on the answer.

Grams tilted her head. "Force her to do what?"

"Get married," she whispered. "Mom told me that she was forced to marry Dad. I figured out later that they married because Mom was pregnant with me."

Grams closed her eyes and leaned back against the next column. She rocked her head back and forth. "How long have you been under this impression?" she asked without opening her eyes.

Lauren looked out at the ocean. "Since I was a little girl." As those words left her mouth, Lauren realized the source of her angst with Grams. For years and years, she'd blamed Grams for the end of her parents' marriage—the beginning of her mother's sadness.

"When your mother told me she was pregnant, I was mad. As any mother would be. The two of them hadn't used protection. She was young, so young. Only halfway through college. She'd just won a scholarship to study abroad in France." Grams narrowed her eyes. "It was your dad who pressured her to get married."

For the second time that night, Lauren almost fell over the banister. "What?"

Grams nodded. "He was old-fashioned about certain things. I told Ellie that she could have the baby—you—and go off to France. I would take care of you until she got back. But your mom didn't want to leave you. Or your dad. That was her choice."

Lauren didn't know what to think or how to feel with this new information. Her dad was traditional when it came to marriage, but apparently not when it came to walking out on his family.

And Grams, wow. Her whole basis for fighting with Grams had been this deep-seated rebellion against Grams doing something she'd never even done.

Did that mean she had to start getting along with her grandmother? Because how boring would that be?

"This must have been like history repeating itself for you," Lauren said.

"Not particularly."

"Come on, Grams," Lauren said dramatically.

"Mom got knocked up. I was a total accident. Now I have an unplanned pregnancy. This has to be déjà vu for you."

Grams leaned against the railing, glancing toward the lighthouse. "Not really. Your mother was only nineteen when she found out she was pregnant. She didn't even know what she was going to major in yet, let alone have an established, stable life. Like you do."

"I guess," Lauren said, considering.

"And another thing," Grams continued. "I really shouldn't say this to you. I promised myself I would never say this."

Grams paused. Lauren waited as long as she could manage, which was a total of two seconds.

"You can't leave me hanging now."

"Fine, but I do feel bad saying this. Your father was a damn fool."

A loud laugh erupted from Lauren.

"You think that's funny?" Grams asked. "Because when I say he was a damn fool, I mean he was a damn fool. Capital D, capital F." Grams laughed as well, before her face softened. "Still, he's your father, and I shouldn't speak badly of him."

Lauren shook her head. "I know how he was. I remember."

"Do you know how Ethan is? Because I do." Grams patted Lauren's leg. "Ethan and your dad are nothing alike. Despite him not using a condom correctly, Ethan is a good man. I like him."

Lauren didn't think she'd ever heard Grams say she liked anyone. Ethan must have really left an impression on her at some point.

Grams put a finger under her chin, raised her head so they were eye to eye. "I didn't pressure your mom, but I am going to pressure you. You love Ethan. He loves you. You're pregnant. Go live a wonderful life with the father of your child."

Grams pushed the box into Lauren's hands. "This contains my diary and letters between me and Cap. Read them one day. You'll understand."

For the first time in she didn't even know how long, Lauren felt wetness tracking down her face. She was crying.

CHAPTER TWENTY-TWO

He hadn't seen Lauren since the hospital.

Restless, Ethan stalked through his house, remembering all the places she'd touched. Such a short time, but she'd left an indelible mark.

He marched into the kitchen, reached into the fridge, cracked a beer open, and downed a large portion. It was tasteless, going down his throat like cotton.

So, Lauren was done with their relationship. "Fine," he said out loud. "Run away." That's obviously what she was doing.

Was she really so unwilling to even discuss their relationship? And shouldn't she have called him when she had those ligament pain things? At least a text message. He was the father of their baby. Didn't that give him some kind of special place?

For a moment, he had to admit that he had no idea what had run through her mind, how scared she must have been, or what he would have done if it had been him.

That moment was brief.

He stormed through the back door, seeking fresh air and relief. Instead, he was greeted by a hot and humid day.

"Shit."

He tried drinking more beer but once again didn't taste it.

It was a different situation than his ex-wife. He

knew that. Yet, it felt similar. Too similar.

Veronica hadn't loved him. Neither did Lauren.

There was something he really didn't want to think about ever. Luckily, his cell phone rang. He'd never been so happy for the interruption.

He saw his mom's name come up on the screen. "Mom?"

"Were you expecting the Easter Bunny?"

He couldn't stop the grin. Olivia McAllister had a sarcastic side that he'd always loved. She was the best mom in the universe. She'd worked hard at the local library while always managing to be at all his stuff growing up. She was also beautiful, funny, and smarter than anyone he knew. Perhaps from all those books she was constantly reading. The only con was that she and his dad had moved away from him when they retired two years ago. He missed them more than he'd anticipated.

"Sorry. I was just lost in my thoughts, I guess."

"Thoughts about the fact that you are going to be a father and you haven't told your mother about her first grandchild?"

Whoa. "Mom? What? How did you find out?"

She snorted. "You live in Seaside Cove. Your dad and I may have moved to Florida, but the gossip train actually has a route between Maine and the South. It's called text messaging. We've been hearing some interesting things about you. Call it mother's intuition if you want, but I just had this feeling that there was something more going on."

"But who told you? Not that many people know."

She laughed, a soft, light tickle. "Do you

remember all those flowers I used to have in front of the house?"

Ethan was absolutely confused as to what was going on and why his mother was bringing up flowers at a time like this. "Uh, yeah, I guess."

"Let's just say that I didn't have a green thumb naturally. I had to be taught how to garden."

"Okayyyy," Ethan said, still not following.

"There's no better gardener in the state of Maine than Rose Josephs."

Bingo. He got it. Ethan had no idea his mom and Grams had been friends.

"Rose became a great friend over the years. But imagine my surprise to hear from her that I'm becoming a grandmother for the first time."

He was definitely in the running for worst son of the year. "That's not how I wanted you to find out."

"The question is, why didn't *you* tell me?"

"Honestly?" he asked.

"That's usually the best approach."

"It happened fast. Really fast. I've barely processed it myself."

"I'm sure you've been very busy with the bar and your friends and dating Lauren. And then breaking up with Lauren."

Ethan's heart sank at the sound of Lauren's name, not to mention thinking how his mother must feel to be hearing all of the events of his life from strangers.

Worst. Son. Ever.

Silently, he cursed himself. He should have known better.

"Technically, I think she broke up with me. Or

maybe we're not broken up at all. I don't really know what the hell we are." He paused, collected himself. "So, you remember Lauren Wallace?" he asked quietly, as if simply saying Lauren's name hurt. In a way, it kinda did.

"I do, and I've always liked that girl. Of course, I haven't seen her in years. Is she still as pretty as she was back in high school?"

"More."

She laughed. "I remember the two of you going at each other constantly. One time, I thought you'd actually come to blows over an English project."

Ethan smiled, remembering.

"Despite that, you had quite the little crush on her back then."

"Shit," Ethan said, unable to come up with a more adequate word or reaction. His mom knew about his crush?

"Language, Ethan Oliver McAllister."

"Sorry," he said sheepishly. "I'm just shocked that you knew about my crush."

"It was hard to miss the little red hearts that would shoot out of your eyes every time she was around. Lauren's done quite well for herself, too. That business of hers is flourishing."

Surprise took over yet again. What was his mom going to say next? Did she know who really shot Kennedy? Could she tell him the real story with Area 51? "How do you know about her business?"

"We're friends on Facebook and follow each other on Instagram," his mom said simply.

Ethan sat back and shook his head. Lauren was connected with his mom on social media? Figured.

"The two of you reconnected and started dating. Now you're broken up. You gonna tell me about this or what?"

What was there to tell? "I dunno," he said under his breath.

"What was that?" his mom asked sharply. She hated when he mumbled.

"I don't know," he said a little too loudly, immediately regretting raising his voice with his mom. "She's pregnant with my child. She kinda freaked out because she thinks I'm going to abandon her, and then she got these sharp pains and went to the hospital and—"

"The hospital?" She gasped. "Is she okay? What happened?"

"She's fine. The baby's fine. She had something called round ligament pains."

He heard his mom's sigh of relief. "That can be quite scary the first time it happens. Rewinding to something you said, though... Why does she think you're going to abandon her?"

"Who knows?" he said stubbornly.

"Ethan Oliver," his mother said with a stern voice.

He gave a half smile. "Middle name for the second time."

"And don't make me use it again. Now, explain yourself."

"I don't get it completely." He pushed a hand through his hair. "Lauren is under the impression that I'm going to just get up one day and leave her. Like I'm going to go off on some adventure or live in Alaska or something."

Olivia's voice dripped with sarcasm. "Now, why would she think that?"

Huh?

"Ethan, you can really be dense sometimes."

"Gee, thanks, Mom. So glad you're making me feel better."

"My job isn't to make you feel better," she said. "It's to knock some sense into you."

"Then, please, continue." He started picking at the label on the beer bottle. When his mom remained silent, he went on. "I thought we were going to have a life together. Live in the same house, raise our baby, be happy. Not for the first time, a woman didn't want that with me, and she ran away."

"Don't compare Lauren to that little tart you married," his mother snapped. "And stop feeling sorry for yourself."

Anger began to rise in his throat. "Shouldn't you be on my side?"

"Not when you're behaving like an ass."

"An ass? Mom, what?"

"I could have told you that Veronica was using you from day one. I would have done that if you'd introduced her to me before you said 'I do.'"

Guilt at getting married without telling his parents washed over him. Had he already called himself the worst son? Did he need to get it tattooed on his chest?

"Remember when your father and I came to visit you in South America so we could meet your new bride? I knew within three seconds of meeting that girl that she was using you to get what she wanted. I don't know Lauren all that well, but I'm sure she isn't using you for anything."

"I know. I'm just trying to make sense of this situation.

"You have no idea what's going on inside her head right now. Or what's going on inside her body, for that matter. Her hormones are going crazy. She's probably having insane thoughts left and right. Her mind is full of excitement and fear and anxiety. Being pregnant is no joke."

"I tried being there for her. That's why I told her I loved her."

"Oh, Ethan," she said on a long sigh. "Think about it from her perspective. She becomes pregnant unexpectedly. Then you tell her you love her. Plus, she's pregnant and dealing with all of that. And working full time." She snorted. "That's a lot to deal with in a very short time."

He hadn't thought of it that way.

"Is it over between the two of you?" she asked.

He pushed a hand through his hair. "I don't want it to be." But it might be. He may have messed this up too much to fix.

"Let me ask you this," his mom said. "If you and Lauren don't work out, what do you plan on doing?"

"I have a friend who might be starting a business in Alaska. He's already reached out to me. You know I've always wanted to live there."

"More travel, more uprooting. What a great choice for a soon-to-be dad. I'm sure your kid will love having a FaceTime relationship with you."

He gulped. Watching his child grow up over

FaceTime and Skype. Maybe getting to see pics on Facebook if Lauren ever friended him. His chest hurt. That wasn't the type of dad he wanted to be.

"Why do you even want to leave Seaside Cove?" his mother asked. "I get why you wanted to travel in your twenties. I encouraged it. See the world. That's wonderful. But now? What is it exactly that you think you need to do?"

"I don't know, Ma. I want to get out there and experience as much as I can. I want to make the most of life."

His mother let out a bad word that he'd never heard her say before. He nearly dropped the phone.

"You don't want to travel. You want to run," she said harshly. "There's a big difference."

He remained quiet, her words and their meaning soaking in.

She sighed, and he knew any anger that she'd just thrown his way had already dissipated. "You want to make the most of life. Well, you now have a woman you love and a baby on the way. Trust me, that *is* life. That's the most there is. Family, love, raising a new generation. You won't find anything more exciting, challenging, adventurous, or exhilarating than that."

She was saying he was running. Wasn't that what he'd just thought about Lauren? What a pair the two of them made. "I hope this kid got your resolve. Maybe even Grams's."

"We should all be as tough as Rose Josephs. Even though we've spent a lot of time gardening together, the woman still scares me, but damn do I respect her." She sighed. "I want to respect you, too. So go out there and make some good decisions."

How did moms always know what to say and when to say it? Was that a parent thing? Would he be like that when Lauren had the baby?

"I love you, Mom."

"I love you, too. Now, get your head out of your ass and get that woman back. And send a sonogram picture to me while you're at it."

He was laughing as they said their goodbyes and hung up. But when the laughter faded, he realized he had some real work to do to get Lauren back. And he had no idea where to start.

• • •

Lauren paced her room, still unable to believe her conversation with Grams.

There was so much to process that she didn't know where to start. Thoughts and ideas about independence and autonomy were mingling with the story of Grams and Cap. Plus, she couldn't believe she'd been wrong about Grams making her mother get married.

As much as it pained her to admit, Brooke had really gotten to her as well. Her sister told her that she had a good man with Ethan. As if Lauren didn't know that. Ethan was amazing. But she was so scared at the same time.

When Gabby came to her bedroom, Lauren was thrilled for the interruption.

"Can you come downstairs?" Gabby didn't wait for a reply, and Lauren had to rush to follow.

"What's all this?" she asked as she walked into

the dining room.

"Your new life plan." Gabby waved her hands with a dramatic flourish.

"I already have a plan."

"Might be time for a new one," Brooke said. "And since we know how much you just love making lists and rules and organizing—"

"And vision boards," Gabby added.

"Right," Brooke said. "We want you to sit down and make a new vision board. Right now."

Lauren took in her sister for a long moment. Brooke didn't flinch. She'd never been one to back down. "Are you still mad at me?" Lauren asked.

"Nah." Brooke waved a hand nonchalantly. "I got bored of that." She snapped her fingers. "Now, stop stalling. Sit your butt down and work."

"When did you get so bossy?" she asked, taking a seat at the dining room table.

"Learned from the best." Brooke grabbed a large posterboard and put it in front of Lauren. "I've taken the liberty of starting for you." On the board was a picture of a gorgeous antique bassinet with loads of ivory lace and delicate pink and blue ribbons. "This is a present from me, the fabulous Auntie Brooke. It will be delivered here in a couple of days."

Lauren's heart felt full. The three of them may be different, but when it counted, they were there for one another. Tears welled up in her eyes.

"As you know, I don't have any money, so I haven't gotten you anything yet." Gabby laughed, her curls bouncing. "But sign me up for free babysitting."

Grams came into the room, arms loaded with magazines. She dropped them in front of Lauren. "For your board," she said, taking a seat at the table. "I don't really get it, but that's my contribution." She gestured to the magazines. "Have at it."

Gabby held up a bundle of different-colored markers. Brooke had a pair of scissors in her hands. Lauren looked from the poster board to the supplies to Grams, then back to the poster board and the beautiful bassinet. A bassinet for her baby. Her and Ethan's baby. A smile broke out on her face.

She got up from her chair and headed toward the stairs. "Be right back." Running to her room, she found what she needed and returned to the dining room.

"What's that?" Gabby asked as Lauren began cutting pictures out. "Is that your yearbook?"

"Yeah, from senior year."

"You can't cut your yearbook," Brooke said as Gabby continued to wear a horrified expression.

"Relax. I'm just cutting out pictures from two pages. Besides, this is just a yearbook, not antique lace or anything."

She used a glue stick to complete her masterpiece. Stepping back when she was finished, she took in her new vision board. "What do you think?" she asked.

Grams, Brooke, and Gabby all looked at it, smiles breaking out on their faces.

Under letters that spelled out M-A-I-N-E were pictures of Lauren and Ethan from high school flanking the bassinet.

Grams handed over the keys to her car. "I think

you know where to go," she said, and Lauren ran out of the house.

She had always deeply believed in the power of a good vision board.

• • •

Thank goodness it didn't take long to drive to Ethan's bar. Lauren had never been in this much of a hurry before, but she'd finally realized the solution she'd been seeking. She was ready to admit her true feelings for Ethan. Out loud. For *all* to hear and know.

This felt right.

The bar must have been packed, because it took her multiple trips around the neighborhood before she finally found a parking spot. She started off walking, which turned into a light jog, and then a full-out run to get inside. To find Ethan.

She pushed open the door in a hurry and…it hit resistance just as she heard an *ow* and saw someone fly to the floor.

Oops. She'd done it again. She hit Ethan in the back and knocked him over.

"Ethan," she said as he looked up, shook his head, and grinned.

"Lauren?" His smile quickly faded, and it broke her heart.

The bar's loud music, which she'd been able to hear from the street, stopped. Every person in the joint turned to watch the two of them. And lucky for her, The Thirsty Lobster was definitely packed. Half of Seaside Cove was huddled around the bar.

Lauren took a long, deep breath. A normal person would tell everyone to mind their own business. However, she'd left normal when she'd first slammed into this bar and reconnected with Ethan.

She was going to do this. Her way. If the town wanted to watch, that was fine. Because she knew how she felt, and she was ready to tell Ethan.

She glanced down as Ethan rubbed his shoulder. After a few moments, he stood. Relief flooded her simply at the sight of him.

He opened his mouth, but before any words came out, she held up a hand to stop him.

"No, let me talk."

"What?" someone called. "I can't hear what she said."

Peggy let out an oath from her regular seat at the bar. "She didn't say anything important yet. She just wants to talk first."

Lauren coughed. "Thank you, Peggy," she said through gritted teeth.

She could feel every eye on her. But the only eyes that mattered were the light brown pair standing right in front of her, waiting to hear what she had to say.

With a final look around the room at their audience, she let out a nervous giggle. "Too bad there's not a microphone."

"We have one." Joe smiled from behind the bar.

She aimed a pointed look in his direction.

"You were going to say?" Ethan crossed his arms.

She clasped her hands together. "Ethan, I..." She trailed off. She walked a few feet to the left, then back again. "Ethan, I came here because…"

"Maybe you want to sit?" he said, gesturing to a nearby table.

"Yes. No. This is fine. We're doing this here. In front of everyone."

"Great, because I didn't pay for Netflix this month," Wendy called. "I need the entertainment."

"I want to apologize to you," she said.

"What did she say?" another voice called.

Lauren groaned. But when she met Ethan's soft brown eyes, she saw the amusement there.

"You're enjoying this, aren't you?" she said quietly.

He held up two fingers close together, almost touching but not quite. "Just a bit."

"You're mean." She pouted.

"You're apologizing. And I keep interrupting. Go on."

"Speak louder," a man called from the other end of the bar.

She faced the bar. "Ethan and I have known each other since forever. In high school, I dated his best friend, and the two of us were frenemies."

"We know all of this already," Stu called.

Lauren grumbled under her breath. "I came back to Seaside Cove for my family. I wasn't looking for romance. Hooking up with Ethan wasn't in my plans." She met Ethan's gaze and offered a smile.

"He's not my frenemy any longer. In fact…I love him."

This declaration was met with *oohs* and *ahhs*. Lauren held up a hand. "But when *he* said he loved me, I wasn't ready to hear it yet. So, I pushed him away."

Peggy and Wendy were shaking their heads. Joe flipped a towel over his shoulder as he grinned at the two of them. A guy she'd graduated with yelled, "Just like a woman."

Ignoring that comment, she continued. "I admit that I didn't handle Ethan's declaration of love very well."

"Doesn't sound like it."

Good grief, every critic in town was here tonight.

"I'm here to apologize to him and…to ask him to take me back." She took in the room. "You've all been gossiping about my family for a long time. Allow me to set the record straight. My father left us. Even though they fought all the time, my mom never fully recovered from him leaving. It was hard."

She walked around the little landing. "I've always been really independent, and I thought I was over what happened in my childhood. But I've realized that I've been afraid of love because I thought loving someone meant losing yourself in the process. That's why I pushed Ethan away."

"Because you love him," Wendy called out.

She felt Ethan's hand on her shoulder. He turned her so she was facing him. "Just to be one hundred percent crystal clear, what exactly are you saying?" Ethan asked.

She stared at him for a long moment before taking a deep breath. "I'm saying that I love you and that I want a life with you here in Seaside Cove. I don't want you to leave and go off on any more adventures, unless I'm with you. I want us to be a family."

He pushed a stray hair off her face. "Because you love me."

"Because I love you."

Everything happened so fast. Ethan stepped toward her, took her face in his hands, and kissed the hell out of her. The bar exploded into applause and whistles.

And Lauren relaxed in a way she never had before in her life. She melted into the kiss, her arms encircling Ethan's neck. She hung on for what seemed like hours, but she didn't care. She would hang on to him for days.

Finally, he broke the embrace. He ran a finger over her dimple. "I'm so glad you keep hitting me with that door. I can't believe you just did that in front of everyone."

She laughed. "There's no hiding the truth in Seaside Cove. And why would I want to hide my love for you?"

She leaned out of Ethan's arms and hushed their audience. Everyone's attention was once again firmly on her.

"Oh, and we're having a baby, too!" She returned to kissing Ethan as more applause sounded.

This time, when they came up for air, Ethan said, "Ms. Wallace, you're dangerously close to breaking a rule or two tonight. Would you like me to make a list of them for you?"

With a grin, she said, "Some rules can be broken, McAllister. As long as I'm breaking them with you."

EPILOGUE

Lauren took in the nearly cloudless sky. A pair of pelicans flew gracefully over the cliff and glided above the ocean. Without warning, one of them abruptly dove into the water for their lunch.

There were people down on the beach today—blankets and towels spread out, children running and laughing, adults lounging with books, a group of teenagers playing volleyball.

It was a perfect August day. Warm but not overbearing. A nice refreshing breeze tickled the hair that she'd left loose around her face.

She followed the path of the wind to take in the gardens. Grams's flowers were even more magnificent this year than any she could remember. Mounds of beautiful colors made up multiple flower beds. Petals hung from baskets on the porch railing and from hanging baskets all over the house. A huge row of white daisies rose proudly under the window that used to be her mother's bedroom.

Daisies had been her favorite, Lauren remembered with a smile.

Her mom would be so happy if she were here right now. Lauren looked to the blue sky. *You are happy, Mom. Wherever you are right now.*

Lauren had officially moved back to Seaside Cove. She and Ethan were living together in his Cape Cod house. For now. They might look for something a little bigger, though, as the baby got older.

The baby. Lauren placed a hand on the small bump of her stomach and smiled. She couldn't wait to meet her little one.

Today, August 5th, Grams had decided to throw a party for Lauren and Ethan. Apparently, she'd also known about the "congrats, you're a great-grandmother!" party they'd been planning—to no one's surprise—and since plans were already underway, Grams turned it into a "congrats to Lauren and Ethan!" party. Lauren loved a good party. And she really enjoyed watching her sisters, Grams, Ethan, Joe, and other residents of Seaside Cove laughing, eating amazing food that Gabby had prepared, and having fun.

Everyone in town had offered to help her move her belongings from Virginia to Maine. Grams and her sisters were constantly checking in on her, too. The irony wasn't lost on Lauren. She'd returned to Seaside Cove to make sure everyone else was doing okay. Instead, she was the one who'd needed the help.

Thank god no one had waited for her stubborn butt to ask for it.

Gabby ran over to Lauren, offered her a peach seltzer mocktail, and threw an arm around her shoulders. "This is so fun."

"You did an amazing job with the food, Gabs. And drinks. You should open your own restaurant."

Gabby snorted. "As an out-of-work actress, I've worked in more restaurants than I can count. I don't think that lifestyle is for me."

Lauren grabbed a bacon-wrapped date and moaned as it melted in her mouth. "But this is soooo good."

Gabby laughed.

"Maybe there's something else you can do with food. You can't deny the world of this talent."

Gabby rolled her eyes, but she was smiling. "I'll consider it."

Brooke marched over to them, her hands flying to her hips. Despite the lovely, pastel visiting-royals-in-the-garden-type outfit she was wearing, she looked absolutely irritated. "What is *he* doing here?" She nodded toward Ethan, who was talking with a group of about five guys.

"You're going to have to be more specific," Lauren said.

Brooke's eyes went wide. "Him. Kai," she snarled. "And his stupid, muddy dog, who seems to just delight in jumping on me when I'm wearing pastels."

"You have, like, a speck of dirt on you, B. Get over it."

"Anyway, I've been thinking about Grams and her long-lost love, Cap," Brooke declared.

"Me too," Gabby said with a faraway look in her eyes. "I wish there was something we could do."

"I still can't believe that Grams, of all people, had that story in her past. It's unbelievable," Lauren said. Her heart continued to hurt when she thought about Grams not being with the love of her life.

"Unbelievable, huh?" Ethan asked, walking over and slipping an arm around Lauren. "Clearly, you three are talking about me."

Lauren leaned up for a kiss. As usual, she melted into Ethan as he rubbed his lips over hers. Her knees went weak.

She was so damn lucky.

"So, daddy-to-be," Gabby began, "getting excited?"

Ethan's grin came fast and true. His whole face lit up at the mention of the baby, and Lauren had noticed he seemed to do that any time someone mentioned their soon-to-be bundle of joy. Ethan was going to be an amazing dad.

"I can't wait to meet him," he said. "Or her."

"I have a feeling it's a girl," Gabby said.

Lauren scrunched up her nose. "I don't really want to say anything, but I kinda do, too."

"Do you care either way?" Brooke asked.

"Nah." She shook her head. "As long as the baby is healthy. Although, I would really like to see Ethan deal with a little girl."

"I will be excellent with either a girl or a boy. They will be spoiled and loved and pampered." He leaned over and whispered to Lauren. "So will you."

She couldn't think of any words to truly express the love she felt for him, so she settled with another knee-weakening kiss.

"Ugh," Brooke moaned. "You guys are grossing me out. I'm going to go call Lucas."

Gabby downed her beer. "I don't think that call is going to go through. Look, Princess is already making a beeline for Brooke and her precious pastel ensemble." She ran off in the direction of the barking dog and their shrieking sister.

"You look happy," Ethan commented, placing a soft kiss on her forehead.

"So do you," she replied.

"You make me happy. You both do," he said with a gentle rub of her belly.

Lauren leaned against him, comfortable and comforted by his mere presence. "By the way, I accepted your friend request on Facebook."

He threw back his head and let out a huge laugh. "About time."

She shrugged with a smile of her own. "Yeah, well, I figured you might want to see all the photos I'm going to post of this little peanut." She rubbed her tummy.

She was beyond happy. She was going to stay in Maine and live with Ethan. They would raise their child with Grams and Gabby around.

Grams.

Lauren eyed her grandmother, who was off to the side, looking toward the lighthouse. Grams had been instrumental in helping Lauren realize her feelings for Ethan. She may think she'd missed out on the love of her life, but Lauren wasn't willing to let it go quite so easily.

Together with her sisters, maybe they could come up with a plan. Maybe Grams and Cap's story wasn't quite over yet.

After all, there were no rules when it came to love.

• • •

Rose stood off to the side, watching her three granddaughters celebrating. She wore what some might describe as a sly smile.

She'd call it *knowing*.

So, Lauren thought she was coming back here to check up on her. She gave a little snort. Please. She didn't need to be babysat.

Now, her oldest grandchild. That was a different story.

Lauren was stubborn, just like she was. She should know. She knew everything about Lauren. Including the fact that the girl would forever do the opposite of whatever she suggested.

Don't go to that bar.

Don't date Ethan.

Don't fall in love.

She couldn't contain the smirk. She'd pushed her in the exact direction she'd needed to go. People could see that megawatt smile on Lauren's face from outer space.

Mission accomplished. Rose silently congratulated herself.

To think, she was about to become a great-grandmother. And she would also bet the deed to this house that Lauren was carrying a little boy. But that was something she would keep to herself, since her granddaughter thought she just knew everything there was to know.

She looked off to the lighthouse in the distance. At least someone in this family had found true love. Although, to be fair, she'd found it herself once. A long time ago.

Only, she hadn't been able to keep it.

The lighthouse held that constant beacon of brightness, as it had for over a hundred years. It was steady and sure. Just like her love for Cap.

Until her recent conversation with Lauren, she hadn't spoken about him out loud...ever. Her love for him, their relationship, their sad ending—none of it had ever come out of her lips. It was a private and very personal part of her life.

However, now that his name had left her lips, she couldn't stop thinking about him. To be honest, she thought of him pretty much every day. But lately, it was more than that. It was a yearning like she hadn't felt since he'd gone missing at sea.

She shook her head, bringing herself back to the moment. Today was a time for celebrating the present and the sweet future ahead. Not for wallowing in the past and the regrets that threatened to consume her.

With a final look at the lighthouse, she turned and walked back to join the party and her granddaughters and the new joy they were bringing back to her life.

Lauren was settling down, and though Rose would never tell her, she was thrilled that she was going to be living here in Seaside Cove.

Gabby was currently showing some of the young kids a dance. A talented dancer, singer, and actress was her Gabby. She'd always been. But as gifted as she was with entertaining, she was an even better cook. Something Rose could definitely push her on. Of course, she needed to get to the bottom of what was happening with her bubbly granddaughter first. Something had happened in New

York. There was a story there and a secret. Rose knew she'd eventually get to the bottom of both.

Then there was her Brooke. Of the three of them, she'd always been the most refined and so-phisticated. But there was fire under all that lace and manners. For an engaged woman, her eyes didn't hold the happiness Rose would expect.

She looked from Lauren to Gabby to Brooke... Yes, she would have to give some attention to Brooke. Although, it would be difficult with Brooke returning to Chicago soon.

Rose would have to work on that, too.

Decision made, she walked back to join her family—the new, the old, and the soon-to-be.

The End

ACKNOWLEDGMENTS

The idea for this book, and the whole Seaside Cove series, was conceived in March 2020. Of course, the world has changed a lot since then. Even in my small corner of the universe, since 2020, I've gotten married, built a house, moved, and had a baby. Phew! Makes me tired just thinking about it. Writing and publishing a book always takes a whole team of people. But this one…and with all those life changes…means I really have a lot of angels to acknowledge.

First, a huge thank you to my editor Lydia whose insightful comments and suggestions truly made this a better book. Thanks for putting up with me and always checking in.

To the Queen of Entangled, Liz Pelletier. Thanks for taking a chance on me, both with this series and way back when I was writing novellas.

Big kisses and sparkles to Jessica, Curtis, Hannah, Elizabeth, Bree, Riki, and the entire team at Entangled. I love all of your energy and your emails make me smile.

I'd like to thank one of my favorite writers, Lauren Layne, for reading this book and sending the most amazing cover quote. I can't tell you how much your kind words mean to me. I want to be you when I grow up.

To Nic, there aren't enough thank you's for everything you do for me. I wouldn't want to go through this journey without you.

Mom and Dad, thank you for, well, EVERY-THING. I truly couldn't have gotten through the last couple of years without you. From cleaning my house to watching the baby to helping us move to babysitting Harry to taking care of me, plus the cooking, the grocery shopping, and the laughs.

Harry, thank you for your unconditional love. I wouldn't be able to write without you curled up in your bed under my desk.

To my darling daughter, Coraline Quinn. You are my joy and the light in my life.

John, this book is for you. Thank you for making my dreams come true.

Return to Blossom Glen, where two opposites must put their differences aside to help the small town they both love...

the
SWEETHEART FIX

MIRANDA LIASSON

Juliet Montgomery absolutely loves her small town of Blossom Glen, Indiana, and everyone loves her. Except for the fact that she's a couples counselor who suffered a *very* public breakup that *no one* can forget. And now her boss asks her to take a step back...which is exactly when the town's good-lookin' and unusually gruff mayor offers her an unexpected job.

Jack Monroe absolutely loves being the mayor of his small town. Except when he actually has to talk to people. Can't he just fix the community problems in peace? Like right now, he's mediating the silliest dispute two neighbors could possibly have. When the town sweetheart steps up and solves everyone's problems in five minutes flat, Jack realizes what this town really needs...is a therapist.

Juliet is able to soothe anyone—other than the surly mayor, it seems. But there's a reason they say opposites attract, because all of their verbal sparring leads to some serious attraction. Only, just like with fireworks, the view might appear beautiful—but she's already had one public explosion that's nearly ruined everything...how can she risk her heart again?

*Find something luckier than catching
the bouquet in this delightful small-town
romance perfect for fans of* Virgin River...

The
MATCHMAKER
and the
COWBOY

ROBIN
USA TODAY BESTSELLING AUTHOR
BIELMAN

Callie Carmichael has a gift for making bridesmaid dresses—some even call them *magical*. Somehow, every person who's worn one of her dresses has found love. *Real* love. And as long as that happily-ever-after is for someone else, Callie is happy. Because she's fully over getting her heart broken...which is why her new roommate is *definitely* going to be a problem.

After being overseas for six months, Callie's only choice is to stay with her best friend's ridiculously hot brother, Hunter Owens. Cowboy, troublemaker, and right now, the town's most coveted bachelor. Only, Hunter isn't *quite* the player she thought. And if it weren't for her whole "no more love" thing, their setup could get confusing *really* fast.

Now, Hunter wants Callie to make him a best man suit—a "lucky for love" kind of suit. But what happens if she makes the suit and he finds true love...and it isn't her?

Three sisters race to the altar in this charming small-town romance from New York Times *bestselling author Ginny Baird...*

second
Bride
down

Aspiring artist Misty Delaney is not about to let her parents' beloved café go under. Not when she can just merge the company by entering a quick marriage of convenience with the rich son of their family's rival. But her sisters aren't having it. They all made a deal: they each get one month to find true love. She can't just *fold*. To make sure Misty gives finding love a chance, they post a "Marry me: Misty!" billboard outside town. Surely that'll give her options?

Watching Misty field marriage proposals from strangers, that she clearly doesn't want, is a big cup of *nope* for café manager Lucas Reyes. He and Misty have been friends for years, but it's time he step up and make his romantic feelings for her known. And what better way to start than by sending her unwanted suitors packing with an announcement that she's already in a relationship. With *him*.

Lucas's little stunt buys an extremely grateful Misty one week to come up with a solution that saves the café *and* keeps her sisters happy. A week during which she and Lucas need to act like they're in love. Except, between late-night stargazing, crashed mopeds, and dancing in the rain, their pretend romance feels almost...perfect. But it's one thing to start falling. It's another entirely to turn one week into forever...

AMARA
an imprint of Entangled Publishing LLC